RELUCTANT MEDIUM

By

G G Collins

Chamisa Canyon Publishing
chamisacanyon@live.com
Attn: Rights & Permissions

Cover Design & Interior by VilaDesign.net
Editing by Jay Terre

ISBN-13: 978-0-9884674-4-6
ISBN-13: 978-0-9884674-0-8 (ebook)

Books by G G Collins

Reluctant Medium

Lemurian Medium

Atomic Medium

Presence: A Rachel Blackstone Paranormal Mystery Short Story

Dead Editor File

Looking Glass Editor

Murder USA: A Crime Fiction Tour of the Nation (anthology, contributor)

Flying Change

Without Notice

Forthcoming

Anasazi Medium

Editorial Kill Fee

AUTHOR'S NOTE

Although there are such ceremonies for returning the deceased, practiced or not, the results, as depicted in this book, are an absolute fabrication by this author. In reality, no spirit person returns, only the essence of the departed. By focusing on the dead, it allows the living to remember them more fully and understand how they might respond in a given situation. Thus, the ceremony helps bring solace and a sense of the loved one to the grieving person.

The Shed Restaurant, La Fonda and Jackalope are the genuine article in the City Different although Jackalope is under new ownership and no longer as described in these pages.

Santa Fe is a real and beautiful city, but this author has concocted places, such as the sleazy downtown motels, which do not exist. A visitor to Tent Rocks would find the layout of the rock formations to be quite different. Of course, no human-sized dream catcher can be found there, right?

ACKNOWLEDGMENTS & GRATITUDE

With special thanks to Terry who acted the part of devil's advocate; and to Tawna, a terrific story brainstormer and wonderful friend. I miss you so much. Dearest Bessie, who gave many of us our start, wherever you are in the cosmos, we miss you too. To Marilyn who is my creative muse and crystal expert, my undying gratitude.

To Cherie and Margarett for reading every page of the rough draft, thanks for your input; to L L Thrasher, a wonderful writer, who improved the manuscript in many ways; to Sally and William Stewart for their generous assistance with real estate background.
And finally, my thanks to the kind and tolerant residents of Santa Fe who routinely open their home to thousands of visitors.

For Terry

For reading & reading & reading again.
Thank you.

Death broke at once the vital chain,
And freed his soul the nearest way . . .

— Samuel Johnson

CHAPTER 1

Bringing back the dead is a serious task. That's why the mask and its construction had been Rachel's sole focus all day. It was important to center one's attention on the process. She attached a photo of herself and her father to the shroud made of cardboard. They had been happy—a rare ski trip together. With string, she threaded one of his cuff links through a small hole on the side. To the upper edge she carefully clipped a note from him.

Rachel learned the ancient ceremony while researching an article about the Hopi Nation. Some Native Americans and followers of eastern philosophies believe one can call back the dead. In her interviews, Joseph, a Hopi holy man, had recounted instances. It was unusual for tribe members to discuss such things with outsiders, but she had written a sensitive portrayal of life within the reservation and Joseph warmed to her. He liked Rachel's sincerity and the deep respect she had for their traditions.

Using notes taken during conversations with Joseph, she would attempt to speak to her father. There were things she needed to know, things left unsaid, and many questions.

Her father's death several months ago was devastating. His car had plunged over the Santa Fe Ski Basin road. After rolling several times it crashed into a tree.

By the time Rachel placed the last few items on the mask, the sun had slid behind Tulsa's Turkey Mountain—hardly a mountain, actually a hill west of the city. Dusk settled snugly around the house. Rachel tugged the worn, soiled shades down to block unwanted light from the street lamp. She nervously pulled at an eyebrow, and then reminded herself she'd be penciling to cover the missing hairs.

She lit a sage smudge stick, waving it about to purify the space, and then placed it in a large terra cotta bowl positioned on the rickety coffee table. The fragrance from the sage permeated the evening air, making it heavier. Lighted charcoal had gone grey in the small pot she used as an incense burner. She took one nugget of Dragon's Blood; an incense used in ceremonies to bring back the dead, and placed it on the charcoal. The incense began to melt into a bloodlike stain. The aroma was musky, almost choking. Indian ceremonial rhythms emanated from the CD player. It was time.

Rachel sat on the braided rug in front of the fireplace. Lean denim-clad legs crossed over the frayed fragments from another generation. With her back to the fireplace, she gazed at the tattered sofa, so over-the-hill she covered it with a white chenille bedspread. A blue lava light—a remnant from the 1960s—softly illuminated the room. It stood alone on one very distressed end table. The paraffin bubbled and surged to the top of the glass enclosure, then fell silently. The pole lamp, a robotic looking thing with three cylinder bulb holders, provided light for an ugly gold brocade chair.

The mask fit awkwardly, but stayed in place once tied with soft shoelaces at the back of her head. In her right hand she held the *paho*, or prayer stick. It had been yesterday's project: a message to the Above Beings taped to a twig found in the backyard. Four colors of yarn—red, yellow, black, white—represented the four winds or four colors of mankind, depending on the source—held it all together. The colorful strands were tied neatly around the finished *paho*.

When her pulse slowed from the preparations and she could brush away the persistent daily concerns, she closed her eyes and concentrated on her father's image, already beginning to recede with time. It swam in the darkness of her thoughts. Three months wasn't all that long ago, but she found it hard to picture his face. There was still too much pain.

She wasn't sure what to do next. Making the mask and prayer stick was easy enough, except for the deep sadness that came with remembering, but now she would have to ad lib. Should she call out her father's name or merely fix on the letters which formed it? Maybe the ritual wouldn't work. Rachel's genetic makeup contained only a small percentage of Native American. The entire effort could be moot.

Indecision tends to allow events to happen instead of taking control to direct the end result. In a heartbeat, the air in the room became stifling. The odor of a spent lightning bolt charged the dust particles and mixed unpleasantly with the sage and incense. Rachel's lungs labored to draw a full breath. Apprehension prompted her to open her eyes. The smudge stick abruptly stopped burning, its warmth extinguished in a small puff of carbon.

Her body trembled as she watched the vapor seep first from the seam where hardwood floor met plaster and then from the intricate crown molding. It poured from beneath the couch like mist on a lake and slid along the wallpapered ceiling, coming ever closer while she watched, fascinated, but with growing anxiety. The hissing began softly, rising to the clamor of a den of disturbed rattlesnakes. Mid-point in the room, the two streams rose and dipped to join in a common countenance. The darkest colors of the miasma collected in an eerie spiral holding pattern, while the particles which reflected light crept away like fog throughout the room, closing off escape.

Rachel watched with macabre captivation although her body readied for fight or flight. Her senses were finely tuned and every muscle taut. The damn dog was barking next door. It was more irritating than she remembered, breaking her concentration. She hoped it would not interfere with what was in motion.

Joseph had not disclosed what would happen, probably because she hadn't asked. At the time, her father was alive and it never occurred to her she might want to attempt such an experiment. A shape began to form in front of her; subtle colors carried on smoke eddy, sluggishly wrapped around a central shaft of air. Fear kicked in. She expected joy at the opportunity to see her father again, but how would he appear?

Rachel hadn't considered that possibility. She willed the confusing ethereal episode away. But the coming proceeded. She could not stop it. What was that movie? *The Monkey's Paw?* A grieving mother wished for the return of her dead son, only to discover him at the door, not as he lived, but as he died in all its horror.

Rachel continued to watch and wait. New sounds began. Like shot hitting a window in a staccato report, small fragments of matter were being yanked from the gaseous haze only to become magnetized to the core of whatever was developing. The room had become so hot she felt clammy.

"Dad?" she asked cautiously. Instead of her father's gentle voice another reverberated inside her head.

"Fool!" It streamed through her mind like a banner trailing a plane. "You dare to intrude in things you do not understand. Once you have opened the gates of heaven or hell, there is no return." Rachel shook her head to clear the disturbing statement. The mask fell, hitting her arm, tumbling to the floor. The cuff link came loose and bounced, stopping near a heating vent. She tried a reality check, reminding herself she was in the living room of her house. Safe. There was nothing to fear, but an occasional mugger or drive-by shooter.

She wanted to stand, but fatigue held her down. Her hand rose to her mouth as a figure materialized. This couldn't be right, she thought logically. Her father looked nothing like this. The man was too tall, too dark. She studied the figure searching her memory for a matching image.

"Where's my father?" Her words were barely audible her mouth was so dry.

"Daddy's busy." The voice was contemptuous. "How did you know I wanted to come back?" She willed her legs to work and pushed herself upright. The twig snapped in her hand, causing her to drop the *paho*. "No!" The scream of rage caught in her throat, thwarted by the mix of odors.

"You're sputtering, Rachel." He knew her! "How is brother dearest? Still looking over his shoulder?" The comment carried a threat.

Before she could think of anything to say, the arrogant spirit hastened to the front door and vanished, *through it*, beyond it, into the night.

Rachel stared at the door, willing it to reveal the truth of what just happened. She'd made a terrible mistake. "Oh, my god," she whispered. "What have I done?"

CHAPTER 2

"**D**amn." It was his answering machine again. "Where the hell is Chris?" Rachel demanded of the phone. "He's the fucking mayor! Someone should know where he is."

It had been nearly an hour since the bizarre occurrence in her living room. She'd called everyone who might know her brother's whereabouts and had come up empty-handed. Apparently, he was not at an evening city government function, so it was anyone's guess. He was known to enjoy a few drinks when he felt put-upon, which he frequently did. Rachel felt he should know what had happened, the threat, but would he believe it?

Indecision once again garbled her mind as the adrenalin continued to pump fear and insecurity through her body. Had she really seen what she thought? Surely what had happened had to be in her mind, yet, she had seen it. Rachel pushed at her cuticles; a habit she deplored because it was a defense mechanism. She had little respect for women transfixed by their nails. Neat, yes. Clean, yes, but painted and pointy? Most definitely, no.

"I have to go there." The corner turned, she raced through the house hauling out a large Samsonite suitcase and an Eddie Bauer duffel bag—a product of earlier more abundant times. She plopped them on top of her unmade bed and opened them. Jeans, T-shirts, socks, sweaters, and her two blazers landed in a heap in the red case. Rachel pushed rubber-sole mocs into a shoe bag and squeezed it between her clothes. She'd wear the running shoes she had on. Running was something she didn't do, but the shoes were comfortable.

A hair dryer, panties, bras, and a night shirt were shoved into the green duffel. She ran to the kitchen and pulled a small Ziploc from its box. "May as well use these things for something since I never put food in them." Back in the bedroom she dropped navy pencil eyeliner, mascara, a Chap Stick, and some sun screen into the sandwich bag. Remembering how dry *New Mexico* was, she added eye drops and a saline nasal spray. The bulging plastic bag, her hairbrush, and a mirror nearly filled the carry-on. Rachel was about to zip it when she had a subtle reminder. Her head was beginning to throb on the right side. She retrieved her pills from the bathroom medicine cabinet which held her precious migraine potions: one prescription to prevent them, and another to stop them if the first one didn't work.

The suitcase was so heavy she could barely lug it across the backyard. The wheels were worthless on the tall neglected fall grass. At thirty dollars a hit, she waited until it was a code violation before overdrawing her meager checking account to have someone cut the grass. For a moment, she worried about being seen by a potential burglar doing a night's casing, but in this neighborhood better to worry about the neighbors. In the shadows of the stately sycamores it was unlikely she'd be seen by anyone. Once she loaded her laptop computer there would be nothing of real value left in the house.

The interior garage light had to be turned on—that might reveal her leaving—but without it, she'd never find the trunk lock. It was a one-car garage and the aging Mercury Marquis barely fit between the unfinished walls. A few rusty gardening tools leaned against the old, silvered boards, compliments of prior inhabitants. The concrete floor crumbled near the edges and several large cracks creased the surface. Even with the measly forty-watt bulb doing its best to illuminate the space, she added another scratch to the dark blue paint while heaving the hard-sided case into the trunk. The Merc had been the only thing she could afford one crazy night when she ran away from home. But that was another story.

Taking inventory, she collected her favorite denim coat and ski jacket. It would be getting cold at night. Once the computer was carefully zipped into its bag, Rachel grabbed her Escape Pouch and pulled the strap over her shoulder. The canvas pouch could be mistaken for a casual—make that very casual—purse, but it easily held notebooks and recorders, and it was washable!

There was nothing else but a few books, a clock radio, assorted dishes, sheets and towels. The house came furnished, dump that it was. Even if she never returned, she wouldn't miss these items.

She wrote a check for the following month's rent, which was due, and dropped the envelope in the mail box, raising the silly-ass flag thingy to alert the postal carrier. With a sigh she called both her employers and left messages on their voice mail. She expressed her regrets. What she really wanted to do was tell them to kiss off, but better judgment prevailed; too many bad endings already.

The kitchen was remarkable in its obsolescence. Linoleum provided the veneer instead of newer sleeker countertops. The Chambers stove worked, but Rachel preferred fast food to home cooking, especially hers. The refrigerator was so old it was embellished with peace symbols and cried "Flower Power." It held two cans of Coke, moldy cheddar, and a solitary apple. With the mold scraped off, the cheese would do for a pick-me-up. She dumped all the ice—which wasn't much—in a small cooler and added the sodas and food.

She heaved the duffel and computer to her shoulder. Already a heavy burden, she picked up the cooler. With her free arm she snapped up both coats and her keys and switched off the light.

There was a long, boring drive ahead of her with only a billion or so trucks for company. She hoped she didn't have to drag the Merc's ass down I-Forty. It could be temperamental. Maturing blue-collar luxury vehicles were like that. Rachel said goodbye to the dark house and let herself out.

Was the retrieved soul lying in wait for her, or had it gone on ahead to wreak havoc in the Land of Enchantment? She suspected the latter. The night sky imparted no answers.

As she walked to the garage a sound she hadn't heard since leaving New Mexico echoed across the neighborhood: the howl of a wolf. *How odd.* Preoccupied, she loaded her car, and forgot the sound that didn't belong.

CHAPTER 3

By daybreak Rachel had intimate knowledge of every truck stop and McDonald's along Interstate Forty. It had been the same song, same verse since Oklahoma City: stop, pee, buy another java—no decaf this trip. She hated coffee, but this was an emergency. It was the middle of the night and she needed to stay awake. The gas-guzzling Merc needed two big swigs along the way. Rachel breathed a sigh of relief as she drove into Amarillo. The gas warning light had burned for the past twenty-five miles.

It was possible to make the drive in about thirteen hours, staying within the speed limits, but Oklahoma roads were unsafe at any speed, so she'd kept it at sixty before pulling out the stops at the Texas border where highways miraculously smoothed out and opened up. Oklahoma roads were notorious. "Made with lumpy shit," her dad used to say. "And you have to pay to drive on them." He'd made reference to the many toll roads crisscrossing the state. No politician was able to explain the state's deplorable highway system, but Rachel had her suspicions.

She had to give the Merc its due. It was comfortable on the highway. It said right on the dash it was "Ride Engineered" and that was no lie. Even over the most pot-holed road, the car cruised like a giant ship at sea, no wave too big to cause a bout of sea sickness. Unfortunately, for women drivers, the interior was designed for men—large men. There were no bucket seats for wraparound comfort, only fabric covered bench-style seating, with controls just out of reach.

The passenger's window rattled at highway speed. In the Amarillo gas station, Rachel pushed a multifolded unpaid parking ticket between the pane and window frame. She hoped it would quiet the rushing wind. Inside the station restroom she absently fingered her shaggy collar-length hair. The few silver strands caught the harsh overhead light and looked great. She'd rubbed off most of her makeup hours ago and appeared pale as a result. Somehow, no thanks to her eating habits, her body remained slim.

Back on the road somewhere in the twilight zone that is the Texas panhandle, she lost all traces of classical music and switched off the radio in frustration. Country music wasn't her thing. All that whining about lost love, accompanied by steel guitars and twangy voices, was too much. Without the disembodied voice of a DJ to keep her company, the darkness enclosed her in a vacuum of urgency. Her foot settled comfortably on the accelerator. The speedometer hovered near eighty. If her luck was improving, there would be only snoozing patrol officers as she sped through the wee hours, and no skulking spirits looking to stir up trouble.

She couldn't figure out what went wrong during the ceremony. Throughout the night she had gone over and over it. Why didn't her father return? Why this dark soul? And, why would it speak in a threatening way concerning her brother? Rachel's relationship with Chris wasn't the most cordial or familial in nature. They had taken on adversarial roles in adulthood. Whether it was due to their radically different philosophies or merely a side effect of her common journalistic bond with their father, she couldn't be sure. She had taken up the pen and followed in her father's rather large footsteps. Her brother, by contrast, had entered politics, and there had always been rumors about his credibility. It made for interesting discussions at family functions.

But her brother's attitude wasn't really her concern. Her father's death and its lack of resolution were. Although the rear of his car was heavily damaged, it could not be determined if it was an accident or deliberate. The police ruled the death questionable, but no suspects or motives were uncovered. Frustration, coupled with grief, left Rachel adrift and estranged from her family. She fled her comfortable life in New Mexico. One of those do-something-even-if-it's-wrong situations.

There was already strain between her and husband Anthony Blackwell after she received kudos from the New Mexico governor's office for her landmark feature on the state's gambling laws. Following that, assignments had been numerous and Rachel spent more and more time away from home. This added more stress to their relationship.

In Santa Fe, she had been a feature writer at its premiere publication, *High Desert Country*. The job was the greatest loss in her furious retreat from the status quo. Her work became a sanctuary from her father's death and the failed investigation. Disappointing her boss had broken what was left of her heart. Julian Brazos was a terrific person whom she hated leaving abruptly, and with an unfinished story. She wouldn't blame him if he never forgave her.

Her brother, Chris, the mayor of Santa Fe, seemed relieved when she left town. Instead of bringing them closer, their parent's death put distance, emotional and geographical, between them.

She'd found an unremarkable place to live, a bungalow in a seedy neighborhood. It once was graceful, but time and a couple of oil busts had depleted its elegance.

She eked out a living working two jobs. A small society rag used her as a stringer. It wasn't her idea of real writing, composing wedding announcements for the well-to-do and covering Junior League events. The pay wasn't enough to make ends meet so she'd taken a position as a morning receptionist at a small PR business. It was the worst of jobs with several executive types dumping their gofer work on her, inexplicably expecting her to simultaneously be at her desk, while running errands, keeping the coffee flowing, and the copy machine busy. What a bitch, but eating was essential.

East of Tucumcari near the New Mexico border, a jackrabbit flashed in front of the car. Instinctively, she twisted the steering wheel to the right to miss the creature. The Merc swerved onto the shoulder and then off, narrowly missing clumps of prickly pear. She fought for control in the ditch weaving and sliding on the dirt and loose stones, swearing at herself for saving the bunny at the risk of wrecking the car. With much effort she wrenched the heavy vehicle to the left, the tires responded, the good earth spewed in its wake. Leaving the precarious edge of blacktop they found purchase back on the pavement.

Her chest heaved from the fright; she slowed, pulled over and stopped. It was cold, but she had to get out of the car. She wrapped her arms around herself for a few seconds trying to conserve body heat.

The chilly air was about to send her back to the vehicle when she heard a voice whisper, "I'd turn back if I were you." Rachel, stupefied, turned toward the open countryside. There wasn't as much as a yard light in sight. "Ooh-kay," she said to herself. "Time to get out of the fresh air." But standing in her way was a filmy slip of something wafting in the breeze. It could be mistaken for a person, but was not identifiable. It repeated, "I'd turn back if I were you."

Alarmed, Rachel glanced about for assistance, but she was shit out of luck and alone on the highway. Having already been frightened out of her wits for one day, she took a different tact. "I've had it with ghosts," she said loudly. "Get lost!" Nothing. The levitating form remained.

Then she heard a growl; soft at first, then more threatening. The sound was near. Rachel stood still and carefully scanned the area around her. At first she missed it, but there it was, a lone wolf, the shadowy form, pale, but fully recognizable. The fur coat appeared dimly illuminated, and was crisply outlined by the darkness. Its eyes were crystal blue.

Her legs felt spring-loaded. She yearned to be all cozy in her car, but the chatty phantom blocked the driver's side. It occurred to her the wolf was not focused on her, but on the vaporous image floating next to her car. The wolf growled again and advanced several feet. Rachel resisted the urge to back away. Her ghostly visitor had enough. Poof, it dissipated like a summer shower in the plains.

The wolf turned to Rachel. She was afraid to run, afraid fleeing would make it chase her. Somewhere in the mainframe of her mind, she remembered one should not look directly at a menacing dog, but she couldn't take her eyes from it. It was no longer issuing warnings. It gazed at her for a few seconds. Benevolently? Then turned and vanished into the night.

Rachel wasted no time. She flung herself inside the car and locked the door. Obviously, she had to lay off caffeine. It was causing her see things.

The Merc sprang to life and she was westbound again. She tried to think of other things, any old thing, to feel normal. Joseph floated into her mind. She met the Hopi shaman just before her life began coming apart at the seams. Joseph was wise, as was to be expected, but he was also calm, kind and happy. He encouraged her to use her writing for good, though she didn't know how to apply that advice yet.

His influence caused her to look beyond the narrower focus of her life to other cultures. Rachel began reading about Native American customs. She found that assembling prayer sticks was a comforting thing to do. Several hung from the sycamore in the backyard of her rental. The Indians believed that when hung outside the prayer would continue the journey to the Upper Beings, so constant praying would not be needed.

The Clines Corner tourist trap was her last stop before Santa Fe. Every imaginable cup, car tag, and Indian trinket was available for a ridiculous price. She passed on all that but gratefully used their rest room.

Highway 285, or the Turquoise Trail, was referred to as a super two in highway lingo. Basically, that's two wide lanes with shoulders. This early in the morning Rachel had it all to herself, which was a blessing because the sun was rising with blinding clarity. She slapped the visor down and pushed on big sunglasses. Between here and Santa Fe she would gain elevation topping out at 7,000 feet.

The area's passenger rail center was in Lamy, for what it was worth. Unsuspecting tourists had arrived there to find no easy way into Santa Fe. Go figure. Fortunately, residents—mostly celebrities—had put together a rail shuttle to alleviate the problem. The Beautiful People couldn't handle inconvenience, especially since Santa Fe was lacking a hub airport. But that had been alleviated too with the addition of a regional jet. No more long shuttle trips into Albuquerque for the jet set. In this case, the effort benefited locals and visitors as well. You couldn't say that about most of the extras which had appeared in Santa Fe over the last decades. Residents and tourists alike paid extra for food, gasoline, and housing as a result of the city's affluent escalation. But the tide had begun to turn with the beginning of the so-called Great Recession. Tourism was down, down, down and the chamber was feeling anxious.

Traffic picked up as commuters left El Dorado for work in Santa Fe or Albuquerque. There were fewer people living here now. El Dorado residents were fearful their water supply could be cut off. In a desert climate water was a precious resource. Rumors abounded but no one seemed to know what would happen. Many "For Sale" signs told the story of uncertainty.

Dread replaced sleepiness as her destination neared. Now that she was here, what exactly was she going to do? Tell her brother she'd brought back a dead person, one apparently with a grudge? He'd commit her in a heartbeat to the home for the very, very nervous. Yet, he had to be warned. Didn't he? "Oh, crap. I'll just play it by ear," Rachel told herself. In the bright light of the new morning some of the panic was wearing off. Maybe there was a logical explanation for what had happened—like a rebound hallucinogenic trip from her formative years? Or a mixture of headache drugs and stress? If she thought long enough, something plausible would come to mind.

Rachel caught her breath as the City Different came into view. Santa Fe is so labeled because of its adobe architecture. After years of living there, the desert city was still a gorgeous eyeful. Snuggled near the base of the Sangre de Cristos the brown flat-roofed adobe houses dotted the hills surrounded by venerable piñon and spreading chamisa. It is no wonder artists and writers find the vistas so inspirational.

She turned off Old Pecos Trail onto St. Michael's Drive to look for a telephone. The fast-food joint wasn't open yet, but she only wanted to use the drive-up phone. A homeless person huddled against the morning cool in the restaurant's cast-off boxes. Most of the businesses along St. Michael's were nice and/or new but this place was a bit seedy by comparison. There was still no answer at her brother's house. "Damn." She slammed down the receiver. It missed the cradle and swung lazily. "You'd think he knew I was coming," she reflected on his propensity to keep her at a distance. "Now what?"

There was only one place to go. No way was she going to show up at Tony's house—her house. That would be too painful. Chloe won by default.

Dear, dear Chloe. They had met years ago when Rachel was sent to interview the owners of the newest real estate venture in Santa Fe. In the last half of the 'eighties, Santa Fe had seen a boom in home sales. The rich from all over the world had to have a piece of southwest paradise before it was all paved over. Chloe "did" real estate. She didn't sell it. She did it, and did it well. Chloe and her partner knew a good opportunity when it presented itself. They left the agency where they were employees and started their own.

It had been like-at-first-sight, although Rachel wondered why at the time. She and Chloe were very different outwardly, but deep in the soul, they were the best of friends. Chloe, in her New Age priestess manner, professed to know that they had been friends in other lifetimes. Rachel thought she was kidding at first and played along. It soon became apparent her friend was serious.

Chloe admired the free spirit in Rachel. Writers, even those with *real* jobs seem to live on air. There's a general misunderstanding about writing—that the pay is spectacular and the work leisurely. *Au contraire.* The big money goes to a few: Rowling, King, Gresham. Writing is never easy, but it is pleasurable work if you're so inclined and can tolerate the hours spent alone. Deadlines provided the most stress, that and uncooperative interviews.

They had begun with an occasional lunch and expanded to weekends in Sedona, Ojai, and Santa Barbara where Chloe had business conferences, and the views or food or both were good—make that great! Chloe enjoyed being included in Rachel's perks and they attended many media events together.

But it was the unfortunate predicaments Rachel periodically found herself in that tantalized Chloe's adventurous heart. The reporter's curious tendency to sometimes enamor, sometimes incite, was what Chloe had come to admire. Rachel, like many journalists, had a tendency to become a sticktight when she thought someone wasn't leveling with her. That made for some interesting, and at times, antagonistic encounters, both of which Chloe delighted in.

Like Rachel, Chloe was a night owl, and since she never left before 9:00 a.m., she'd still be at home. Luckily, her house had plenty of room for unexpected guests.

Rachel took Galisteo to Paseo de Peralta, which acted as the city's loop, almost encircling downtown. Chloe lived off Gonzales in a dazzling house with views galore. From the enormous windows in front she could watch the sunsets. The deck which traversed the back of the house allowed glimpses of the ski trails on towering Mount Baldy. Some evenings the mountains would wash red in the sunset, hence their name Sangre de Cristo—Blood of Christ—mountains.

The private road off Gonzales was dirt—Santa Fe slang for never graded gravel, full of potholes and washes—and led to half a dozen houses. Chloe's was all but hidden in the trees and shrubs. A piñon limb scraped the side of the Merc, leaving its imprint forever. "Damn, Santa Fe is no place for a car the size of a UPS truck!" Rachel admonished herself.

There was a pleasant crunch beneath her feet as pebbles twisted and turned on the path to Chloe's door. Rachel poked the door bell.

Chloe Valdez was clearly not Latino, as her first husband had been. The raven-haired beauty was all French. She had kept the last name because she liked the juxtaposition and Rachel thought it was probably good for business in this area of Hispanic traditions. This morning Chloe's waist-length locks were tied at one side of her neck. She was made up, which always included deep red lipstick on full lips. Her skillfully arched eyebrows rested above brown eyes of fire making a stark contrast to her fair skin. That was Chloe, a mix of contrasts.

"Holy shit!" Chloe shrieked. "Why didn't you tell me you were coming back?" Toned arms wrapped Rachel in a stranglehold. Enthusiasm was one of Chloe's attributes; she could energetically love or fight with the best. She pulled back, seeing the look of exhaustion on Rachel's face. "Good, lord, Rach, come in. You look like you walked from Tulsa."

"Thanks." Rachel rubbed her face as though checking for stubble. "I hadn't planned on making the trip." She entered the expansive foyer, stepped on the wool Oriental rug, then walked through the house on Saltillo tiles. The skylights in the hall bathed light on several paintings by local artists of worldwide renown. The living room provided a white backdrop for Chloe's eclectic tastes. Another rug, larger than the one in the hall, was surrounded by oddly shaped furniture. The canary yellow and teal chairs resembled inverted party hats. Black pillows accented the bright colors.

Chloe pulled back a stool at her kitchen bar. "Sit down. You want coffee?"

"No!" Rachel softened her voice. "No more coffee, thanks. Could I crash for a while? I haven't slept all night."

"Sure. Are you okay? You look like you've seen a ghost; pale as me."

Rachel started at Chloe's observation. "You wouldn't believe it. After I sleep, I'll tell you about it."

"Help yourself to a guest room," Chloe said. "I'm glad you're here. I've missed you." Rachel was engulfed in a silken hug and kissed on both cheeks, European style.

* * *

Rachel pushed back the comforter several inches so she could look around the room. The only light came from the window, filtered by sheer curtains. At first she thought there was smoke hanging in the air, but she didn't smell any. A mist clouded her vision. She could feel the vapor on her skin. And that awful feeling that she wasn't alone.

A quick glance at the reading chair next to the bed reassured her that no one was sitting there. Upholstered in white, she could be certain. Relieved, she was about to pull the covers up when she saw movement at the foot of her bed. It was as if someone had waved a scarf. If it was Chloe, she would have been silhouetted and exposed, not gauzy. But Chloe wouldn't be prowling about her house, she would have knocked.

You've had a long day. Go back to sleep. Good advice. Take it. Rachel sunk back into the covers, sighed and closed her eyes. That's when the floor board creaked.

CHAPTER 4

There it was again, an undeniable sound. Chloe's house had tile in the common areas, but the bedroom floors were covered in hardwoods and Mexican rugs. Rachel reached out from under the covers and switched on a lamp. Light flooded one corner of the room. She slowly poked one foot out and then another. The floor was warm. Chloe's flooring hid heated tubing beneath the tile and the hardwoods.

Rachel stood stiffly waiting for the next shoe to drop, so to speak. Every sense on alert, she felt the incident over. She marched across the room and turned on another light, and another. Nothing. The bathroom was empty as well. An odor hung in the air. She couldn't identify it.

You're losing it Rach. Time to let it go. She crawled back into the plushy bedding. About to turn off the last lamp, she hesitated. *Won't hurt to leave one on.*

* * *

Chris Woods slammed out of his posh five-bedroom home in the foothills north of Santa Fe. It was midafternoon and he was pissed. So the bitch had gone home to her mother, and taken the kids with her. Fine. That was three less problems he had to deal with. He was immediately struck by a pang of guilt. His boys were special to him, especially Christopher, his namesake. The child's face reflected his own. He climbed into the dusty black Pathfinder, dragging one expensive pant leg along the running board. Angrily, he swatted at the offending grime. In Santa Fe living on a "dirt," albeit gravel road, was desirable, even envied. Chris thought it stupid. Nothing escaped the dust.

There had been five messages from his sister last night when he returned home to find his wife had packed and left. What on earth did Rachel want? She marries a good guy, has a great life, then a few months ago she up and leaves. What kind of sense did that make? Women!

He'd tried to return her calls, but there had been no answer, even at 2:00 a.m. No surprise. Rachel had been squirrelly since their father died.

When he reached downtown, he parked in his reserved spot at Santa Fe City Hall, grabbed his briefcase and entered the building.

"Good afternoon, Mayor," said the building receptionist.

"Hello," he grumbled. Chris could never remember her name, probably because the girls never stayed. It was a crappy job and everyone wanted to move up. In his office he took the stack of message slips his secretary handed him, closed the door, and dropped them unread on his desk.

Was his wife's latest escapade going to cost him politically? He had to think. "Hold my calls," he barked over the intercom.

"Sir," his secretary replied cautiously. "Your sister is here."

Damn. She must have driven all night. No wonder he couldn't reach her—didn't even have a cell phone. What the hell was so important? Just what he needed; another female problem. He wanted to send her packing, but instead asked his secretary to show her in.

"Rachel, this is a surprise." Indeed. He performed the perfunctory hug and stood back to read the extent of the emergency. She looked tired but didn't seem to be in any real anguish.

"How are you, Chris? Sorry about not calling, but it seems I'm here."

"Nonsense," he lied. "Never too busy to see my sis." His face revealed his mood. It was not becoming or welcoming. He added suspiciously, "What's up?"

"Oh, nothing really." Rachel could lie too. "Did you get my messages?"

"I tried to call you back early this morning, but didn't get an answer. Something wrong?" he asked. His sincerity had dried up and blown away years ago. Politics seemed to do that.

Rachel thought a moment. Something was definitely up with her brother. Frustrations of the job? Chamber on his back again? Police chief? She could only guess. Then there was his rather volatile relationship with her sister-in-law. Chris' infidelities were common knowledge. The good-old-boy membership regarded him as a bit of a folk hero and therefore covered for him when it came to his wife and Santa Fe's citizenry.

She wasn't quite sure how Chris had become such a jerk. Their mother died when they were small children so the blame couldn't be placed on her. Their dad had been an honest, kind, all-around nice guy. But something went astray with Chris. The no longer honorable—was it ever?—profession of politics had drawn him like a magnet. Santa Fe was a small town in many ways. Everyone knew the mayor and soon Chris saw doors open to him, from the best tables in restaurants to free tickets to the opera. What other candy had tempted him?

She answered his question. "I look tired because I drove all night to get here. No, nothing's wrong. Just got in the mood for a visit." This was obviously not the time to break the news about bringing back the dead. In the first place, he wouldn't believe her. Probably no one would. Rachel wasn't sure she did.

"Your new employers—I forget how many there are—don't mind you taking a vacation right away?" Chris said and immediately regretted it, a little. Things had been tough for her recently, partly due to her own instability as he saw it. Anyone who became a writer obviously needed a complete head examination. Although their father's income as a journalist had been adequate, there hadn't been many extras for the family. Chris still smarted from what he saw as a life denied.

Rachel detected the note of rancor and *the look*. The one Chris always gave her when he was indulging what he saw as her neurotic tendencies. Chris' false concern for her emotional well-being had been made clear to her. "They don't mind," she lied again. "I know you're busy. I'll see you later."

The relief on his face was almost palpable. "By the way, how are Jennifer and the kids?"

"Oh," he paused. Did she detect the slightest outbreak of perspiration? "Great."

"Good. Well, I'm staying with Chloe. Got a few hours sleep there this morning. Let's all get together for dinner."

"Sure." Total lack of enthusiasm.

Outside, Rachel stepped into a perfect day. Not a cloud cluttered the pure azure sky. Something was going on with Chris. Her guess? Domestic problems. She figured Jennifer had finally dumped him. "Never kid a kidder, bro."

CHAPTER 5

The office of *High Desert Country* was located in a rundown office on a narrow one-way street off Agua Fria. Rachel made the short left turn with little room to spare. The bulky Mercury had to inhale as it squeaked between the shabby liquor store and the high curb.

Rachel had visited many magazine and newspaper offices. For all the presumed glamour of the publishing industry, their offices never seemed to reflect any of it. *High Desert Country* was widely read throughout the southwest and western states. The glossy mag had won numerous awards for photography and writing. No one would ever suspect this from looking at the unremarkable building.

Why talk with Julian? She told herself whatever she was chasing could take awhile to find. It was purely guesswork that Santa Fe was the place to look. In the meantime, she needed some income.

The last time she saw Julian Brazos she had given him her hasty notice. He had been angry and disappointed. The anger she understood. The disappointment hurt. She had left him high and dry with a partly finished assignment. Unprofessional? You bet. All she could do was apologize. Pretty lame to someone who had helped establish her career.

She remained in her car after shutting down the engine. The parking area was enclosed with a coyote fence, six-foot lengths of trimmed branches, bark intact, held together vertically with wire. The warm air felt good right after turning off the AC but the bright sunshine was fast turning the car into a stuffy oven. Rachel leaned against the steering wheel while idly running her index finger through the dust on the dash. It was as if something alien guided it, but still a nice brain-dead activity.

Would Julian talk with her? She hadn't bothered calling him, afraid he wouldn't see her. A cool breeze rushed in when she opened the door, pushing out the warm air. Rachel drank it in, hoping for a sustaining rush of courage. The emotion she felt was anything but courageous. The wind seemed to carry with it a foreboding. She turned away from it. She should have faced it straight on because it would have put off seeing what she had unknowingly written on the dash. Scratched in the dust on the navy vinyl was the word "fool." She had even underlined it. It was the second time in less than twenty-four hours that the word had come up.

Rachel wiped away the dust casting the word aside. She slammed the car door and stood in the bright day, feeling chilled. This would teach her not to mess with ancient Indian ceremonies. They were probably booby-trapped so they'd backfire if done by someone less than a full-blood Native American. With effort, she shrugged off the fear that was spreading throughout her body making her feel anxious.

The magazine office was located in an old adobe house—like everything else. The City Different was actually the city same. Virtually all houses, offices, and stores were made of adobe, or materials made to imitate it, and painted some color of brown. No buildings were allowed to be higher than five stories so as not to block the majestic views or soar over the state Capitol building.

The flagstone walk trailed off to the left of the entrance to a pleasant corner. There, one could sit on an uncomfortable wrought iron bench and watch or feed the fish swimming lazily in the small pond. Russian olive trees provided a whisper of shade and silvery beauty to the quiet garden nook.

A few hardy summer flowers continued to bloom in pots at the front door. Inside, most of the interior partitions had been removed, leaving kind of a stucco warehouse look. Framed Santa Fe Opera posters hung from the walls. Stella Dallas—her mother was a big Barbara Stanwyck fan—still manned the reception desk. Julian hadn't changed anything since Rachel left. The Steelcase desks—midcentury (the last one) government issue—were as she remembered them, scattered about at odd angles. He'd picked them up for a song when the city bought new furniture under her brother's leadership.

Light tapping noises carried from the back where someone was hunched over a computer working on deadline. Rachel didn't recognize him—probably her replacement. The thought made her momentarily jealous.

On the break table, stale coffee had formed a dark line in the glass pot. The sight didn't help her queasy stomach as she thought about talking with Julian. Packs of generic stevia, Splenda and Sweet'N Low littered the top. Piles of magazines and newspapers cluttered the reception area. Hardly anyone ever sat there. She felt like an intruder in this place where she had once belonged.

Stella, intently watching a soap opera on her old-school five-inch TV, had yet to detect her. The door had been left open. Rachel didn't even cast a shadow when she entered. Julian didn't seem to mind that Stella was addicted to television. As long as she answered the telephone and got the phone numbers right. Stella was flat-out beautiful. She obviously worked out—probably in front of a TV. Her short blonde hair was flawlessly styled, her attire professional. Stella was the only person in the office who dressed up. Jeans and T-shirts predominated with the rest of the crew.

"Rachel, how wonderful to see you!" Stella declared upon noticing her. "Thought you were gone from these parts forever." She quickly walked around the desk and hugged Rachel.

"Hi, Stella. You know how it is. Can't stay away." The older woman's smile was contagious and it made attractive crinkles around her eyes. "Is Julian here?" Rachel asked conspiratorially.

"Yup. Even in a good mood last I saw him. Want me to buzz?"

"Maybe I should just go back to his office—not give him a chance to say 'no.'" Stella winked. Rachel took that as okay.

Julian was a native Santa Fean, a big man, not overweight, but hefty. He had mostly gray hair including his beard. As she studied him from the open door of his office, he grimaced at a spreadsheet covering most of his desk. Rachel turned away, thinking this might not be the best time, when Julian cleared his throat. "Only cowards sneak away," he said.

Shit. He was going to be a cad. Rachel figured she had it coming. Time to face the music. "Hi, Jule. You looked busy so . . ."

"So you thought you'd avoid me?"

"Pretty much."

"Come in, Rachel. Sit." He pointed to one of two brown director chairs. The other one was full of page proofs. Several file cabinets lined the short wall of his office. They perfectly matched the desk right down to the scrapes and dents. More stuff stacked there. Only about four-square-feet of floor space remained. "What brings you back to SF?" He leaned back in his chair with hands clasped behind his head. The chair protested, even older than the rest of the furniture.

"I, well . . ." she stammered. "It looks like I'm going to be here a little while—legal stuff." Total crock, but maybe he'd buy it. "Wondered if you had any work you could throw my way. Purely as a stringer," she added hastily.

"Geez, how about finishing that story you were working on when you left?" She expected him to smile, but he wasn't teasing. Still pissed.

"Okay, I deserve that," Rachel said. "Any other shit you want to throw at me?"

"I only give second chances once," he said sternly.

"Okay," Rachel replied, feeling like a jerk.

His lips turned up softly. They were forgiving her. She blessed Julian a thousand times. Even though their ages were similar, he was a father figure. She hated to disappoint him.

"Nah, that's enough. No sense overdoing it. Can't offer you your old desk—replaced you, you know—but then Carl up and quit last week—although *he* gave two weeks' notice." A look in her direction meant to inflict guilt. It worked. "Take the clean desk. Here's a media kit on the new housing compound for finer families."

He lifted a silver folder from beneath the spreadsheets. "Do an interview for the city page. I can't help but wonder why someone wants to build this with the real estate market crashing. Course, there seems to be no end to the number of people with tons of money and no sense, all wanting a ridiculously large adobe house."

It was a puff piece and she knew it, but she was willing to pay the price. At least Julian hadn't turned her away.

"Okay. I'll get on it tomorrow," she looked at him for approval. He nodded, going back to his bookkeeping nightmare. "Jule. Thank you."

"*De nada.*" He waved her away, not one for outward displays of emotion.

Rachel fled to the outer office and sat down at the only desk not heaped with paper and used cups. Tears threatened. She pursed her lips tightly together and quietly said thank you for Julian.

CHAPTER 6

The following morning, after some uninterrupted sleep, Rachel felt almost normal as she prepared to leave for her interview. The good folks at Pueblo Blanco were only too happy to make time for an article in *High Desert Country*. Hard to believe the developers hadn't realized the name smacked of elitism, if not downright racism. She supposed there was a small chance they didn't know it meant the "white people," but she doubted it, always the cynic.

There was blame enough to go around in New Mexico. For every bigoted Anglo there was a Native American or Hispanic counterpart. Some Pueblo tribes had been publicly outspoken about their intention to take tourists' money—all the traffic would bear. Some sightseers returned the *favor* by exhibiting boorish behavior during religious tribal ceremonies. It seemed almost no one came off as completely without prejudice or at least lacked understanding.

Rachel checked her satchel for an extra pen. Her notebook and tape recorder rested in the passenger seat. Good. She felt in control again. Interviewing and writing was her lifeblood; exactly what she needed.

She headed the Merc out on the always busy Highway 285, toward Taos. Rachel hated this road. The driving was fast and most drivers were short on patience. Fortunately Camino Tierra was only a few miles north. After driving through the ranch style gate that announced to all their arrival at the exclusive soon-to-be-walled compound, Rachel ate dust behind a truck for close to a mile.

Dump trucks were hauling in topsoil for the golf course. Just what Santa Fe needed; another water eater. The city's water resources—much of which depended on snowmelt—were limited. Overdevelopment had already cost the city dearly in consumption. Why did people move to a desert climate only to plant grass and other nonnative plants that require daily watering? Why not stay put? If you want a grass yard, Santa Fe isn't the place to live. Now some idiot developer, who likely resides in a different region or country, was building another golf course that would require constant watering.

Rachel had an idea for the story—an exposé on irresponsible developers. She quickly canned the notion. Julian would fire her if she strayed too far afield.

At last, the truck stopped, the dust cleared, and the complex came into view. A massive Spanish style building took center stage. It must be the office and common use facilities. The imposing porte cochère gave the unfortunate feel of a nursing home. She could envision Gramps being pushed across the grounds via wheelchair. That ought to bring in the buyers. Here the drive was paved in cobblestone—definitely not New Mexican! Winding streets angled away from the main structure. There were six completed homes, according to the press kit. Each represented a different floor plan. Exterior elevations in Spanish, the familiar Pueblo adobe and the less used Territorial style covered all the bases for southwest design.

At least the designers had the forethought to leave the native piñon trees, juniper, and chamisa. Some effort had been made to build the structures around the existing flora. Rachel was certain the fauna—coyotes, lizards and other wild creatures of the region—would not be as welcome. The honeyed folks of Pueblo Blanco had better keep their poodles firmly in hand or Mr. Coyote would make a meal of them.

She parked beneath the huge overhang, seeing no sign telling her not to, and checked the press release for the name of the spokesperson. The PR guy was listed as Alexander Robbins.

The inside of the cavernous foyer was tiled in yellow ochre clay squares. It was an attempt to imitate authentic Mexican tile. It didn't fail entirely, but the tile patterns repeated. The ceiling formed an exaggerated arch, giving the space the feel of imminent escape by flight. The walls were so white it required sunglasses in the bright light to admire the paintings of Pueblo dwellers, probably the only natives to cross the threshold except for service workers. There were several large palms—very Las Vegas—scattered about, perhaps to fill space so no further expenditures on art would be needed.

Rachel heard hesitant typing from down the hall. She followed the sound to a young receptionist who struggled with a new computer. She frowned at a large open manual and pecked at a few more keys.

"Hi," Rachel said.

"Shit!" The girl jumped from her seat, the new, still-covered-in-plastic chair banged into the white wall behind her, leaving the first dent.

"Sorry, didn't mean to scare you."

"Oh, I'm sorry. It's this damn, uh, blasted computer. We didn't have this kind in school." No doubt a fly-by-night business school Rachel thought or she'd know how to work it. Remembering her reason for being there, the girl added a beleaguered, "May I help you?"

"Rachel Blackstone, *High Desert Country*." The girl batted heavily mascaraed lashes in total discombobulation. "The magazine. I have an appointment." This child was truly short a brick. "With Alexander Robbins." Did she have the entire picture now? Rachel was asked to wait while she bounced out of the room—to get her interview? Sometimes, one could only hope.

Robbins could give Sean Connery a run for his money in a few years. The balding man had striking silver hair around the lower half of his head, piercing blue eyes and one killer smile. A fit fifty, but with a few too many muscles, his handshake was firm but didn't break any of her bones. Outfitted in worn jeans and a plaid shirt, with cuffs rolled up, Robbins looked cool.

"How do you do." It wasn't a question but the patrician voice and engaging eyes said he was interested. "Please excuse the casual dress. I've been playing with trucks today. Haven't done that since kindergarten. If you come this way, I'll show you the model first."

Rachel folded back her notebook and began running tape. Most people weren't good interviews. Some lacked experience, others were self-conscious, and then there were politicians! She suspected Robbins would be concise and articulate. He had that confident nature about him.

They entered what looked like a recreation room. It was large, plain, with many windows, and would likely remain unused. An architect's model of Pueblo Blanco was laid out under a glass box. The plastic lawns were green. Rachel suppressed the comment that really wanted to come out. "This model will be moved to the front entrance tomorrow," he said. "There will be 100 homes here upon completion." An enormous housing addition for the city, Rachel wondered where all those flushes would go? Robbins pointed to the complex model with its tiny houses and regionally incorrect trees. Guess the architect didn't have any chamisa or piñon in his box of imitation foliage.

"One-hundred? Can enough water be supplied to support that many people and all this added vegetation?" Oops, great way to start an interview, with a hostile question.

A look of annoyance passed quickly across his face and was gone. "Oh sure, that's all been worked out with the city." Rachel wondered how, and made a note. Robbins pointed out all the lovely amenities of Pueblo Blanco. Yes, there would be a terrific golf course designed by a washed-up former pro. Two swimming pools would accommodate adults and children. More water. A minuscule playground adjacent to the kiddie pool rounded out the amenities. Perhaps the developers didn't want to encourage people with kids to live here.

The rec room would be used for informal entertaining according to Robbins. The really uppity stuff would take place at the other end of the building in a yet-to-be-finished banquet facility. Rachel thought she should try an attitude adjustment, but damn, she hated this snobby crap.

She uh-huhed in the right places. One of the nice things about taking notes was that it prevented her from responding to things she should keep quiet about. It was also useful when bored to tears while covering yet another "fabulous" event referred to as a rah-rah city piece.

After touring the tiny scale development they walked across the dusty street to one of the model homes. It was lovely. An interior decorator had done his or her best to make a good impression. But it had that elegantly unlived in look that no house should be caught dead wearing. Rachel thought a pair of dirty socks lying on the floor and a three-week stack of newspapers would give it a homier feel.

Robbins did his spiel. It wasn't the hardest sell she'd ever heard but it was well-rehearsed. He didn't seem right for the role of marketing. In her experience, fast-talking bleached blondes with cigarettes dangling from their lips pitched these places, carefully avoiding mention of astronomical maintenance fees in favor of a constant assault of fast-food facts concerning home ownership and its many tax blessings.

Boiled down, this was just another thrown together, three-bedroom, million-dollar house with nothing going for it but a pretty facade and location, location, location.

"With the downturn in the Santa Fe real estate industry," Rachel began carefully, "how can the developers justify such a large expenditure for new housing?

Robbins blinked, but he was quick. "Our latest studies indicate an upturn is expected within a few months just in time for the spring selling season."

How convenient. "May I have a copy of that report?"

His mouth turned down at one corner. Irritation. He didn't want to go there. "Sure, I'll be happy to get that for you." He lied. Rachel knew that line. All reporters knew it.

He recovered and a few minutes later Rachel concluded the interview. With the glossy media kit and Robbins' perfect description of a surreal planned community; she was certain she could write another aren't-we-lucky-to-have-this-in-our-midst story for the city page. Now, a little investigative journalism would have been interesting, but this was so much bullshit.

She was scheduled to meet Chloe for lunch so she gunned the Merc—it protested; she insisted—and let a truck eat her dust this time.

30

CHAPTER 7

The Mercury squeezed between two expensive cars along the Second Street studio district. In Santa Fe, haute vehicles were standard, but they must be dirty—at least on the outside. These qualified. This part of town was home to Hollywood sorts who deigned to come to the only desert in the world where the food was as good as the views. Some bought mega bucks homes in the high hills or in Wilderness Gate, stayed a few years, but found that the lack of a major airport complicated their jet-setting ways.

Rachel looked with disdain at the mess in her car. She would have preferred vinyl seats to the cloth—easier to keep clean. It was still trashed from her ghostly midnight pursuit. Empty plastic bags, paper cups, crumpled napkins had conjoined with discarded reporter notebooks, newspapers, and assorted pens. It was not likely to be put to rights anytime soon. The remains of a lone grape lay in a cup holder. It had finished its life in the food chain as a raisin. Chloe would refuse to be seen with her anywhere near this heap.

The California cuisine restaurant had found a happy home with film and television types frequenting the neighborhood. Wheeling and dealing went on over tabletops due to the numerous movies and series television filmed in the region. The place sold the hell out of radicchio salads dusted in white pepper and sprout sandwiches gently ladled with Béarnaise sauce. No green chile cheese burritos were on the menu.

Rachel stood inside, waiting for her eyes to adjust to the dim light. Chloe was easy to spot dressed *a la* Santa Fe: candlestick skirt, silk blouse, denim vest, and boots. Her body dripped with turquoise jewelry. Egad, even a cowboy hat rested on her beautiful shoulders, held in place by the chin string. She wore *the look* when she worked. Even more noticeable was her companion, a drop-dead-gorgeous man who sat across from her. There was something familiar about him. Before she could think what, Chloe saw her.

"Rachel, please join us." While Rachel crossed the room—very much aware he was watching, but not rudely looking—Chloe pulled a chair from another table, causing a noise like a fingernail on a chalkboard. She seemed not to notice, but the rest of the room did. The man stood.

"Hi, Chloe. Am I interrupting?" Rachel hesitated to sit down without asking, though it perturbed her slightly that Chloe had asked someone else to lunch without telling her, however handsome he might be.

"No, not at all. I'd like you to meet Logan Masters. He's here in Santa Fe filming his TV series. Perhaps you've seen it?"

But of course he was Logan Masters! Rachel tried to rearrange the frown on her face into a sweet smile. "How do you do?" Rachel shook his proffered hand, stifling an adolescent reaction that threatened to surface.

Logan Masters was a long-time favorite with Rachel. She'd watched his several successful series. Realizing she was about to salivate, she tried a turn at conversation. "I've caught a few episodes of your new show." Oh, god, she'd just admitted missing most of them. He thanked her for watching. "Do you enjoy filming in New Mexico?" There, much better, almost a grownup sentence.

"Very much." His was the kind of perfectly modulated voice that would live on in commercials and narration long after his acting career had come to an end; smooth enough to catch your attention, sincere enough to believe. "I like it so much," he said, "I'm thinking of buying a house here."

Oh no, the reporter kicked the star struck female out of her body, another fabulously wealthy actor determined to run up the price of housing in Santa Fe. Rachel stared; fearful her next comment would be insulting. When the silence had gone on for longer than any of them could stand, Chloe saved the moment.

"Logan," first name basis, "is considering building a darling," they all were to realtors, "house in Pueblo Blanco where he's an investor."

Of course he was. Rachel wished she could afford to buy a house at all. When she thought of the dump she rented in Tulsa, it made her choke. Of course, she and Tony had a nice house in the foothills but she wasn't going back and it would soon be Tony's house.

"That's a great spot to live," Rachel tried. A great spot, no shit. "I hope you'll be happy here." Trite.

"Well," seeing her distress, Logan said, "I must be going. We've an afternoon filming schedule. Thank you," he cast those deep brown eyes on Chloe, "you've been most helpful. I'll call you after I've talked with my wife. She's excited about the new place.

"Nice, to have met you."

"My pleasure," Rachel said. Finally, something human.

Chloe smiled brightly until he left the restaurant then smacked Rachel on the arm. "What's the matter with you? Haven't you always told me how much you like Logan Masters? Geez, Rach, could you have been any more dopey? Couldn't you have lied and told him you'd seen everything he's ever done—which you have!"

"You caught me by surprise."

"Surprise. Yes, it was a surprise—for you. Dammit, I thought it would cheer you up."

"I am cheered up." Rachel changed the subject before she passed the pissed off stage. "Julian gave me my old job back. Well, sort of. I'm temporarily employed while I'm here. I did my interview at Pueblo Blanco this morning."

"What did you think?" Chloe shifted back to the realtor.

"Another really expensive place to live in Santa Fe."

"Santa Fe's real estate market is going to hell in a hand basket."

"So I've read."

"This summer the *touristas* didn't show up in droves like past years. Fewer visitors translate to fewer buyers."

"Funny, Chris hasn't said anything."

"Your brother, the mayor, wouldn't. You might as well know," Chloe's voice softened. "Some people are blaming him for the downturn."

"Chris? What did he do?"

"Some say he's anti-tourism."

"Some? You?"

"I didn't say that," Chloe said. "But you know he can be caustic at times." Yes, she did. "He's been forthright in his opinions about what he sees as the degradation of the city by tourists. Sometimes that doesn't go over well with visitors who have received yearly full-color multipage invitations from the convention and visitors bureau. In some ways I agree with him; for instance, the pilfering of flagstone from the Plaza. Course, can't blame that totally on tourists, nonetheless it is primarily visitors who have done it. The city had to plant grass so many stones walked away.

But, if visitors stop coming, Santa Fe's economic health will go down the *retrete*." Chloe also spoke Spanish, especially when miffed. French, if she was truly provoked. "It's the city's chief source of income and Chris is wrong to scare off that much money. Better to take an educational stand instead of an accusatory one."

The waiter, who had been patiently unobtrusive while Chloe concluded her vituperation, asked, "Would you care to order now?"

"No!" It was a duet. He slunk away. He'd probably take it out on some unsuspecting diner.

"Gee, look at the time," Chloe said. "I've got an appointment. See you tonight?"

"Sure," Rachel said. "And, Chloe, I'm sorry I spoiled your surprise. Thank you."

"No big deal." She was gone in a whirl of skirts and fragrance. Rachel coughed. "Shit, I hope that doesn't give me a migraine."

"Excuse me?" It was the waiter again.

Rachel didn't have the heart to leave without buying something. "I'll have lunch—to go."

CHAPTER 8

Lunch was a moveable feast. It moved all around the car. The iced tea to go was too large to fit in the hole of the plastic console affair. It went over when she pulled onto Cerrillos—better known as motel row—and made a wide stain on the carpet of the passenger side.

This is the least *different* part of Santa Fe. All the so-called affordable motels cling to the edge of the street for several miles. Devoid of much character, many accommodations look no different from those in Little Rock or Syracuse. One-size-fits-all. The budget-minded traveler seeks refuge here. The discerning can find good restaurants along Cerrillos, but most are connected with a motel or national chain and not given to native foods or charm. If one was tired of culture and yearned for homogenized Americana, this was the place.

Traffic was thick and fast, and horns blew often. Rachel cursed herself for going this way, cursed Santa Fe drivers, who were notorious for not using turn signals and driving well over the speed limits. When she made a precarious left onto Guadalupe the sandwich took flight and landed at her feet. One slice of bread lodged under her driving heel. Better not to say what happened to the mayonnaise. "Shit." Now she couldn't even eat it. She missed Johnson Street and hung a belated right at McKenzie, then backtracked to Marcy. Although Santa Fe has outgrown its Burro Alley identity, the street system in the downtown area has not. That's part of the allure. Cars inhabit every available parking space; the larger ones stick out and threaten to snare the unaware fender.

After making several trips around the block she found a spot big enough for the Merc, but it was in front of the post office. She'd have to hike across the city lot. Hunger gnawed at her. In desperation she picked up the slice of bread facing upward and scarfed it. There were a couple of swallows of tea left in the bottom of the overturned cup. She washed down the bread with it before she choked.

Tall trees shaded the federal building and the post office in the parklike setting. Office workers picnicked on the grounds and lovers kissed on the soft grass, oblivious to others. Two children played with a puppy while their mothers watched. She crossed the busy, one-way street as cars jockeyed for the far left lane and the letter-drop boxes.

Chris would not be delighted to see her again. After his reception yesterday she'd probably get tossed on her ass. She was right. Her brother wore a pasty smile. His face was red, as if he'd just stopped yelling at a flunky.

"Rachel, we've really got to stop meeting like this." Humor often cloaks the truth. "I've got to leave for a meeting."

There was no point in putting on niceties. She plunged right in. "Have you had any strange, uh," now that she was ready to talk, it wasn't easy to articulate, "phone calls or visitors?" That was a close as she could get. Coming right out and asking if the dead had made an appearance, say for lunch, would not garner anything but disbelief and a quick trip to one of the many mental health professionals in town.

The red of his skin deepened. Self-control? Not one of her brother's well-developed traits. Suspicious of her visit in the first place, she was complicating matters by asking stupid questions.

Chris had been standing next to the authoritative mayoral desk; he quickly assumed the power position behind it. Tanned hands gripped the edge so tightly his knuckles whitened. Her brother took a long breath before he spoke. Rachel stayed in place. "Could you be more specific?" was all he said, but his tone was not friendly.

Specific? Had he known, specifically, the exchange would have ended right there. Rachel tried, "Two nights ago something happened in Tulsa." Perfectly true. "I thought I saw someone, but I can't be sure."

"This *someone* precipitated the nocturnal drive? Who the hell was it?"

"That's it. There was something familiar, but I couldn't put my finger on it."

"Rachel, you know, I'm the mayor." News flash. "I don't have time for guessing games. You come in unannounced, twice, and expect me to drop everything and pursue an inane conversation. Go back to Tulsa or find something here to entertain yourself."

"I already have," Rachel said, feeling petty. "Julian gave me a job until I'm ready to leave. I'm working on a story about that new residential development outside of town."

"What?" Startled. "Which one?"

"Pueblo Blanco. Why?"

"Just curious. Rachel," the tired parent tone. "Try to stay out of trouble."

"Trouble? What trouble could I possibly get into writing a story?"

"Do you want the entire list?" He had her there. Her irreverent style had vexed several people around town but Julian loved it. The more letters of protest he received, the more successful he viewed the piece as long as it didn't alienate an advertiser.

"Gee, Chris, why don't you get down and dirty?"

"If I have to."

"Fine, but if I were you, I'd keep an eye out. Something is going on."

"Rachel. Have a nice day." She was dismissed.

"And you, brother dear." Rachel smiled sweetly. "My best to the family."

"Uh-huh." His face contorted. Bingo. She left with deliberate steps. Domestic bliss had plummeted off the Richter scale. Chris was up to his old tricks.

* * *

The public rest room was a pit: Paper lay in small heaps on the floor, faucets dripped, liquid soap spilled in small pink pools on the counter made of broken tile. The air was about as breathable as that in an outdoor toilet. Only the finest hotels seemed able to keep public facilities clean. She went through the routine: tug enough reluctant paper off the roll to cover both sides of the seat and then hover perilously while simultaneously aiming for dead center. No girl grew to adulthood without being taught the holding pattern. Rachel flushed with the toe of her shoe—some guests before her hadn't. After washing her hands, she opened the door with the paper towel in hand, glanced around—the trash receptacle was across the room. The crunched mess landed behind the door with a growing collection. When would people ever learn to place the can near the door? Who the hell wanted to shake hands with half the city?

She went over the confrontation with her brother. Shit, he'd been some kind of assistant to Mayor Baca when the poor guy keeled over from a heart attack. Chris had been in place to move into the mayoral office. It's not like he'd worked all that hard to earn the trust of the community, promised a Mercedes in every drive, or devised a plan to ensure every citizen made a buck more than minimum wage. Jerk.

Deep in thought and meandering through the hallway where cross-ventilation was creating a cooling breeze, Rachel became aware of something disturbing. There isn't a woman alive who hasn't sensed fear while walking down a city sidewalk or rural country road. It's the sixth sense that alerts the brain, readies the body, and shouts, "You're in danger!" Rachel continued walking slowly, seeking the waiting enemy in her peripheral vision. Nothing. He had to be behind her. Sticky perspiration stung her armpits and gave a slimy feel to the back of her neck.

Once, in a safety class the instructor told her students, "If you feel someone behind you: Stop. Turn. Look them in the eye." It seemed like excellent advice at the time, but right now she didn't want to know who was following her. It was part of the same logic that says until someone tells you about a death, it can't be true. She kept moving.

Her ears couldn't pick up a sound other than her own footsteps and a phone ringing somewhere down the hall. The odor brought her to a dead standstill. She fully expected to feel the impact of another person. It didn't happen. The acrid smell of an electrical short sickened her. Rachel remembered it clearly from the awful manifestation in Tulsa. The wall stopped her body as she flung herself against it. There was no one. Not even a city employee on his way to a meeting. She was all alone.

The scent of electricity dissipated. Her sweat-stained skin cooled in the drafty hallway. As her heart slowed, she wished she knew what the hell was going on.

CHAPTER 9

The office was locked. Everyone had taken an even longer lunch than Rachel. She navigated the stone path through the courtyard, brushing against the large chamisa on the way to the fish pond. Kneeling near the edge, she reached into the cool, still water. The dozen or so fish rushed her, expecting feed bag time. Their tiny mouths sucked at her fingertips, tickling. The key was still there under the same moss covered rock at the bottom of the pool. Julian never changed. Half the town knew where this key was *hidden*.

At her computer, writing the story, Rachel felt in control. Here, in her element, no problem was insurmountable. There were always words to explain it. She tapped out the lead, wrote the intro and moved on to the interview. These rah-rah pieces were fairly easy. One had to tell only what it was, and how it benefited Santa Fe, even if she was uncertain it would. Then, throw in the stats, in this case sizes, prices, and don't forget those maintenance fees. This piece was less challenging than many.

In some cases it was up to the reporter to write the story, more or less, from stilted press releases and glossy brochures. Rachel had been known to walk around a business, facility, or arts venue after a difficult interview in an effort to soak up some reality. Sometimes it worked.

Early in her career she'd been assigned to interview a man whose long-time business was retailing fringe market goods. These items encompassed everything from temporary tattoos to soft-core porn greeting cards to drug-related paraphernalia. When she arrived on schedule, he made a show of forgetting the appointment, cursed his employees for no reason, and proceeded to jump up and down throughout what could be loosely called an interview. She suspected he had been sampling his own illegal substances. Rachel took the best notes she could from the indecipherable data that belched forth and wrote a very short article. Want good coverage? Lay off drugs and alcohol before talking with reporters. It's also better not to make passes. Bad karma.

Julian and Stella returned. Julian nodded as he walked by her desk. He rarely disturbed an employee who was working. Stella had no such compunction.

"Welcome back." Stella's smile was a little sly. "Just here temporarily, huh?"

"Right," Rachel said. "I've got to tidy some loose ends."

"I see."

"No, really."

"I said, I see." The smile broadened and Stella's eyes were lit with a combination of high jinks and understanding. It said she knew something she wasn't telling. Stella crossed the room to make a fresh pot of coffee. Rachel thought nothing she could say would change Stella's mind. Let her think what she wanted. Once her little brush with the spirit world was resolved, she would be back on the interstate headed east. Maybe she could even get her jobs back. Or not.

She was rolling, already on page three, leaving only one space between sentences. It was something about newspaper and magazine work that was a complete contradiction to old lady Sontag's— her ninth grade typing teacher—stern instructions to space twice between sentences. After sometime spent behind the reception desk at the oil company it was hard to keep the proper spacing in mind.

Rachel needed another notebook. At the back of the offices, a hall led to the unisex restroom, referred to as the *copy room*. It accommodated a rickety photocopier, and shelves for supplies that usually weren't stocked. If using the toilet, it was mandatory to lock the door. Fortunately, Stella had the foresight to have a curtain hung to block the view of the throne. Rachel grabbed a notebook and left.

The stucco walls of the office were painted a soft lilac. All the woodwork was high-gloss red—Julian meant to keep the staff awake. The windows were bare with the exception of unused yellowing shades rolled to the top. The floor, old brick saturated in some kind of poly coating, was meant to make cleanups easy. Despite that, it hadn't been swept for some time. A fine dust could be detected in the sunbeams. Paper in various sizes and colors littered it in a comfortable mess.

Undisturbed, Rachel finished the rough draft in a couple of hours. Everyone had come back from lunch. After her recent introductions to surreal spiritual hoodoos, it was nice to experience normalcy.

Part of being a journalist type was the uniform. It was a blessing not to have to dress in power bow regalia, the female equivalent of a man's tie. Not that Santa Fe was that sort of place anyway, but writers were expected to look funky, and Rachel was happiest in T-shirts all year. In winter she topped them with a jacket; summer called for vests. Walking shoes were always *in* with her. She preferred flat shoes whenever possible—in case she ever needed to beat a hasty exit. That interview hadn't happened yet, but she was willing to bet it would before she hung up her notebook and vanished forever to where writers never die, they just make up a new life.

She would let the article cool overnight and look at it fresh tomorrow. There was some fact-checking she wanted to do before filing it.

Her thoughts turned to the story she would like to write about Pueblo Blanco. Did her brother know about the development? Maybe—if he was over his mad—he could open a few doors for her at city hall. Sure.

CHAPTER 10

Two blissfully quiet days had passed without any unwelcome visitors. Rachel was running late. The gallery showing began at seven. Chloe specifically told her to be there, but Rachel had eaten a leisurely dinner by herself. After a sizzling plate of carne adovada and a margarita, she was fifteen minutes behind and had not yet straightened out her life. Tomorrow she would meet with Tony and see how the settlement would go. She dreaded it, and at the same time wanted it over.

Canyon Road is the Santa Fe equivalent of the Louvre. The winding street was chock full of cars. Rachel drove past the zillion or so art galleries and restaurants twice before giving up and parking in a pay lot.

She hadn't bothered to change clothes after work. The upside to that was she didn't have to slog through the gravel lot in dress shoes. The downside was her friend would be embarrassed to have such an unfashionable companion. Canyon Road was all uphill this direction. Rachel was breathing hard by the time she reached the New Man Gallery. She stopped to catch her breath and take a look around. The gallery was another old adobe house converted to white space for *objets d'art*.

The crowd was monied—mostly new money. A few were in tuxedo and evening dress. The courtyard was filled with mingling bejeweled aristocracy. Rachel's attire garnered a few raised eyebrows as she entered through the elaborate iron gate. To justify her lack of finery, she pulled out her notebook. How gratifying to watch the upper crust relax their troubled brows. Ah, the media was here. That, they could deal with. A couple of people nodded discreetly in her direction. They would sleep peacefully tonight with headlines and society pics dancing in their heads.

Inside, Chloe was wrapped in layers of deep purple silk. It might be a dress or fabric straight off the bolt. Rachel couldn't be sure. Chloe's hair was slicked up with mousse into a Spanish dancer's knot. All she needed was a tiara. On Chloe it seemed a perfectly normal way to wear hair. On anyone else, Rachel for instance, it would have looked asinine.

The woman with Chloe was the gallery owner. Her photo appeared regularly in the local papers, even *High Desert Country* had run a story on the successful business owner. Rachel had drawn Vivian Smythe's anger when she had pointed out in the article that New Man Gallery seemed to exclude women, at least in name. Vivian had a talent for choosing the next up-and-comer. The rumor mill said that artists had to audition, that might explain why most were men. Although Vivian's face wouldn't launch a thousand ships she was working her way through a thousand painters and sculptors, and they didn't seem to mind the way she looked. Her jet-black hair—at age seventy, drawn on brows, and spiky eyelashes were all a part of the persona she had created. It worked for her, even though Rachel couldn't suppress a shiver whenever she saw her. Vivian reminded her of the wicked witch of the west—or southwest.

The gallery owner, upon sighting Rachel, had to go check on the real guests. "Something I said?" Rachel inquired after reaching Chloe.

"She's never gotten over that story you wrote about the gallery," Chloe said. "You're late."

"It was a perfectly good article. I might add, the first one written by any SF publication. She was delighted when I showed up for the interview. She just has an underdeveloped sense of humor. Besides, I'm not actually late. You know parking's a bitch."

"Yeah, especially when you're late."

Rachel ignored Chloe's jab. "You look gorgeous."

"Thank you." Chloe smoothed the fabric clinging to her breasts. Rachel noted the effects of a push-up bra. "Careful, one false step and they'll hit you in the face," Rachel whispered.

Chloe frowned. "I notice you, well, didn't dress up."

"It's okay." Rachel pulled a pen from her purse. "Everyone thinks I'm here to report on the show. I'm perfectly acceptable in that role. Who's the latest find?"

"Pedro."

"Pedro?"

"Just Pedro," Chloe said. "No last name."

"What does Pedro, no last name, do?"

"Geez, Rachel, look around. He's really good."

In fact, Pedro was quite good. Rachel left Chloe to talk with one of her associates, while she looked at the large paintings hung strategically and lighted perfectly.

Rachel collected fragments of conversation as she walked around the groups of people eating *tapas* and washing them down with champagne and sangria. She wrote each in her notebook . . . *exactly the right aggregate of flawless form and light . . . the appendages support the parable in ways that even the average person could understand . . . vibrant colors lend sustenance to the notion of eternal life . . . concept and logic exist in timeless flight . . .*

One never knew when conversational jewels like these could round out an idea; perhaps a piece on ludicrous discourse at an art showing.

"Make any sense to you?"

At first Rachel wasn't sure the question was addressed to her, but the man standing next to her didn't seem to be with anyone. At that moment, she wished for a push-up bra and uncomfortable shoes. Logan Masters held a glass of sangria in one hand, a gallery guide in the other. There was an unmistakable twinkle in his eye. The same one he used so effectively in his television work. It could break hearts and wreck homes.

"Mr. Masters, how nice to see you again." A better effort than earlier.

"My pleasure, I assure you. I think you're the only person here I've met. Please call me Logan."

"Chloe's here."

"Is she?" Logan looked about the room. "What do you think of this Pedro?"

"It's nice work. Good use of white space. His splashes of color, particularly the yellows and reds, leap off the canvas. And yet, the paintings are somehow restful." Pedro's efforts were reminiscent of a child with his first box of crayons but it was a look Rachel liked. Some artists were so uptight, one emotion that always comes through loud and clear in art.

"I agree. I think I'll buy one for my new house. Are you covering the opening for your magazine?"

Flustered, Rachel thought of punting, and then went with the truth. "I was running late so I came as is. I'm playing reporter." She showed him the page with the guest's comments.

Logan had an infectious laugh, irreverent but genuine. In a few seconds their mirth began drawing attention. People, in gallery correct attire, moved to a safer side of the room, making hushed dismissals of the two barbarians. Rich actors were usually accepted in this circle, but only if their behavior was a fitting echo to those in the know.

Rachel and Logan convulsed onto a wooden bench. Logan carefully placed his glass out of harm's way and asked, "May I?" indicating he wanted to look at her notebook. She handed it over and watched while he wrote down three more descriptions beneath her own. That brought on more laughter.

They agreed to leave the stuffiness of the gallery for the cool, dry evening outside. The odor of chamisa hung in the evening darkness. It reminded Rachel of the sickly sweet milkweed plant. In small doses it was fragrant, but up close, it was overpowering. Several roses still bloomed in the protected courtyard, mixing their bouquet with the night air.

In the moonlight Logan looked like the movie star that he was. Rachel had to be careful not to stare. Before they parted, she asked for an interview and Logan obliged. They agreed to meet for a lunch interview on the set.

CHAPTER 11

Goodbyes weren't Rachel's favorite thing but they were a necessary part of life. It didn't seem to matter whether someone died, left or faded away; there was a hole to fill. She had grown weary of some women's unquenchable need to talk about closure, a psychobabble term Rachel deplored. Sometimes shit happened. Either a door closed or it slammed shut. Nor did she care that travails made one stronger. She already knew she was strong.

Rachel's philosophy for life's little traumas was to clean up the mess and get on with it. The conviction was good. One notable exception was the death of her father. She couldn't help but feel the police had not done everything possible to discover the reason for his death. Not knowing would haunt her for life.

Consuela Gomez was getting out of her car as Rachel pulled in at the Winters Winters Winters law firm. Why they didn't call it Winters and Sons, or at least use commas, was baffling.

In the parking lot, Rachel shook hands with the short, round woman with wild hair. Consuela's hair was so thick it couldn't be parted. The curly tendrils waved in the windy day like soft cork-screws. With every bouncy step she took, the coils grew more tangled.

"Good day for a divorce settlement?" Rachel asked.

"Good as any," Consuela responded somberly. "How are you, dear?"

"Considering the state of my affairs, not all that bad." It was part wishful thinking, more virtuous than doing the pity-party scene.

"Not to worry." Consuela touched her arm. A Jewish mom at heart despite her Catholic upbringing, Consuela always tried to make it all better. "I've already worked this out with Nicholas. It should be pretty cut and dried."

The office of the Winters clan was lawyerly. Appropriately stuffy leather furniture and expensive paneling predominated—no O'Keeffe prints here. Brass barometers and nautical scenes hung from the walls.

With lawyer in tow, Rachel was whisked past the congested waiting room and into the inner sanctum. Tony Blackstone spoke quietly with Nicholas Winters, the eldest of the family. Winters saw them enter.

"Ah, here they are." He was a jovial kind of man with stunning silver hair brushed straight back and pulled into a ponytail, perfectly correct for a Santa Fe attorney. He stood and reached out an expensively tailored pinstriped arm to shake their hands. "Do sit down."

"Hi, Rachel," Tony said. He seemed sad but looked great. Tony was a film producer—not much Hollywood stuff, but independent films, PBS programming and a few commercials. A good living, he'd liked it until a few years ago. He looked very West Coast in a navy silk T with matching suit. His face barely lined; he cut a striking figure. His black hair was cut fashionably short, but he fussed with it anyway.

"Hi" was all she could to say to this man she'd lived with for a decade. Tony didn't want the divorce, though he had agreed not to fight it.

Winters read a bunch of attorney mumbo jumbo. Rachel didn't listen; Consuela would. The gist was that Tony would buy her half of the house, give her half the contents and the Jeep. Since there were no children, there were no custody arrangements. They didn't even have a pet.

"Excuse me," Rachel interrupted Winters. "All I want from the house is my desk and personal items. I don't want any of the furniture or the Jeep."

"Rachel," Tony implored her. "I want you to have the car. If you don't take any of the furniture, how will you manage? All you've got is that old car and your laptop."

"I'm living in a furnished house so I don't need the furniture. The car may be old, but I like it and . . . it's all mine." The day she knew she had to go; Tony had kept the car keys to prevent her from leaving. She had been determined, and had taken a cab to the bank where she closed out her savings account, bought the first car she saw for sale and fled. When she reached I-40, she flipped a coin and turned east. She could just as easily have gone to Phoenix.

"Rachel," Consuela had on her lawyer hat. "You are entitled to these things. If you don't want them, then sell them and keep the money."

"Thank you, all of you," Rachel said, "but I really don't want them. A simpler life with less stuff is working for me. I'm not ready to clutter it up again."

Tony and Winters moved to the hall and talked it over. Rachel was aware of their hushed tones. She knew Tony wanted to take care of her, to be fair. But life wasn't fair. If it was, people wouldn't die, fall out of love or make mistakes.

Rachel wanted only to get out of there. She felt her resolve draining away, remembering the good times with Tony. Consuela read the confusion on her face, patted her hand and asked if she was sure. She was. She did love Tony, but the time had come for her to move on.

The two men returned and offered additional money in lieu of the car and contents.

"It's not necessary."

"Rachel," Consuela said, "take it."

"Okay," Rachel gave up. She'd do anything to get out of that office. "Do you need me anymore?"

"No," Winters said kindly. "We can handle it from here."

By the time she walked down the carpeted hallway, through the ostentatious waiting room, and out the front door, tears were imminent. She reached her car just as the impulse to kick something came to her. Her foot left a small indentation on the door.

Her toe hurt like hell and the telltale throb of a migraine surfaced on her forehead.

"Damn. Why is doing the right thing always so painful?" she moaned as she rubbed her head. There was the mistaken idea that if one rubbed the affected area it would disperse the pain or stop it altogether. It only worked on lesser hurts.

The inside of her car smelled bad thanks to the recent lunch spill. It needed a more thorough cleaning than the quick wipe-up she gave it. She lowered the window and collected her thoughts. Most of the time there was no right or wrong decision, only different paths. She couldn't worry if one path was somehow better than another, merely take it and see where it led.

It led back to the office.

She cranked up the radio. Some occasions required loud music. From time to time, she angrily wiped a tear, but wouldn't give in.

CHAPTER 12

What a bummer. Rachel had no idea that divorce felt so final. More work on her housing article didn't move her. A time-out was in order. She pulled on her jacket and grabbed her bag from the back of the chair. Julian looked thoughtful as she passed his open door. He fiddled with his beard when distressed.

Engrossed in escape, she barely noticed the impact with the office photographer, graphic artist, and all-around fix it wizard.

"Hey, Rach. How are things hangin'?"

Sheldon "Shorty" Smith was a survivor of his misspent youth. Only part of his brain had been fried by drugs. The creative side, according to Shorty, had been enhanced to the max. His long, curly brown hair seemed unaffected by time. Small round glasses rested on his nose. Shorty was a genius when it came to a camera or a graphics screen. Best of all, he kept the archaic photocopier running. *High Desert Country* would have coughed up several thou' for a new one by now if it were not for Shorty. Fortunately, Shorty, who was lanky and not particularly short, didn't require lengthy conversations. His attention span rivaled that of a four-year-old.

"To the left," Rachel replied. He probably hadn't noticed she'd been gone or thought she'd been on vacation. "How's tricks?"

"Done'em all. No new horizons." He playfully jabbed her arm, causing his camera strap to dislodge from a bony shoulder. By the time he reached his desk—the one piled high with 10-year-old stuff—the camera had been rescued, discarded, and forgotten. A new motorcycle magazine had arrived and he was madly flipping through it.

Traffic was light as she drove to Chloe's. When she reached the drive, the piñon scraped her car again. She halted with a crunch of gravel, pushed back the door, and trudged around the car to the offending tree. It felt good to snap the small limb, so she broke it into several more pieces. She reassured herself it was already dead. She had done the poor thing a favor. The Merc would surely appreciate keeping the remainder of its paint.

The front door of Chloe's house was standing open. Rachel stomped up the steps and called out, "Chloe, it's me. You in there or is this a burglary in progress?" It was only slightly funny. Burglary was a rather popular hobby in Santa Fe. Few people who worked in Santa Fe made much money. The first guy to carve a howling coyote was probably doing all right if he invested well, but the average working person was squeezed like an orange at breakfast. Only a few took up stealing to make ends meet.

Chloe came rushing from the back of the house. "Geez, Rach, you scared the hell out of me.

"No, we haven't been robbed but when I came home the whole place smelled like an electrical fire. You know, that, oh shit, what is that smell? We studied it in chemistry, do you remember?"

Rachel remembered it from only yesterday during the close encounter at city hall. She remembered it from her living room in Tulsa. Chemistry class had given it a name: magnesium, an element, atomic number 12, used in pyrotechnics for its bright white light. Electrical shorts had always smelled like magnesium to her.

"The house is all right," Rachel said. "I think we better talk."

"Okay?" Chloe said, her eyebrows rose in question. "Let's go outside while this airs." She locked the front door but left the remaining doors and windows open. On her way through the living room Chloe pulled a silver box from an antique secretary.

They settled on the with the view of the mountains. Shade was inching its way across the recycled material planks. An unpleasant atmosphere occupied their corner of the world.

"So," Chloe said, "how big a problem is this?" She held out the box, lid open. Inside were joints in three sizes. "Small, medium or large?"

"Let's think positively," Rachel said. "Medium."

Chloe produced two sterling silver roach clips and a gold-plated lighter from Cuba her first husband had given her. They lit up and settled back. With the second hit Rachel began to relax and tell her story.

"You know I've never agreed with the non-conclusions made by the police about Dad's death." Chloe touched her friend's knee consolingly. "I don't believe he fell asleep while driving down the ski basin road. The results of the . . . ," she could hardly speak the word, "autopsy, showed no indications of a stroke, heart attack or anything else. It wasn't late at night, and besides, Dad was a night person like me. He didn't nod off at the wheel at 8:30 in the evening, nor would he drive carelessly anywhere, but especially not on a road known for its curves and blind spots."

"I agree, sweetie," Chloe interjected, took a drag, blew it out and continued. "I've always thought there were some pieces missing in the story. The theory of being forced off the road by kids seemed plausible to me. Kids don't seem to have anything better to do these days."

"He was supposed to meet me at my house," Rachel said. "I was waiting for him. There was something he wanted to tell me. He said it was important, but he wouldn't give any specifics, except to say it would alter our lives. What's that supposed to mean?"

"I don't know Rachel, but it could have been good news."

"Right, it could have, only he sounded kind of grim. Anyway, the car was so damaged that the investigators couldn't prove or disprove the run off theory."

"But who would want to run your dad off the road?"

"Precisely. Who? No one. Later that night Mario Peña's house blew up," Rachel continued. "Of course, that's a great deal more spectacular than a car accident. Hell, more than 45,000 people die in auto wrecks in this country each year. No big deal, right?"

"If it helps," Chloe said, "the police never solved the who or why of Mario's house being destroyed. It was odd. I always thought Chris and Mario were friends, but Chris didn't use his clout to push that investigation."

"He told me he didn't want to antagonize the police chief," Rachel said. "They've never gotten along. Chris said the SFPD would do a better job if he stayed out of it."

"The paper reported that Mario was presumed dead in the explosion, but there was never any proof of that," Chloe added. "It must have been one powerful explosion to leave no evidence that someone had been in the house," she said doubtfully.

"Or lousy CSI. At any rate, Dad's inquiry got deep-sixed. Because of that, I haven't been able to put it behind me."

"Rachel, give yourself a break. It's only been a few months. It can take years to get through the grieving process, especially in a culture that doesn't recognize mourning. Add your breakup with Tony and you've had an emotional blitz."

"I know, but geez, I usually don't do stupid things just because life hits hard once in a while."

"Stupid? What did you do that was stupid?"

"There's an Indian ritual," Rachel paused so they could both change gears, "that's supposed to bring back the dead."

"What?" The look of empathy fled Chloe's face, replaced by one of intense interest and slight shock. "What have you gotten into?" She took a long drag.

"I thought if I could talk with Dad, everything would become clear. He'd tell me he swerved to miss an animal, or maybe a tire slipped off the pavement causing him to lose control. Maybe he'd even tell me how great the afterlife is and clear up some other questions I have in the here and now."

"What happened?" Chloe prompted.

Rachel recounted the phenomenon that occurred by the glimmer of her lava light, how her attempt to talk with her father had failed, and her compulsion to return to Santa Fe.

Chloe listened quietly. Her eyes were wide with astonishment. She was already on the edge of her seat and it crossed Rachel's mind she might fall.

After several seconds of silence Chloe could contain herself no more. "That's amazing! I've heard of things like that. Hell, everybody in Santa Fe has. You know this place has the whole battery of New Age specialists and masters of the unearthly sphere. But to have actually experienced a . . . uh, rendezvous with a soul!"

"Chloe, that's not all." Rachel held out one hand to slow her friend's racing hypothesis.

"There's more?" Chloe was incredulous.

Rachel continued with the incident along I-40 where the second sighting took place, the words it spoke telling her to go back, and how the wolf scared it away. Then, she ended with the creepy feeling and the odor in the city hall building.

"Rachel," Chloe grabbed her hand, squeezing it in excitement, "not a soul, but . . ." she thought for a moment."A bona fide shape-shifter! That must be what it is. You know, like on that show, *Supernatural*. Sam and Dean deal with this kind of thing all the time."

Rachel watched as Chloe's imagination worked overtime and quickly took a puff to smooth out.

"God, Rachel, what if it gets into places via the wiring?"

"Wait a minute," Rachel implored her friend, who was now standing. "What if it . . . what if it was a . . . flashback? You know, to my wasted youth."

"You're telling me you drove across three states in that heap of yours chasing after a flashback? That's *loco*," Chloe stated. "Even you wouldn't do that, and you've done some pretty strange things, but we won't get into that right now. This . . . this is much more interesting." Rachel could almost see the wheels turning in Chloe's gorgeous head. "Don't you see what you've done? You've opened some kind of spiritual portal and you've, well, come out a medium!"

"A what!" Rachel exclaimed. "No way, we are not going there."

"I think we already are there," Chloe replied. "And the wolf; wolves can be spiritual guides. Didn't you think it odd he was alone? Wolves run in packs. Some Native Americans believe the wolf is a pathfinder," she went on breathlessly. "It's also thought the moon is the power ally of the wolf. The moon was full that night! Maybe he came to protect you."

"Hold on," Rachel said. "Let's not get carried away. We don't really know anything."

"But you said the wolf growled at the spirit, frightening it away. It didn't behave aggressively with you. It allowed you to go on your way. I'm going to leave a window open tonight, in case it wants to come back. That way, it won't have to go through a light switch or something."

"Chloe, stop. Before we go off half-cocked, shouldn't we entertain the possibility that at least one of these things might not be a friendly?"

Chloe turned on the heel of a boot, having walked the length of the deck during her dissertation. Her hands clasped over her waist, holding the clip with two fingers. "Rachel. Who was it? Who was the soul you chased after? Do you know?"

The sun was quickly sinking over the Jemez. In a few minutes all the scary corners of this part of the world would be dark. Rachel thought of the doors standing open, the windows pulling in the cooling air. What else might enter with it? She'd gone this far. She might as well confess all. Probably Chloe would laugh and they'd both feel better.

"I think it was Mario Peña."

Chloe didn't laugh. She inhaled sharply.

CHAPTER 13

The following morning at breakfast, or at least what Chloe considered the morning meal—real coffee, papaya juice, and rice cakes—they discussed what might have happened that night in Tulsa.

"When I interviewed the shaman, I couldn't tell if they actually brought back the dead or if the intense concentration on that person helped you to know what they would say if still living. As I said last night, I'd worked on the prayer stick and the mask for a couple of days. Hell, Chloe, I don't know if the smudge stick was spiked and caused me to hallucinate or if this thing really happened. I wasn't under the influence of anything at city hall, and you didn't even know about this when you came home to a house reeking of an electrical short.

"Since Chris had been chummy with Mario I tried to reach him immediately, but I think he was out seeking carnal knowledge. If I had managed to bring back Mario it seemed likely he'd head for Santa Fe. Odd thing is why did I feel it was imperative to get here?

"Oh no, look at the time. I've got an interview with Logan Masters." Rachel slugged back one more swallow of juice to wash down the rice cake.

"Use your reporter's wiles to determine if he's happily married," Chloe said. "If not, I'd be interested in making him my third husband."

"You say that as if you're collecting."

"Better than stuffed animals."

"I'm off to the set."

"First channeling—now you're going Hollywood." Chloe wore an endearing smirk.

"Later."

* * *

The set where the Logan Masters' series filmed was south of town off the legendary Turquoise Trail. Rachel wasn't sure why it was legendary except that fortunes had been won and lost in the mines along the trail. The several small towns along the highway had at one time boomed and later gone bust just short of becoming ghost towns. Thanks to the Santa Fe effect and southwestern art, the villages were enjoying another sort of boom.

At the marker for the ranch where much of the filming was done, she made a left off the blacktop. The Merc bumped grumpily over a cattle guard. Not a guy in uniform, but the mess of pipes and spikes in the road which livestock adamantly refused to walk over, eliminating the need for gates. A barbed wire fence stretched in both directions from the guard. Nary a tree grew here to shade the hide of a solitary cow if it were to graze nearby.

She made another turn and followed the tire tracks. Stubborn grass grew between them and tickled the belly of the Merc. Sandia Peak dominated her rearview mirror for a few minutes. Another turn in the cow path brought a few foothills into view. Miles away they would compress and merge with the Great Plains.

Logan Masters was playing a southwestern P.I. How this differed from his portrayal of a Los Angeles private cop or a New York detective, Rachel could only surmise. The formula was pretty much the same, only the character name and clothes seem to change. Logan had a successful television career with several hit shows and a couple of dozen movies to his credit. He was the darling of the Lifetime network and fit most women's idea of a hunk.

His characters were both macho and sensitive, and don't forget, educated: the impossible man. Masters' personas were equally at home in a shoot-out or at the ballet. And his dialogue was always witty.

Once waved through by security, the *Jake Weathers* set was only a few hundred feet ahead. It was a jumble of faux buildings and nondescript trailers and a mangle of parked cars. Nothing grew here. The ground had been trampled to dust. There were several wardrobes hanging outside, *a la* sidewalk sale, undoubtedly gathering dust—more authentic. Three cameras were mounted at various locations around the town of facades. Black director's chairs with the *Jake Weathers* logo stood in jumbled groupings. Cables ran everywhere, a gauntlet for the unwary. Two tables, heavy with doughnuts and coffee, were popular hangouts for those who were in-between scenes. A small throng of extras munched, awaiting their turn at discovery and fame. How they would ever keep their figures eating that stuff, Rachel could only wonder.

Waiting, from what little experience Rachel had with location filming, was the norm. Her ideas of glamour were quickly decimated the first time she visited one of Tony's shoots. It seemed the director, camera people, and actors walked around and talked, then waited for hours while set designers, gaffers, and lighting crews did their thing.

A makeup artist who hadn't bothered to paint herself pointed out Logan's trailer. It was one of the white ones. The only distinction his had was a bay window; so much for star treatment.

Logan answered her knock with his characteristic smile. She fought it, but it warmed her heart. He invited her in and offered her a place on the window seat. Morning light filtered through horrible curtains—beige material with yellow and orange tassels hanging in two horizontal lines. Apparently no expense had been spared for the leading man's trailer. She'd heard on some entertainment *news* show that he preferred it that way.

Rachel pulled her tape recorder and pad from the shoulder bag. A round dinette table stood between them. A teapot and several chipped cups littered the top, along with a stack of scripts and an assortment of pens and pencils. Down the short hall, the only bed was made. A change of clothes lay across the burgundy coverlet. The tiny kitchen was neat. Only a hand towel hung askew. This wasn't a living space, but more of a waiting room.

"Okay if I tape?"

"Sure. Want some tea?"

"Yes. It smells wonderful. Assam?"

"Very good. A tea drinker."

"Cold, hot, real or instant. Just not flavored or herbal."

"Instant?" He wrinkled his nose. It was charming.

Rachel dumped some sugar in the hot brew and stirred, thinking about her questions. She'd tried to think of something original, but with someone who'd been doing interviews for twenty years, he'd probably heard them all. She sipped the hot dark liquid cautiously. "Delicious."

She pushed the record button and popped the first question. Logan didn't hesitate. He promptly sketched out his formative years and his breakthrough into acting. Rachel knew he'd told it all before, but starting with something familiar helped put people at ease in the interview process.

Much to her embarrassment she didn't begin taking notes. She was captivated by this man's easy smile and his willingness to do an interview with a regional mag when *People* and *E!* were making regular requests for stories.

He had flawless skin. Rachel detected just the slightest bit of cosmetic surgery, but not the pull-it-up-tight-and-cinch-it-down variety. This was a careful nip and tuck by a skilled doctor. It was not an effort to make a middle-aged man look twenty again, but enough to ward off any sagging the camera might expose in HD. The average person would never get beyond the sensuous brown eyes. They had magnetic power. The lines around them, the result of years of filming in the sun, crinkled wonderfully when he smiled.

"You aren't taking notes," he observed.

Rachel stumbled out of her contemplation of Logan Masters' features. "Oh, I . . . I'm taping." Could she say nothing mature around this guy?

"I was a journalist for a few years prior to becoming an actor," he said. "I did that once and later found the tape had unraveled. That was one tough assignment. No notes and a ruined tape."

She immediately glanced at the tape recorder and smiled sheepishly. "Good advice," she mumbled and started scribbling. *He knew all along!* Knew, she had been staring like any other groupie. But, she'd never heard about his journalism days. She quickly followed up with a question. However, Logan owed her one awkward moment and she intended to collect.

CHAPTER 14

Back at the office, Rachel found a message slip on her desk. It was from Chloe asking her to call, with a P.S. from Stella saying that Chloe was very excited.

"Rach, I have great news."

"Don't keep me in suspense."

"I got a new listing today. It would be perfect for you. Can you take a look at it this afternoon?"

"What?" Rachel asked, confused. "You want me to look at a house? Have I worn out my welcome already?"

"Nonsense, you can stay forever, but this place is you, and within your price range."

"Chloe," Rachel started, "I have a price range? You remember I'm not staying?"

"Right, Rach, everyone believes that. Will you meet me?" Rachel scribbled the address. "Okay, but I'm not staying."

"I'll bring lunch," Chloe said.

She moaned as she hung up the phone. Lunch was sure to be cucumber sandwiches and scones. She'd have to get a green chile cheese burrito on the way back to the office.

"Going house hunting?" Stella had been listening again. In an office this small it was impossible not to. "That's fun."

"Just making Chloe happy."

"Uh-huh," Stella said as though equipped with omniscient powers.

"I'm not staying."

"I said, uh-huh." The receptionist was trying not to smile smugly, but her eyes gave her away.

"I repeat," Rachel paused for emphasis, "I'm not staying."

"Okay with me," said a young man. Rachel hadn't met him so she asked, "And you are?" The guy walking in the front door looked young enough to still be in high school, but he was apparently old enough to hold a job if the briefcase was to be taken as a clue. He had close-cropped blonde hair and blue eyes. He wasn't bad looking but the frown and furrowed brow gave away a thorny personality.

"Rachel Blackstone, and you?" she offered her hand but it wasn't necessary. He brushed past her.

"The boomerang reporter. I've heard about you. I got your job, and I'm not giving it back." His spine was very straight as he walked away from them. He placed his expensive attaché on the desktop and aligned it exactly along the edge. The boy reporter flipped open his notebook and sat down to work.

"That's John J. Connor, the Third," Stella whispered.

"Really?" Rachel said. "There are three of them?"

"One would assume so," Stella replied, "but, it's a little scary to think about especially since he's very conservative."

"Julian . . . hired him?" Rachel couldn't believe it. *High Desert Country* had been a bastion of liberal idealism for as long as she could remember. "What *was* he thinking?"

"Told me he wanted to shake things up, and he was the only applicant with any published credits." Stella added with a conspiratorial flare, "He's also his nephew."

"Nuf sed. But why not *The National Review?*"

"No openings?" Stella surmised

John J. Connor, the Third, sensing he was being gossiped about, glared at her briefly from the corner, and then returned to his assignment.

"Hope Julian can handle the fallout," Rachel said. "I'm off to lunch. See you later."

"Happy house hunting."

* * *

She met Chloe in the South Capitol area. It was an old neighborhood composed mostly of small houses wedged between the state capitol building and Cordova Road. The location was good. Several of her favorite restaurants were nearby and it would be an easy commute to the office, if she were staying.

Chloe had a basket from a favorite caterer, the Palate Pal. "How'd the interview go, Rach? Is Logan Masters happily married? Is there hope?"

"We didn't get into that," Rachel responded. "It was difficult to stop looking at him and take notes, like a good reporter. I'm afraid I embarrassed myself again."

"Again? Really, Rach, you've got to get past the sophomoric infatuation and act like a full-grown person."

"Like that's possible for either of us."

"Have to agree with you there," Chloe said. "Every now and then I hear these grown-up words coming from my mouth and wonder who is talking. I certainly don't feel like a mature human being."

"That's because you aren't," Rachel barbed. "We're both unconventional, you know, Bohemians."

Chloe was thoughtful for a moment. "I can live with that." She changed the subject. "Now, let's take a look at the house. They're willing to sell most of the furniture if you want it," Chloe continued without taking a breath. "Terrible tragedy."

Oh great, which must mean someone was murdered in the house, Rachel thought.

"I know what you're thinking," Chloe said, "but it isn't like that. The guy who lived here was killed in a work-related accident. His parents reside in Arizona and need to sell the place quickly."

The house was a typical adobe structure, flat roof, stucco walls painted brown. The windows were trimmed in darker brown, but the door was turquoise.

Rachel half listened. The basket Chloe toted looked to have something more substantial than the cucumber sandwiches she expected. She guessed Chloe had gone all out and chosen chicken salad. Maybe they could eat before touring the house.

"I'll just leave this here." Chloe placed the food on the front step in the shade of the *portal*. The house looked small because it was nearly hidden by trees and gardens gone wild. What began as a flower bed had been allowed to go feral. Asters were blooming profusely, but hibiscus, hit by frost, was limp. The stucco had some cracks which Chloe referred to as superficial. Rachel guessed that meant the walls were not in imminent danger of collapse.

"It's a two-bedroom, one-and-a-half bath home with an absolutely darling," there was that word again, "kitchen nook that would be perfect for your home office." Chloe had morphed from her friend into super real estate agent. She tried to imagine what the action figure would look like; definitely a cape, but very fashionable. She went on and on about appreciation, points, and loan sources. "Even you can afford this house with your settlement. It's a steal at Santa Fe prices." Rachel zoned out.

The house did have its charm in that fixer-upper way. It would take paint, elbow grease and time to make it homey. There was no foyer, just barge right into the living room. The recliner would have to go. But the hardwood floors would stay. A nice dining room would have a pretty view of the street once the jungle was tamed. The kitchen, although old, appealed to her. Most of the world didn't live in houses with outlets placed precisely at two-foot intervals. She didn't need such *necessities* either. It was cozy and warm, a place she would want to be. It had the requisite Saltillo tile. The cabinets were painted a sage green. There was a dishwasher. Good. Not that she dirtied all that many dishes, but still welcome. The bathrooms were a bit grungy but tiled in soft beige and trimmed in teal with an art deco flare.

"What do you think? Rachel?" Chloe asked. "Don't decide yet. You've got to see the patio." She pulled on the kitchen door, which screeched in protest. There was a tiny back porch that acted as a vestibule. A shopworn broom was its only occupant. They exited into the backyard. "Isn't it lovely?" Chloe did her arms-open-wide, a la Julie Andrews' mountaintop air embrace, as she stood on the flagstone.

Rachel had to admit she liked it. The walled courtyard was lined with more tangled growing things. A large cottonwood shaded the terrace and much of the house. Several iron chairs waited for someone to scrape the peeling paint from their arms and legs.

"Okay, it's nice," Rachel answered. By this time Chloe had let her arms rest alongside her body. Rachel felt something against her leg.

"What's that?"

"Oh that," Chloe said, "is the cat."

"Cat?!"

CHAPTER 15

After eating a finger-sized chicken salad sandwich, with the crusts cut off, and a small plastic bowl of fresh fruit, washed down with some kind of sparkling water, Rachel crammed down a burrito with extra cheese. This time the washing down was accomplished with a Coke. Momentarily she imagined the cholesterol clogging her arteries, but the thought moved on.

A red 4Runner cut her off in traffic and she honked. The driver gave her the finger. "Asshole," she muttered.

She had to admit that the house had its charms. Chloe knew her taste, or lack of it. But, was this what she wanted? Her rent in Tulsa paid for the next month, she had time to think. After she understood what was going on with Mario Peña, the Sooner state might look like a haven. Chris obviously didn't want her hanging around.

Going back to Oklahoma wouldn't be all that easy. She had a place to live, but it was a fair bet the jerk PR company wouldn't take her back—but there were numerous jerk PR companies. Some other crappy clerical job would present itself. Perhaps the society rag would keep her on. If not, it would not be so easy to replace.

When she reached the office, Stella had a large envelope for her. "Your attorney dropped this by," she said and handed it to her. It was marked "Important" and double underlined.

Rachel dropped it on her desk and sat down. Consuela thought it urgent enough to make the trip herself. Rachel tore open the envelope.

It wasn't what she expected. A note from Consuela was inside, along with some papers addressed to her in her father's hand. In her almost unreadable scrawl the attorney had written, "This is from your father. It got misfiled with your divorce case. We didn't find it until after our meeting with Winters. Please accept my apologies."

Tears filled Rachel's eyes as she looked at her father's handwriting. The emotions that hit her were so strong she couldn't find the anger for Consuela's assistant. It was a gift. Part of him had lived on. Alone in the office but for Stella, who was watching a soap, she began to scan the contents.

The papers were notes, some handwritten, mixed with typed letter size sheets. Rachel quickly read some of the entries. They concerned housing and office developments in Santa Fe County.

A dozen or more were listed with publicity contacts. Alexander Robbins was the contact on each one. That wasn't altogether odd because he might be a publicist specializing in residential and office real estate ventures.

Rachel began reading the typed notes. Her father found that none of these undertakings had ever made it to completion despite the fact that all city and county regulations had been approved. She wondered how he discovered this and what the implications were?

From his comments she understood that each of these enterprises had been launched by the same developer, ABC Development, Inc. Not original or descriptive, but easy to remember. That too, wasn't overly strange. A large company in the business of developing land into living and working space could have hundreds of projects going around the country or even beyond. But the coincidence had been a little too intriguing to an old newsman like her dad.

On the last page he'd written several questions: "No project completions. Reason? What's going on? Is city hall involved? Chris?"

The last two annotations puzzled her. What made him think that someone in city government might be involved? Was he going to ask Chris for help?

The day not over, another visit to the city offices might be fruitful, specifically the planning department. She hoped her brother had gone home early. It was preferable she not run into him.

It was 4:20 and the meter on Lincoln Street had expired. Grudgingly, she plugged a couple of quarters. It was all she had and she didn't want to mess with the new parking meter that demanded credit cards.

The planning office was typically governmental. Fluorescent lights produced a harsh glare causing faces to take on a ghoulish green cast. One tube blinked constantly. A counter made from unfinished plywood had a temporary-permanent look. The counter sported a dull faux marble Formica finish in boring beige. Industrial green paint overlaid with years of fingerprints and unidentifiable smudges provided the backdrop for black and orange—like Halloween candy—plastic chairs, the kind that hook together to form a straight line.

A sign hanging from the ceiling instructed her to take a number. Another overly photocopied sign threatened to turn her out in the street was she to cut in front of someone in line. A third edict ordered her to take a seat in the chair closest to the door. There was also to be no smoking, no weapons, no cell phones, and no loud talking. Shirt and shoes required.

"Gotta love government," she mumbled.

Friendliness aside, she picked up a soiled square of formerly white construction paper with the number "1" on it. With her thumb and forefinger she carefully avoided the gross edges. Rachel preferred to stand but feared no one would wait on her if she didn't follow orders.

There appeared to be no one around. With no bell to summon help, she feared she'd wasted coins in the meter. But, she'd give it a few minutes.

A large woman eventually lumbered into the room. She wore a dress that looked like a tent, in a bright optical pattern that only accentuated her size. Her hair had that overprocessed look resembling straw. Light blue eye shadow in luminescent streaks graced her lids. Distress registered on her face the moment she locked eyes with the only occupant of the waiting area. Rachel took the high road and chose to believe the woman was concerned that she'd been waiting too long. Instead of approaching Rachel, she yelled to someone unseen.

A petite girl appeared from the boneyard of back offices. The veteran employee spoke to the diminutive soul in a stage whisper while pointing at Rachel who felt the beginning of a frown curling around the corners of her mouth. It was at that moment she became certain that the benefits and retirement packages for the government employed couldn't possibly be worth thirty years of being rump deep in paperwork, regulations, and dissatisfaction.

The ingénue had that fresh-from-school look that lasted a few years for most new women. Her honey blonde hair hung in tendrils around a heart-shaped face in the latest imitation of a currently popular TV starlet. A natural flush accentuated her cosmetic blush. Doe eyes were still bright with great anticipation of a wonderful life on the brink of happening. Rachel had the urge to warn her, but it was better to let nature take its course than to ruin the fabulous aura of newfound freedom that would shatter in a short time.

Hot pink cherub lips smiled honestly. "I'm Betsy. May I help you?" It sounded as though she meant it.

Rachel figured it was safe to stand up now and approach the bench, uh, counter. "Yes," she handed the child-woman the tarnished number one. "I'm Rachel Blackstone with *High Desert Country*." She fished one of her cards out of a pocket and handed it to Betsy, whose eyes flashed with excitement at the mention of a print medium.

"Wow. I started to take journalism in college, but there was this really cute prof in business, so I took marketing instead."

"Uh-huh," was all Rachel could think to say.

"It worked out okay, though, 'cause you have to do all that writing in journalism."

"Right." Rachel was tempted to pursue this line of conversation but since she only had 60 years—give or take—left to live, and elected to let it ride.

"I'd like to have the name of the company who's building Pueblo Blanco."

"Ooh, awesome," she droned on. "I've never done that before."

"Just my luck," Rachel muttered.

"What?"

"Oh, nothing. I was just thinking out loud."

"I'll be right back," Betsy said. "It's my first week. I have to ask Alice where to find this."

Yes, do go ask Alice, Rachel's thoughts jumped to the Jefferson Airplane hit. She was tempted to launch into her version of *White Rabbit* but figured her logic and proportion would be viewed with distrust here in Wonderland. Instead, she whistled the tune and was rewarded with a look of disapproval from Alice.

Betsy returned, triumphant in her success. She dropped a folder on the counter and read: "ABC Development, Inc."

"You're kidding?"

"No." Betsy, concerned, looked closely at the document as if clarity would reach out and touch her. "That's right. Here," she turned it toward Rachel, "you can see for yourself."

Certainly Betsy had been present in class the day the alphabet was taught. She was correct. "Address?" Rachel waited.

Betsy screwed up her fresh face. "It's a box number."

"Shit," Rachel said. Betsy ignored the obscenity as Rachel wrote down the P.O. number. Box numbers weren't the best lead, but the only one she had.

"Thanks," Rachel said. "You've been a great help."

Betsy beamed, having done her new job perfectly.

"You can also get this information on our website."

"Thanks." Rachel was thoughtful as she walked back to her car. She hoped Chloe was eating in tonight. There were a few questions she wanted to throw her way.

CHAPTER 16

C hloe was in—in her room experiencing a late afternoon delight. Rachel could feel herself blushing as she, a fist poised to knock on the bedroom door, realized that Chloe was not oohing and aahing over a new outfit.

Retreating to the kitchen, Rachel considered the selection of microwave dinners, thumbing her nose at the reduced calorie, low fat feasts encased in paper boxes with photos of food that actually looked good. "No fat, no flavor," Rachel whispered in disgust. It was time for a green chile cheeseburger—everything in New Mexico came with green chiles, allegedly even breakfast cereal. She grabbed her keys and made tracks to the nearest hamburger joint, the Casa Chile Burger. Home of the biggest plastic chile in the state, and a sign that proudly claimed: "More than two-dozen sold."

She placed an order and then walked outside to use a pay phone, one of the few left. She dialed the number of the Hopi Indian reservation headquarters in Kykotsmovi Village, Arizona; affectionately known as K-Town. It rang several times. Rachel was about to give up—it was after hours—when a woman answered.

Rachel identified herself. "I'd like to leave a message for Joseph." The Hopi were known as the Peaceful People, they needed to be since their reservation was encircled by the Navajo who had at one time menaced the gentle corn farmers. The Spaniards had made several efforts to convert the Hopi, but gave up because of their remote location.

The woman said that she would give Joseph the message. Rachel knew it could be days, even weeks, before she heard from him. His house was located in the far reaches of the reservation. He preferred to live according to the old ways. It was a house-house; four walls and a roof. No phone. She didn't know if that included electricity or a bathroom because she had interviewed him at the Hopi headquarters. Rachel hoped he could elaborate on the ceremony she had performed so poorly.

The burger, with extra chile, was a perfect accompaniment to the sunset she watched from one of the outdoor tables. The sun died in a rush of color while Rachel wondered how she could have left New Mexico in the first place.

It all came flooding back; the day her world fell apart. Tony had returned from Los Angeles after completing work on a documentary about the reintroduction of wolves into the western states. It was the wee hours. Rachel was writing a story for Julian in her home office. That day, she'd received word the governor would be honoring her for the state gambling piece. She was still high from the news and from the three celebratory margaritas she'd drained with Chloe. Tony was in one of his moods: jet lag, bad day, malaise, who knew? But he wasn't happy—a nearly chronic state.

He was inebriated as well, but instead of being pleasantly high, he was down. Her award made him even gloomier. It seemed they'd been working towards this moment for years. As a couple, they began madly in love, grown contented, and moved on to long periods of unhappiness. Time didn't seem to mend hearts, only deepen the blemishes.

Tony had never been a fun drunk, but early on he rarely imbibed. Rachel blamed the unrealistic pressures of a semi-Hollywood lifestyle for his increased alcohol intake. The move from documentaries and commercials to high-profile films hadn't materialized. Tony was at an age where careers in filmdom ended. With only a few silvers, he'd begun coloring his hair—something Santa Feans weren't known to do. He worked out more than he worked, and even had an eye job two years earlier, all in the hope that he could still pull off the promising up-and-comer.

Rachel had avoided the entire state of California because of the impossible expectations people in the entertainment industry had. No one was allowed to age gracefully in that business. Actresses often began having cosmetic surgery in their twenties. Those who weren't lifting were augmenting or having nonexistent fat cells sucked from their gravely thin bodies. It was a little easier on men, but many underwent the same torturous regime as women—even those whose jobs were behind the camera.

After Rachel told him her good tidings, Tony had poured another drink, taken a big swig and thrown the rest at the wall of their dining room.

She'd heard about people who just cracked, never understanding what it meant. It was a combination of breaking heart, disappointment in someone you loved, and the realization that time doesn't heal everything. Sometimes you have to pick up the broken pieces not too small for individual transport, and get your bruised soul away from the hurt.

Rachel thought she was doing that when she fled. In a hurry, she snapped up the Merc for $600 from a used car lot on Cerrillos. She arrived in Tulsa with less than a thousand dollars.

By the time she'd made the utility companies and her new landlord resplendent in deposits, she was nearly penniless, with no job, in a strange city. She found herself depressed and lonely—a bad combination.

For two weeks she'd stumbled from one interview to another until she landed the two part-time jobs. Chloe told her Tony was calling but Rachel steadfastly refused to allow her to divulge her number.

A few summer insects, bereft of a calendar, buzzed the streetlight in the early autumn darkness. They better join the migration or hibernation to avoid a fatal showdown with frost. She cast a glance at the ski basin hoping for fresh snow. Within the next couple of weeks the aspen would turn golden. Rachel loved the fall season. The turning leaves looked like flames licking the green pine forest. They were stunning for a moment, then gone with the mountain winds.

She assumed it was safe to return to Chloe's. Rachel backtracked to her car by way of the restaurant trash receptacle. With disgust, she considered cleaning all the rubbish from the car's interior but it seemed like too much work. In a couple of minutes she grabbed all the larger items and shoved them into a nearby trash bin. Compromise. It looked better.

Rachel made sufficient noise while entering Chloe's house so she wouldn't catch her friend indisposed. She sat at the kitchen bar sipping something—it reeked of peppermint. There was no sign of the other half of the rendezvous. She greeted Rachel warmly, offering to share her tea. Rachel accepted knowing she'd have to chase it with something harder—at least caffeinated. The herbal stuff would choke a goat, but she sipped it politely.

Rachel filled her in on the package from her father and the trip to city hall. "What do you think?"

"There is one odd thing about the location of that development," Chloe said. "Three years ago a left coast developer tried to get something going out there. I don't remember if it was housing or an ashram. Anyhow, the planning request was turned down." Chloe posed with her index finger and thumb on her chin as if they would help her think. "Was it an endangered species or some kind of easement problem? I don't recall. Anyway, the whole thing was nipped in the bud."

"I have an address for the developer," Rachel said. "Unfortunately, no phone, FAX or e-mail. I'll check for a website. If nothing, there's always snail mail. Maybe they'll care to enlighten me about the project."

"At this point," Chloe yawned. "It's about the only option you have. Let me know how it turns out. I'm going to bed." Chloe left Rachel to finish the tea. As soon as she was out of sight, Rachel poured it down the drain.

CHAPTER 17

"**B**y the way," Chloe said from the hall. Rachel felt guilty as she looked at the empty pot. Too late. There was no way to hide her stealthy actions. "Your actor friend, Logan, called today." Chloe eyes registered Rachel's offense as she reentered the kitchen. "He's sending over a pound of peppermint tea. He heard it was your favorite."

"I, uh," Rachel cast about for a way out. "Sorry, I wasn't going to drink it."

"You think I don't know that?" Chloe said mischievously. "You're a hopeless junk food addict. Actually, he wants to take a little trip to Pueblo Blanco to see what headway they've made. He's an investor as you know."

"Let me know what you find," Rachel said.

"Uh, he wants to go with you."

"With me?"

"Why are you surprised?" Chloe asked. "You guys were getting along famously at the gallery opening the other night." She paused for effect. "Rach, he's great looking, a nice guy and a celebrity—and you're available."

"He's not." Rachel had to admit to herself she was interested.

"It doesn't have to be a lifelong commitment." Chloe had a wicked grin. "Have some fun. You deserve it."

"I'll call him in the morning, from work, but it's strictly business."

"Right." Chloe winked.

* * *

"Stella, looking good," Shorty said the following morning. Shorty and Stella had a love affair of sorts. Not in the literal sense but there is something about opposites and attraction. They'd worked together since Julian opened the doors.

"Hey, Rach," Shorty jabbed at her, "Why don't you get a Santa Fe-sized car?" He'd beaten Rachel through the office door, because he rode a motorcycle and didn't have to fit a car the size of an RV into a parking space.

"Very funny, but I'm beginning to like the Merc. It has character."

"Yeah, two parking spaces worth of character." Shorty lumbered off to his graphics while Rachel stood wishing she could think of a flashy comeback.

"Hi, Stella, any messages?"

"One from Logan Masters. He wonders if he can pick you up at nine-thirty?"

"That's okay. I'll give him a call."

"Logan Masters, the actor?"

"Right you are, Stella. The very one."

"And you're not going to tell me what it's about?"

"Nothing to tell. He's an investor in Pueblo Blanco and I'm writing a story on it."

"I see."

It was too early for Rachel to fence. "You do look awfully sharp today, Stella."

"Flattery will get you off the hook."

At her desk Rachel confirmed their meeting time on Logan's voice mail. After finding no website for the company, she wrote a letter to ABC Development requesting an interview with the developer and slipped it into outgoing mail.

Outside, she blinked back the bright sunlight and enjoyed the warmth on her face. A black Range Rover with tinted glass pulled along the curb. Logan popped out and with a smile, ushered her politely into the passenger seat. It was a totally cool vehicle, would go anywhere, but didn't.

Rachel asked how the *Jake Weathers* filming was going. Logan chatted comfortably about his current leading lady, who'd never been anywhere remotely near the countryside. She was having some adjustment problems—like walking on something besides concrete. Somehow a lizard had found its way into her trailer, putting the filming schedule back half a day. Despite his amusement at her attack of vapors, he told the story without animosity. The actress would go back to California with no hard feelings.

"So, why did you want to see Pueblo Blanco today?" Rachel asked. "Not that I'm complaining, but why with me?"

"Haven't been out there since the big invitational soirée they threw a couple of months ago. Since you're doing a story on the place, I thought you'd be the logical one." He paused as the Espanola valley opened before them. It was breathtaking even to those who'd grown up with it. The colors were reds, pinks, tans revealed by centuries of wind and water. Father Time had indeed been good to this valley. "Wow!" he said. That's worth the trip. I came after dark last time. And," he resumed his line of thought, "you're good company." He gave her a sidelong grin from behind the wheel.

Rachel wasn't sure how to take the attention, but had to admit it was encouraging to know that at least one male thought she was worth spending time with. Considering her brother's reaction to her return and the heartbreaking split with her husband, it was a boost to her lagging self-esteem. She wouldn't be sharing this tidbit of awareness with Chloe, however, fearing a marathon of psychobabble interpretation. For now, it was kind of cozy to sit in a car with a man like Logan Masters.

When they passed through the gates of Pueblo Blanco Rachel was caught off guard. "Geez, the other day when I did the interview there was all kinds of activity. It looks deserted today."

"We'll know soon enough," Logan asked for more speed and dust flew behind them as the Rover responded. They pulled beneath the porte cochère of the office and community center.

It's obvious when a building is vacant. Even if the papers and mail are gathered, there are subtle clues about absence. The sidewalk leading to the big front doors had a scattering of small sand. The carved panels of the doors were dusty as were the windowsills on either side of the opening.

"Looks like they pulled up stakes." Rachel said, skimming the surface of the glass with her index finger, and then wiping the dirty finger on her jeans.

"Yeah, the lights are on, but no one's home," Logan replied. "Let's go around back."

"Not much more is done than when we were here for the investor party," Logan observed as they walked.

"When I was here for the interview," Rachel said, "there were trucks in and out, but I didn't pay attention to what they were doing. There are six finished houses," she pointed out unnecessarily, "and several slabs. My understanding is most developers have to sell X-amount of units before they can begin building."

"They may have hit a snag with one of the construction crews or are awaiting supplies," Rachel added. She didn't know how much Logan and the other celebrities had invested so she tried for some reassurance. "That kind of thing happens all the time. Our house was supposed to be built in three months. Nearly a year later we finally moved in."

"That's odd," Logan said. Rachel followed his line of vision. They had been slowly walking toward the model houses when he'd picked up on something. "See the tire tracks in the dust. Looks as if someone has pulled into the garage, but I don't see any indication they've backed out."

Rachel agreed with his appraisal. "Good, maybe that means someone's here. I'll try to raise them." There was no answer to the doorbell or her knock. "Guess we're wrong."

"Well," Logan said, "I'm not a real P.I. I just play one on TV." They were laughing as they walked back to the Rover, but the face that watched them go was not.

CHAPTER 18

They returned to the quiet residential street outside the magazine office. Mrs. Brazos' dog lay in the sun getting some zzz. The old black dog's tail wagged occasionally as if to say that at least one ear was aware of what was going on. Mrs. Brazos was a remarkable lady. She'd taken the staff of *High Desert Country* to raise. Her husband was dead and she'd outlived both her children so she turned her maternal instincts to residents on her street. Rachel and her co-workers had often, and at great length, sampled her goodies for *Cinco de Mayo, Día de los Muertos,* Christmas, and just because she felt like cooking.

Little Davy Williams was doing his best to skateboard along the street. At one time pavement had completely covered the road but time and lack of funding had made it a potholed mess. That made his route more challenging as he zigged and zagged around the miniature craters, much like ski moguls in reverse. He was barreling by so fast he didn't notice the TV star watching him.

Logan pulled over and parked parallel on the shoulder. He jumped lightly into the ditch while Rachel stepped out into the street.

The Smiths lived next door to Mrs. Brazos in this multiethnic area. They had retired to Santa Fe from New Jersey. The couple had made an effort to learn Spanish so they could talk with new friends in their native language. Rachel loved them. Mrs. Smith was sitting in a small porch swing under their back *portal* watching her husband tend his garden. He was raking imaginary foreign matter from the scrupulous bed of fall flowers. His homegrown bouquets often adorned the reception desk of the magazine office.

Rachel walked into the middle of the street so she could say hello to the Smiths. She was about to wave when the sound of a car caught her attention. It careened around the corner and accelerated, moving fast from the wrong direction on the one-way street.

With only seconds to get out of the way, Rachel dove toward the ditch. She landed with a thud and quickly rolled into the shallow trench covering her head with her hands. The car sped by barely missing her and leaving choking dust in its wake.

Shaking, Rachel got to her feet and began brushing the dirt from her clothing, but immediately remembered Davy.

The child passed them moments before the car appeared. "Logan, Davy!" She pointed at the boy's back, but Logan was already in pursuit, yelling at Davy to get off the street. Mr. Smith dropped his rake and followed. His wife stood clasping the white embroidered handkerchief she always had in her possession.

All Rachel could do was hope the driver would slow down or the two men could somehow avert an accident. The black Cadillac lurched to even greater speed. Rachel tried to see through the heavily tinted windows, but could only make out a single figure from her view of the back.

Her attention was held by Mrs. Smith, who had left the security of the porch and was running as best she could on arthritic legs. Everything about her showed fear: posture erect, mouth open, hands clenched. Her handkerchief lay on the ground. Rachel began running to see what was happening.

When Rachel rounded the Rover, she could see that a tragedy would not be avoided this day. The car hit one of the potholes. The driver lost control. Mr. Smith was caught between the car and a wall.

In the distance—it seemed much farther than it actually was—she could see Logan had reached Davy and picked him up safely. Rachel's moment of gratitude for this was cut short as she watched in horror as the Cadillac flipped over, skidded on its roof toward Mr. Smith. Despite the terror, he was sure to be experiencing, he still had the wherewithal to try to get out of the way, but the wall blocked his escape.

Mrs. Smith screamed as she watched a part of her die. Rachel covered her ears as if that would block the screeching slide as the Cadillac hit a parked car and then crashed into the wall. Metal crunched, resisted, and gave way at impact. There was no explosion like in the movies. As the cars settled into their new shapes, the windshield could stand the strain no longer and disintegrated into a thousand pieces. There were soft rustling sounds as the event ended.

Rachel stood transfixed by shock and realization. A moment later she was moving, running to stop Mrs. Smith from seeing her dead husband.

Love sealed with time can be strong. The couple had been married for nearly fifty years. They had lived through the customary ups and downs of a marriage, survived the losses, and managed to grow closer. Rachel raced to stop her. Mrs. Smith's face was twisted in pain as her chubby form ran toward her mate. She was so pumped with adrenalin that she nearly knocked Rachel aside.

"No, let me go," raged a tortured voice. "I must help him." Even from where they struggled Rachel could see Mr. Smith's upper body caught between two unforgiving pieces of metal. No one could help him.

"Please, Mrs. Smith." What was her first name? Something her husband had said once—he grew some kind of flower because it was his wife's name. Lily! "Lily, please stop. We can't help him. It's me, Rachel, please stop fighting me." The woman's body sagged in her arms. Rachel helped her to the ground, turning her away from the horror just feet away.

Logan ran to see if he could help the old man. Rachel believed the injuries to be massive. Mr. Smith's flowers would bloom on their own next year, if at all.

A crowd gathered. Julian sprinted down the street from the office. He wrapped his big arms around them both. Lily Smith wept. Sirens wailed in the distance. Logan checked the carotid artery on the unknown occupant of the car, as viewers had seen him do many times on his show. He shook his head as Rachel held onto the trembling body of the new widow. She turned to Julian, whose face was fixed in disbelief. He blinked back tears and rough-ly brushed them away with a burly hand.

Rachel could smell gasoline. The rancid odor mixed with the dust, death, and confusion as they awaited those who could clean up the mess and make death official. But there would be no one who could explain why it happened.

CHAPTER 19

T he following morning, Rachel gazed out a window of the office. Sleep had been elusive. She was exhausted, not so much from the lack of rest, but from the violent accident and loss of sacred life. The office mood was solemn. The ruined cars had been towed away. The street had been washed clean of blood. Everything that could be done had been. The fixable things were the easy part. That left why? Why had the driver gone the wrong way and at such a high rate of speed? Was he drunk, insane, stupid? There were no immediate answers.

Rachel checked her messages and found a solitary slip. The note left no name or number, just a rather odd line, "Drop the piece." Stella's two-cents worth scrawled below told Rachel the caller had been mysterious and not particularly polite.

Fine, whatever that meant. Piece of pie? Piece of shit? Well, that couldn't be it, but she was in no mood for cryptograms. Piece of work? She was working on two stories, only one officially as-signed by Julian. Did it mean the story on Pueblo Blanco? Besides the PR guy at the new housing compound, who knew or cared, besides Julian? Rachel wadded the paper and tossed it. The caller must have gotten a wrong number.

The twelve-page manuscript on Pueblo Blanco was complete or at least as done as it would ever be. She attached it to an e-mail and sent it to Julian. The walk to the back office was short. Julian stared out his tiny window, clicking his retractable pen. "The story is finished. I just sent it to you. I think there's another story there: misuse of water resources, development madness, something askew." He seemed preoccupied.

"Did you read the morning paper?" Julian asked, but didn't turn from the window.

"No. Why?" There was rarely anything of serious note to read in the Santa Fe paper—unless it happened elsewhere. They ran the police calls, which were usually not serious. Rachel liked to read them. Once someone had broken into a resident's RV where they had eaten cookies. During the summer the largest water consumers were reported by name, gallons consumed, statement amount and penalty fee. Water was almost more important than crime in this desert city, particularly because it was dryer than it had been in decades.

"Apparently, the guy driving that Cadillac had a criminal record." Julian turned and the expression on his face worried Rachel.

"Crime is everywhere," Rachel said, "but Santa Fe doesn't have much opportunity for felonious sorts. The casinos are owned by the Pueblo Indians. The race track is outside of town, but there is a flea market outside of town too."

"Stella told me you received an odd phone message" Julian said.

"Yes, that's true. Do you want to see it?"

"Yes, please."

Rachel returned to her desk and picked up the white plastic trash can. She fished the wadded slip out and smoothed the paper. Retracing her steps, she presented it to Julian.

"Well, doesn't look like much," he said.

"I figure it was left with the wrong office." It hadn't made sense to her when it arrived and it still didn't.

"Stella said that *he* specifically asked for you."

"He?"

"She thinks it was a man, or a woman with a low voice." Stella could remember things for months that the average person would forget by the time they cradled the phone. It was one of the reasons Julian valued her so much. "You know," Julian crossed his legs wearily, "The college paper I worked for received threatening notes from time to time. We ignored them because we thought all the dangerous shit was happened in the large cities."

Julian was a long way off; probably back on campus in Denver where most students had been interested in the powder on the slopes. "But?" Rachel nudged.

"But." He leaned back in his chair, placing his hands behind his head, thinking. "But, sometimes we should pay attention to weirdoes, because they can be dangerous. The problem is, you never know which one it will be. Suffice it to say, the newspaper office was set on fire and two lives were lost: the custodian, who happened to be the father of five, and a student reporter. Probably, killing was not the intention, but that's not the way it worked out."

Rachel sank into the empty chair. She had the feeling this story got worse. "Did the police find the arsonist?"

"Yeah, a kid named Alec Robertson. He was mad at the world. He took umbrage to an editorial we wrote about a U.S. military buildup. I helped put him away by investigating his background and writing a piece for the *Rocky Mountain News*—my first entry into the world of paid print. One of those back country boys raised on God, guns, and guts. His grandfather boasted at the trial that he could fire a gun before he learned to walk. To listen to these folks testify about overthrowing the government and the casualties it might inflict was bloodcurdling. He swore in court that he'd get me."

"My god, Julian, has he ever been released?"

"Yeah, about a year ago. I held my breath for a while, but decided he must have forgotten or had other insurgent fish to fry.

"The thing is, Rachel, I gave up crime reporting after it became clear to me just how many nuts are out there. Ten years at the *Washington Post* and three with the *Chicago Sun Times* made me aware of something." Rachel waited quietly while he paused. They had known one another long enough to be comfortable with the silence. "You spend a lot of time with these crazies," political correctness out of print was not always Julian's thing, "and some of it begins to rub off. It's a little like being a cop. You see so much suffering. You get to a place where it seems normal—even logical. Eventually, it's a way of life."

"What are you telling me, Jule?"

"That I'm taking this note seriously. I'm giving it to the police."

"Jule, is that really necessary?"

"You said it yourself. You think there's another story to Pueblo Blanco."

"I'm talking about water shortages and maybe a little graft and corruption. Hardly worth killing over."

"Nevertheless."

"Even the Santa Fe police have better things to do than read screwy messages." Julian frowned so Rachel stopped the short speech she had been constructing in her head that this was nothing. "What's next?" She changed the subject. They'd visited the badlands long enough.

"How long are you going to be here?" Julian smiled slightly, his happier face returning.

"Long enough to do a couple more stories, I guess."

"Here's a new gallery opening—like we need another." Julian handed her a glossy press pack. "And how about the yearly ski basin report? When do they expect to open?"

"The basin employs soothsayers now?"

"Rachel, you know the drill. Everyone wants to wax their skis and dream of packed powder. And, here's a new restaurant opening."

"Doesn't a stringer normally do that?" It wasn't that she was too good to review food—she loved food—but it seemed he was deliberately trying to give her lightweight projects.

"That would be you, would it not?" Julian raised his bushy, flyaway eyebrows.

Technically he was correct. She was stringing, since she had not been reemployed by *High Desert Country* as a full-timer.

"You'll like it," Julian teased. "They specialize in carne adovada burritos."

"I feel the need for an early lunch." She grabbed the media package and sprinted out of the office.

* * *

"Your man made a big mess," said the voice over the phone. "No one was to get killed. This was a scare job."

"Accidents happen."

"Not when I'm paying." Silence. "Do you have any idea who you're talking to?"

"Yeah, I do." There was a sharp click. The line went dead.

CHAPTER 20

Rachel punched in Chloe's number. Voice mail. She left a message, hung up the phone, and waited. The funny thing about death, even violent death, is that the world doesn't seem to notice. Someone's life ends and the sun rises, birds sing, and people go about their business. Somehow, Rachel thought it felt wrong to go right back to work, but brooding didn't seem like a proper tribute either.

The car warmed in the sunshine. Cars zipped by the gas station in characteristic blurs. She wished she'd gotten something to drink. By the time the phone rang she'd slumped over, close to a nap.

"Hello!" She grabbed the phone to stop another ring. "Chloe?"

"ESP?" Chloe asked.

"Near death experiences do that, I hear."

"You okay, Rach?"

"Yeah, a little shaky, but okay," Rachel said. "How about lunch?"

"Oh, god, we're talking greasy, aren't we?"

"It's free. I'm writing a story on the place."

Chloe didn't miss a beat. "Where? I've got to finish some paperwork, but I can be there in thirty."

Rachel gave her the address on Cordova.

It was more like fifty minutes, but Rachel had planned for that. Cordova runs through a largely residential part of town. There is a sliver of a park at the intersection with Galisteo. Rachel pulled over and watched some kids play among the trees. Their mothers sat on a quilt nearby, talking and giggling. All was right in their world. When Chloe's Mercedes flew by, Rachel started the Merc and followed.

It was early for the lunch crowd so Rachel parked next to the Benz. She saw Chloe's frown at her lush car keeping company with an aging Marquis. Her friend looked fabulous—denim and a silver belt. Sometimes Rachel was envious, but turning out like Chloe was work, something she preferred not to do.

The place resembled most restaurants in the city: white walls, southwestern art prints, pale finished wooden tables and cushions covered in flame stitch fabric. It was moderately priced by Santa Fe standards—almost affordable to the average person. It had all of Rachel's favorite New Mexican dishes, but what was in short supply in Santa Fe were eating establishments that specialized in the kind of dishes the rest of the country ate. She rarely tired of carne adovada, chile rellenos or huevos rancheros, but once in a while she craved fried food untouched by the food police. But as long as she was here, Rachel was quite happy with New Mexican specialties.

They settled at a back table which overlooked a terrace still in the process of being assembled. Light washed through an opaque skylight, giving life to the large plants hanging from the *vigas*, large hand-hewn timbers that held up the ceiling.

"If the food's any good, this would be a great place to send my less fortunate clients," Chloe said.

"If they like fern bars," Rachel groused.

"Some people actually do," Chloe commented. "But I fear you are right. It's like traveling halfway around the world and staying at a Holiday Inn."

"I have to keep an open mind," Rachel came back to the present. "I'm doing a story."

"It sounds open to me," Chloe said.

"Thanks a lot."

"Don't thank me yet, but I may have some information on that company you're trying to reach."

Interested, Rachel urged her on. "How so?"

"Fella I met today is an attorney. We were talking about Pueblo Blanco—he'd already looked there—and he said he'd heard through the legal grapevine the company's a shell."

"Really?"

"Truly. So whoever has ownership of the development can hide, pretty much indefinitely, behind an attorney. You probably won't get a reply to your inquiry—remember the address was a P.O. Box? If these folks don't want to be found, they probably can't be, barring an indictment."

"Which I don't have—and would involve police," Rachel sighed.

"Which you don't have. You do have the name of the attorney, who—I emphasize this—who might have created the company."

"I do? Chloe! My dearest friend in the world."

"Oh stop, you know how I hate gushing." She feigned modesty.

"Don't I," Rachel faked agreement.

"Here's the guy's name." Chloe pushed a business card across the table as if they were making a top secret microfilm exchange in Cold War U.S.S.R. "My new acquaintance says this lawyer does this kind of work on the side while running a more respectable practice in the open."

"Will it self-destruct?" Rachel whispered.

"If it does, we have to disavow all knowledge of your actions."

"Seriously, thanks. I'll give him a call later."

"I make no promises," Chloe said. "The guy may not talk—probably won't talk. He's bound by all kinds of ethics, you know."

They finished lunch, then Chloe ran off to her next appointment while Rachel stayed and did a twenty-minute interview with the owner. She'd waited until after eating before revealing her identity. The food had been mediocre but as Chloe had said some people liked it that way. She'd concentrate the story on ambience. Julian didn't like to be unkind to local business. It could create ill will and hurt advertising revenues.

She returned to the office where she wrote a quick draft and saved it for completion later. When Julian went to lunch, she dialed the lawyer's number. While it rang, she debated whether to claim her media position or try to fake it. His receptionist answered before she could decide so she went with the truth.

"Victor Chavez, please, this is Rachel Blackstone with *High Desert Country* magazine."

"Mr. Chavez doesn't speak with reporters."

"Even when we're featuring Pueblo Blanco, a development he's involved with?" She hurried on. "It's going to be our lead story next month."

"Just a moment." Rachel waited. The fact she'd been placed on hold told her she probably had the right attorney. "Mr. Chavez," the receptionist returned, "is out of the office right now. If you'd like to leave your number I'll be happy to give him the message, but I'm unfamiliar with this development."

"Does that mean he isn't working with the company who's building it? Geez," Rachel played the perplexed reporter, "I'd hoped to get his take on this. It would balance out the article."

"I work with every client that Mr. Chavez accepts," the receptionist said a bit snooty. "I'm certain I would know about this if it was one of his." Uh, the old kiss-off.

"Okay, we'll just have to go with what we've got, accusations and all." She gave her something to think about. "Thanks, I appreciate your, er, help." Rachel left her number and hung up, confident it was the right attorney, and hoping it was the right approach to draw him out.

CHAPTER 21

Having lost the battle, but not the war, on the lawyer front, Rachel chose the ski story over the gallery because it was the farthest drive and the one she dreaded the most. Her father had been killed on the road to the ski basin. She hadn't driven it since then. It was time for her to get over the hurdle.

Rachel took a right onto Artist Road, which made a bend uphill and became Hyde Park Road. It took about thirty minutes to make the drive, if you drove the speed limit. The mountains rose to 12,000 feet above the city, which was already more than a mile high. The first several miles were easy with only a few turns, but soon after that the two-lane road got serious with switchbacks and ear popping rises in elevation.

It was near Big Tesuque her father died, crashing through the guard rail and falling to the rocks and trees below. Originally, the theory had been he'd lost control of his car. But later, when it was determined that no drugs or alcohol were involved a closer look was taken. Another set of tire tracks suggested the possibility of an accident or foul play.

She drove by Big Tesuque without looking at the picnic sites she knew were there, or the lonely stream fed by snow melt. There were two trails along the stream with many places to stop and reflect. It had been one of her favorite places.

The Merc sputtered past Aspen Vista, which marked the last leg of the trip. Rachel made a mental note to have the car tuned up for the elevation, and then remembered she wasn't moving back and discarded the notion.

The parking lot of the Santa Fe Ski Basin, which would shortly be packed with snow and four-wheel drive vehicles, hosted only a half-dozen cars today. By Thanksgiving—the basin's traditional opening—there should be a nice base if the expected snows arrived. That didn't always happen and season lift ticket holders had been disappointed during light precipitation years.

This afternoon the quad lift—called the Super Chief—was being put through its paces. Crews were doing repairs on the steps leading to the ski facilities, replacing railroad ties that would support the metal steps. A new coat of paint dried on the walls of the building. Rachel had spent many happy times here skiing, but seldom with her father who was usually working. News stories usually aren't convenient and don't respect weekends or holidays. During the summer and fall the lifts ran so people could see the spectacular view from the summit and appreciate the golden aspens.

The basin's PR person was eager and met Rachel on the huge deck. Gorgeous and well-dressed, Lisa Johnn should have been a confident person. Instead, she made sure right off that Rachel knew of her qualifications, having just graduated with a master's degree in marketing—with honors! Reassuring. Rachel thought marketing jobs must be tough because people came and went quickly.

True to expectations, the ski basin expected record snows—*Farmer's Almanac* or prophets? On the schedule was the popular Winter Fiesta, several benefits and skiing workshops, along with competitions such as the Bump Run and snowboarding events. A two-story addition would add 12,000 square feet to La Casa Lodge and a new black diamond slope was ready for the first dare devils. Rachel finished the interview and made arrangements for photos. Shorty had a library of ski photos but he might want another excuse to leave the office.

She put the car in second gear and began the winding trip down. The aspens were just teasing at the color to come. To visit Santa Fe in the autumn was to fall in love. With the winds of spring and summer monsoon behind it, the area could show off.

Ideal skies, colorful trees and a slower pace made it the perfect season. Rachel loved winter too. Most out-of-state skiers drove north to Taos, where the most challenging runs were, and left Santa Feans to their mountain. But winter's cozy quiet could be interrupted with periods of icy wind. Summer's dusty roads were replaced by mud. Cleaning shoes became the area pursuit.

Deep in thought, Rachel almost didn't notice the odor while making the sharp turn into Big Tesuque. At first she thought the Merc's brakes were overheating. The gauges were normal. Relieved that she wouldn't have to pull over, she made the third turn of the snaky section of road, but the stink persisted.

"Shit." She slowed and opened the window. Maybe she could clear the car of the smell. A glance in the rear view confirmed an empty highway. The picnic grounds were deserted. "Better pull over and check under the damn hood." What she knew about what went on under the hood of newer cars could be written on her thumb. She'd been a bit of a gofer as a child when her father had made minor repairs on his classic car, but computers and other high-tech engine parts had left those days way behind.

Beneath the hood looked much as she remembered. Rachel was adept at checking fluid levels but that roughly covered her mechanical abilities. There was nothing apparent. No smoke, steam or oil escaped their intended domiciles.

"Funny thing," she wondered aloud, "that smell seems to be everywhere. And I must be going nuts talking to myself!" She reached to slam the hood when memory kicked in and she froze. Rachel turned on her heel to look again. There was nothing but a fabulous view of the valley below and the blue Jemez Mountains in the distance. She looked back the way she had come; nothing and no one. Not even a car coming down from the basin. "Just me and the ozone layer." But she couldn't bring herself to laugh. She felt paralyzed to do anything at all. Gooseflesh tickled her skin as she stood indecisively.

"This is ridiculous!" She closed the hood with a bang. The door remained open as she had left it. The aspens quaked as a deep rush of wind pushed at them. Had it been a month later they would have spilled like a rain of golden doubloons. It took with it the fragrance of a lightning stroke and carried away her misgivings. Rachel thought this time the phenomenon could be explained. The wind could come up quickly in the mountains. A storm could strike out at the mountains while all remained calm in the city below. But that didn't explain the keys.

They were not in the ignition. Nor did they lie in the seat. A hasty inspection of her pockets revealed nothing but a rumpled tissue and an ancient movie ticket. Rachel retraced her steps but found no sign of the keys on the ground. "Great. This is just great." She was certain she left the keys in the ignition. That's why she'd left the door ajar, so she wouldn't lock herself out.

The fear crept back. There was plenty of cover off the road, albeit steep to maneuver. Feeling very exposed and vulnerable Rachel got back into the car and locked the doors. She would have to wait for someone to go by, flag them down and get help. At least the odor was gone. A horrible and unbidden picture flashed through her mind—a body slumped over a steering wheel. Her dad? She shook her head to clear the image. When her eyes opened, she noticed the keys lying on the floor of the passenger side.

Holding them in her hands, they seemed warm as if touched by the sun, but they had not been. She fumbled, but managed to insert the keys in the ignition. The car roared to life on the first try. Rachel struggled with the gear shift, found "Drive" and the Merc charged onto the road.

CHAPTER 22

Sun Dancing Realty was located off Paseo de Peralta near Canyon Road. The sprawling former hacienda had been home to several businesses previously including a bookstore, restaurant and a boutique but because it wasn't on either of the well-known streets, shoppers and hungry people hadn't found them. When Chloe's mentor and fellow realtor, Anita Lopez, bought the rambling rundown building, many in the industry figured it to be an albatross; especially after she hit up her millionaire husband—now ex—and completely renovated it into Santa Fe's most high-profile real estate agency.

With Lopez at the helm and Chloe the best-selling agent in the city, inside a year everyone knew where their office was. Sun Dancing was the real estate authority for celebrities and the well-heeled. It was high-end real estate all the way, listing property in Wilderness Gate, the expensive historical east side, and the north hills including Tesuque. For nearly a decade, Santa Fe had been the hot place to travel and live. Even modest homes were priced out-of-sight to many natives. This made for considerable resentment toward wealthy outsiders intent on having a piece of Santa Fe style. Things were changing, and so was Sun Dancing. Rachel knew Chloe and the agency would survive. Chloe always did. Failure was not in her vocabulary.

She pulled in front of Chloe's office. It was quiet this late in the day. A few cars, all top dollar models, were parked under the tall cottonwoods. The old hacienda was painted one of the fifty-some city approved colors of brown. Windows were trimmed in azure, to ward off bad spirits. The massive front doors were original panel works with antique hardware. Cosmos and asters bloomed along the authentic adobe walls, the flowering clumps broken up by piñon and landscape boulders. The *canale,* Santa Fe's version of a rain gutter, cast a late day shadow over the flagstone path leading to the entrance.

Inside, elegant hand-chiseled wooden columns led to the lobby. The receptionist desk was impressive set against a backdrop of bright white stucco covered in art work. These were the real thing, insured to the hilt. Rachel crossed the imported Spanish tile that paved the wide hall. Pine benches, built by a craftsman in Taos, ran the full length, many draped with Indian rugs. A receptionist, whose name Rachel couldn't remember, was on duty. After Chloe hired her, she'd made a point of saying that the woman was not only "right" for the agency because of her elegant look but also extremely efficient and capable. She was probably the highest paid clerical worker west of the Mississippi. Rachel greeted her and walked on by to Chloe's office.

The only office larger than Chloe's belonged to Anita Lopez. Rachel's rental in Tulsa would have fit within the confines of Chloe's work space. She was talking on the phone, exuding orgasmic tones over a house—make that a "very special" house. Rachel walked in at Chloe's exuberant waving and took a comfy chair across from the handcrafted desk. The office consisted of three areas: a work zone with desk, computer, and wood file cabinets; a roll-up-the-sleeves conference spot with a table and chairs for eight people; and the chatty we're-just-good-friends-in-my-living-room corner complete with comfort foods, refrigerated designer waters, flowers and cozy throws. Three red telephones, the hot lines as Chloe referred to them, were within easy reach wherever she might be. Chloe was never without one. Each of her home bathrooms was equipped with one too—with several lines. Rachel thought phones in the toilets akin to hell.

After a few more gushing minutes Chloe put down the phone. "Hi, Rach, *¿qué pasa?*"

Rachel told her about the visit to the ski basin, with emphasis on the strange occurrence during the return trip.

"Holy shit! You know what you need?"

Rachel was afraid to ask, but did.

"A life navigator," Chloe said with conviction.

"Say what?"

"A life navigator. They're great, and many of them are acquainted with Indian lore too. I swear you're dealing with a shapeshifter who digs the smell of magnesium."

"What exactly are these navigators?"

"Think of them as therapists. People spend thousands of dollars on therapists every year and don't think it's strange. That's what these counselors do, help you navigate through life. What could it hurt?"

"I'll think about it," Rachel said. "In the meantime, could you do me a favor?"

"Most likely." Chloe's eyebrow rose in anticipation.

"Remember telling me about the development which didn't? You know, where Pueblo Blanco is going up."

"Sure. What do you want to know?"

"What prevented it from coming to fruition? Can you find out?"

"Affirmative. I'll make a call." She reached for a phone.

"May I use one of the others?" Rachel wanted to check in with the office before it closed.

"Sure. Any line not lit."

Stella answered on the second ring. "Rachel, glad it's you. Your Hopi friend called. He was on a provisions excursion from the backside of the reservation."

"Shit, I missed him. Did he say anything?"

"Man of few words, my dear, but he did mention he'd be back in a couple of days—wasn't specific."

"Thanks, Stella." Rachel was disappointed. "Anything else?"

"Not a thing, hon. Got to go. Julian's threatening to lock me in."

Rachel sank back into the plush cushions of the sofa and waited for Chloe to finish her call. What happened today? It was easy in the safety of Chloe's office to dismiss the whole thing. It could be stress. Surely, all of humankind's stressed out numbers were not finding themselves extra sensitive to magnesium. The moment she saw the keys on the floor of her car Rachel would have confessed on a national talk show to her belief in the supernatural. Damn, she wished she hadn't missed Joseph's call.

Chloe hung up. "Easement problem. Soil didn't pass the perk test for septic system. No sanitary lines, no easement."

"Was there a mistake? They must have one now."

"Far as I know there haven't been any changes in this area. They might have gotten a variance, but it's hard to believe."

"There must be a reason. Chloe, you're the expert."

"Well, gosh, Rach, that's only a little pressure." Chloe massaged both temples. "I thought you were finished with the story. What does it matter now?"

"I just want to focus on something other than the mess my life's in."

"Hmm." Chloe tented her fingers in thought. "There's always the old standby."

"Yeah?"

"Bribery."

"You mean a government official?"

"It happens. Now," Chloe changed the subject, "I want to know if you've given that precious house any consideration? It's not going to last long. I showed it today."

Rachel hadn't taken a single moment to think about the house, so she lied. "Of course, but Julian's keeping me pretty busy, and there was that horrible accident. You know, Mr. Smith's funeral is tomorrow."

"The paper said the driver of the car had a criminal background. What do you suppose that jerk was doing there?"

"That's bothering Jule too. He even gave that screwy message I received to the police. I think the incident reminded him of a tragedy that happened while he was in college; kind of a post-traumatic thing. Everyone at the office is upset about it. Geez, nothing like that has ever happened in our neighborhood before. The asshole was driving the wrong way, fast. He didn't care about the law or the people."

"Rachel," Chloe changed the subject back to her, "what are you going to do? Do you know? And, no, I don't want you to leave, but staying in purgatory isn't going to get you anywhere."

"Honestly, I don't know. Going back to Tulsa would be easy. It wasn't much of a life, but it was all hers, and in time it could be terrific. Staying here would be harder—more baggage to deal with. I can add Tony to that heap. Getting along with Chris has never been easy so I expect it won't improve. Did you know his wife left with their kids right before I returned?"

"He plays well with others, doesn't he?" Chloe said, dripping sarcasm. "Half of Santa Fe hates him, the other half is tolerating him until election time, but somehow he manages to get what he wants anyway."

"There's not much chance he will change," Rachel said. "Dad had given up on him. They saw each other on holidays, at funerals and weddings. Can't say as I blame him.

"In answer to your question, I don't know what I'm going to do."

* * *

Pipe bombs were simple. The newly completed one was ready for deployment; the target chosen. The timing needed to be more accurate this time.

CHAPTER 23

L ily Smith's husband had been a veteran. Abe Smith was laid to rest in the National Cemetery across the street from DeVargas Mall. Heavy clouds made it an appropriately depressing day.

Rachel was a sun fan. Having lived in beautiful, albeit overcast Portland, Oregon, she had found that during the winter, one could experience days, even weeks of nonproductive cloudiness. Spring in Oklahoma brought severe thunderstorms, but watches and warnings haunted the other seasons as well; tornadoes one day and six inches of snow the next. In Santa Fe, one could enjoy sunshine more than 300 days a year. Rachel had come to know a cloudy day in Santa Fe as mostly sunny—with an occasional cloud drifting overhead. Today wasn't one of those days, but a bona fide overcast day.

Lily Smith was inconsolable. Her only child, a grown daughter, had flown in from New Jersey for the sad occasion. Stella said that Lily might sell her home and live with her daughter.

Everyone from the office attended except the nephew, John. Since he didn't know Mrs. Smith, Julian asked him to hold the fort. It didn't bother him. From all appearances, he preferred staying as far away from other people as possible. It showed in his stories. He was too detached in his telling and completely devoid of any emotions. That meant he couldn't identify with the hopes or traumas of the people he interviewed.

Shortly, Abe Smith would be just another white marker in a vast sea of headstones. The graveside service was proving too much for Rachel. There hadn't been enough time since her father's memorial service. She walked slowly away from the small gathering, to her car. It was better she return to the office and help the nephew. He was bound to screw up, given his people skills.

She elected to park a few blocks away from the office. Walking would help clear some of the sad reflection. Missing someone you've lost is pointless and yet it's all there is left to do. Joseph Conrad was correct when he wrote, "We live as we dream—alone." Some pain and loss are so intense, they cannot be shared.

The police had kept the phone message but didn't hold out much hope it would be helpful. Despite the fact that the driver had been a criminal, it was believed the man did not intentionally kill Abe Smith or himself. It was a straightforward case of reckless driving. No big deal, it just claimed two lives.

The office lot was deserted. Rachel immediately felt a flush of anger. Had wonder boy left his duties for something more fun? Nah, it was unlikely he knew fun. She spotted his silver sports car down the street. He'd been the last to arrive that morning so there hadn't been any spaces left.

Julian's office provided the only back way out of the building. He used it when he needed to make a quick escape. Rachel's blues were turning to mischief as she considered sneaking up on the nephew, maybe even catching him in the act of going through personnel files or some such fireable offense.

It was a tight squeeze along the back fence with perhaps three feet separating it from the wall of the building. Overgrown lilacs tumbled down the chain link fence, scratching at her face and arms. River stones formed a walk of sorts, laced with beer bottles and aluminum cans. One chamisa grew defiantly from beneath the adobe wall. In full bloom, the yellow flowers smelled to high heaven. Rachel stifled a sniffle. Julian would have to be desperate to take this route in or out of the building. She hadn't used it more than a couple of times.

Her key slipped into the lock but it struggled with the seldom used tumblers. It scraped, she turned hard and hoped the key wouldn't break off. When the lock obliged, she found the door stuck and had to yank it open. The whole thing made such a racket, there wasn't much hope of surprising anyone.

Once Rachel had resolved her conflict with the door, she found the office quiet. She stood in Julian's room and listened. The silence was so intense; Rachel thought she could hear her own heart. Oddly, the birds had stopped their chatter.

The last few days of her life had heightened her instincts. There it was again—that feeling of something amiss. But, there was no ominous scent. Then she heard the low growl of a wolf. It seemed quite close. Rachel turned and looked out the open door just as the filmy figure crept by. At the same moment, she saw the word, *run*, as though projected upon a screen in her mind. She shook it off.

Rachel took a couple of stealthy steps and emerged from Julian's office. John was oblivious to everything. His headphones pumped music into his pale, fuzzy head. If he hadn't heard the noise Rachel made getting in, he could not have heard the telephone ring. He'd done no work.

While this annoyed Rachel it wasn't what bothered her most. She couldn't help but feel a strong desire to leave. The presence of the ghostly lobo concerned her. It had shown up before on the lonely highway and sent the spirit packing. She couldn't be certain of its intentions. John jumped from his seat when he realized he wasn't alone. The headphones tugged off his head and landed in his now empty chair.

"You scared the hell out of me," he spat. "What are you sneaking around for?" Rachel cut him off with a quick movement across her throat.

"Something's wrong," she said.

"Yeah, you." The nephew was pissed about being caught goofing off.

"Shut up," Rachel said. "I don't give a shit what you were doing, or not doing. Let's get out of here for a while." Standing, in this usually happy place, feeling so frightened was worse than peculiar.

"I don't have to do anything you say." It was junior journalist again. "I'll tell Uncle, er Julian. We left our posts because his easy come, easy go reporter had a hormone swing."

"Listen, you little punk," she glared at the twenty-something product of nepotism, "if you want to stay, suit yourself, but I'm taking a powder for a few minutes." She left the way she had come. When she reached the back door, she felt the shudder which seemed to precede the bang of the blast—almost like the ground rumbling prior to an earthquake. For a few moments her hearing was replaced by the other senses. The force shoved her down. She fell in slow motion, arms out to protect her body. When she landed, her hands fell on broken glass. They stung with fresh blood. Rachel was certain she screamed, but couldn't hear herself. Her nose took the final punishment as plaster dust rushed through the office, engulfing her and then blowing past. The last thing she wanted to do was to go back inside, but the prickly kid was still in there. Momentarily she froze on all fours wondering when she could hear again.

Humans are a strange lot, prone to rescuing others, even those they don't know or particularly like, while risking their own lives. Rachel pushed herself up to her feet, and brushed some of the plaster dust from her clothing. She tasted blood as she carefully nursed the lacerated finger. It occurred to her, it might need stitches.

The building stood. From where Rachel was, it appeared unharmed. The dust was clearing but it didn't take much to cause respiratory problems. She ducked down and went back through Julian's office covering her mouth and nose with her hand. The main work area was also still in one piece, but there was a lot of debris in the entry and Stella's desk was nearly hidden in chunks of stucco.

Rachel found John on the floor behind his desk crouching in the corner. She touched one shoulder. "Are you all right?" She could barely hear her words.

John must have heard her. He quickly opened his eyes and jumped to his feet. "I'm fine. No thanks to you."

"Jackass!" Rachel suppressed the desire to shake some sense into him. She turned her back on his scared face.

The phone didn't work, so she picked up John J.'s cell phone from his desk and dialed nine-one-one. The dispatcher said the police were on their way. She walked through the mess and looked where the foyer had once been. Whatever the cause, the front door and several feet of wall on either side were gone. The plaster from the ceiling was still sifting rivulets of powder onto the floor.

"You better get away from there." John was regaining his composure.

"If you're scared, stay where you are," Rachel retorted. She yawned allowing her ears to pop. Her hearing was returning. "The damage has been done. It's over."

At first she didn't notice the staff had returned. Julian, Stella and Shorty stood; mouths open, gazing in fixed disbelief at the gaping hole. "Welcome back," Rachel said.

They slowly filed through the opening. Stella carried her purse over her head, an attempt to avoid contaminating her coiffure.

"Lord, love a duck," Shorty commented in characteristic understatement.

"Are you two okay?" Julian asked Rachel and John J.

"Yeah, no thanks to her." John pointed at Rachel. "She knew about it." Everyone turned to stare at Rachel.

CHAPTER 24

"What the hell happened to you?" Chloe demanded upon seeing her friend walk through the kitchen door.

"I'm okay," Rachel held up a bandaged hand. "There was a little explosion at the office today. My finger took seven stitches. Everything's all right."

"Right? Everything's all right? You're injured in an explosion and it's all right! What's going on?"

"My hand was cut on glass as I dove for cover through the back door."

"A fine distinction. Do go on."

"The police say it was a small bomb."

"My god, a bomb? I thought we were talking about an accident. Rachel, things have gone from strange to dangerous. First, there's the supernatural thing you conjured up, then those other encounters, the awful car accident, and now a bomb. Matters have gotten out of hand!" Chloe was close to hyperventilating.

"It is getting to be a lengthy list," Rachel said. "My rational side wants to say it's a random event or maybe the nephew pissed off the wrong people, but the reporter in me says there's the possibility it could be tied to my interest in Pueblo Blanco. I'd swear they're hiding something, but why go to the media for publicity if you can't take the scrutiny? Although the story I wrote amounted to nothing more than a free ad, Julian's going to axe it. Hope he's feeling generous and offers a kill fee, otherwise I don't get paid for my trouble."

"Getting paid is the least of your problems," Chloe said. "I think you're missing the big picture."

"Big picture?"

"Yeah, you're too close to all this."

"Oh, really?" Rachel's hand hurt. She was tired and didn't want to hear some metaphysical reasoning why her life was a total piece of shit.

Chloe opened her mouth to speak, but the telephone rang before she could go on. She picked up the phone hanging next to the refrigerator. "It's for you," she said.

"Damn, would you please take a message?"

"You'll want to talk to him," Chloe said from the arched doorway. "It's your medicine man friend."

"Why didn't you say so?" Rachel rushed passed her.

"I thought I just did," her friend answered with minor annoyance.

Rachel snatched the phone. "Joseph, I'm so glad to hear from you. How did you find me?"

Joseph answered slowly, not one to speak without thinking, "The magazine telephone was out of order. I called Mr. Brazos."

Rachel momentarily felt like a twit, but this was no time to let embarrassment get in the way of information. "We had a little trouble there today."

"Yes, a bomb would be a little trouble," Joseph said. Rachel could feel the slight smile working its way across the lines of communication.

"Joseph, remember when we discussed calling back the dead?"

"Of course."

"Well." She hated to admit what she had done, but she needed Joseph's help. "I tried it." There was no reply so she rushed on. "I don't know what went wrong. Maybe it's because I'm not full-blood Native American. Maybe I just didn't know what I was doing. Whatever, I brought back the wrong person."

Rachel waited until she was certain Joseph had covered the phone and was laughing his ass off. "Joseph," she whispered, "did you hear me?"

"Yes. I'm thinking."

"Okay." She didn't want to break his train of thought. She could almost see him rubbing his chin. Joseph had a great face, one of those touched by time and wisdom, and how his eyes could twinkle. Rachel thought they probably were doing just that as he pondered her quandary.

"Whom did you call back?"

"My father. He was killed a few months ago. I thought if I could talk to him . . . " Rachel stopped as the tears came. Great gasps of grief escaped. "One . . . moment." She covered the phone, closed her eyes to the tears and made herself gain control. "Joseph, I'm sorry."

"Your grief must be great," Joseph paused giving her a moment. "Who came back?"

"A man who reportedly was killed in an explosion the same day my father died," she replied. "He was a friend or associate of my brother."

"This man is evil."

"I . . . don't know." She thought it a question. Rachel wiped her face angrily. She had to get it together.

"He is. No good spirit would interfere in this way."

"What are you saying?"

"The old ways are dangerous to the novice."

"Joseph, what can I do?"

"Things are set in motion that we cannot change. Listen to your spirit guide."

"What spirit guide? I don't have one," she felt desperate.

"We all have spirit guides," Joseph said as if he were talking about everyone having a TV. "Yours will become apparent."

"That's all? Can't I send him back? Joseph, you don't understand. Strange things have been happening. I smell magnesium and then peculiar stuff occurs. There are others."

"Others?"

"Yeah, well, there was something along the interstate one night that told me to go back, but a wolf scared it off."

"Wolf?" Joseph asked. "A single wolf? And it frightened the other soul into leaving?"

"Yes, why?"

"I believe you have met your spirit guide."

"You mean Chloe is right?"

"The woman who answered the telephone?" he asked.

"Yes, she said that wolves could be guides."

"They are some of the best. You must let it help you."

"Can't I just send this . . . ghost . . . back?"

"It may come to that, but only you can see this through to conclusion. If you listen closely to your wolf friend and your instincts, they will help you. Try not to think logically. This life is not of this world." Then Joseph added, "I must warn you, the spirit is likely to grow stronger. You must be vigilant. I will make a *paho* for you immediately. It will provide you some safety."

"Stronger!" Rachel felt forlorn, "I'm in over my head as it is. What if I can't see it through?"

"You can. You would not have attempted the ceremony, if you could not. You are a believer."

"Joseph," she could not bear to hang up. He seemed the only person in the world who could understand her dilemma. "I'm scared." The reality of the situation was taking hold of her. She picked at the tape encircling her finger, found a loose end, tugged at it, made her hand throb. "I'm not sure I can deal with this. And, how will I know when it's over?"

"When it is gone, you will know. Be careful and have faith."

"I'll try. May I call you again?"

"Of course."

"Thank you." The tears were being pushy again.

"Go with your Great Spirit." He was gone.

Rachel slowly hung up the phone. She turned at Chloe's touch and cried in her arms. "What am I going to do?"

"We'll think of something," Chloe said. "We always do."

* * *

Joseph turned from the phone at Hopi headquarters. Through the window he gazed southwest to the Coconino National Forest.

Humphrey's Peak stood more than 12,000 feet. Soon skiers would be skimming its slopes. Further to the north lay the Grand Canyon. Today, it was sure to be congested with visitors from around the world.

Through these benign thoughts Joseph's brow furrowed. His friend was in serious trouble. He had not wanted to frighten her, but he feared for her. A spirit who would use such methods to return is dishonorable and treacherous. Before he left for home today he would ask a family member to find him if she should call. For now, he would construct a prayer stick for Rachel. Then it must be left to the Upper Beings.

CHAPTER 25

Rachel and Chloe talked for hours. While Chloe had been supportive, they had reached no real plan of action because so much was not known. When Chloe left for a late showing Rachel decided to take a bath. What she really wanted was a joint, but she didn't care for smoking alone. A Xanax would have to do. She rummaged through her things but had no luck finding the pills. In her bathroom the bubbles piled higher and higher in the tub. The last thing her body wanted to do was calm down. Perhaps problem-solving action would be more satisfying? She turned off the water and walked back into her room.

Rachel picked up a smudge stick of dried white sage held together with red string. When burned, it purified the physical and spiritual presence of the user. She pulled lengths of yarn in four colors from her supply. She wrote a quick prayer for courage and protection. Outside, in the light that poured from the windows she searched for a small twig. Rachel carefully wrapped the small piece of paper containing the prayer for safety around the stick and fastened it with the yarn.

She felt it necessary to be away from her friend's house so as not to bring any evil into her home. In this part of Santa Fe there were large areas of undeveloped land between houses, but no fences to delineate the property lines so that vistas were not obstructed. In a hollow area against the hill and surrounded by piñon, Rachel brushed a dusting of snow off a large rock, placed the sage and lit it. The pungent fragrance perfumed the evening air.

What she was about to do, she knew nothing about. Her inner voice was urging: "Do something!" It was not comforting she was afraid it would be wrong thing.

The preparations made, she resisted the urge to sit, wanting to be ready for anything, such as hightailing it out of there. As she cradled the prayer stick, her hands shook in the cold. There were gloves in her jacket pocket but she wanted nothing that would hinder movement. Every sense was heightened as she thought about what to do. What would it be like, meeting the devil? She shivered. There would be no mask this time. She had nothing of Peña's personal effects. It probably wouldn't work anyway. She hadn't heard of this kind of calling back. It was her invention.

Clouds lingered. The night sky was lit by only a few of the brightest stars. The white earth provided the most illumination.

Doubts rose again and again. The only supernatural expert she knew was Joseph. No ghost busters. Nine-one-one wouldn't respond. She was in this up to her neck and had no one to blame but herself. Rachel concentrated on the burning sage. The delicate leaves curled and blackened as the smoke crawled along the twigs. She felt isolated, vulnerable.

Her breath emerged in misty puffs as she remembered Mario Peña. Never one of her favorite people, his arrogant exterior seethed with anger. Unfortunately, he always seemed to be near her brother. Knowing Chris, she wasn't all that surprised by the company he kept.

The familiar odor announced his arrival. It fairly crackled in the air, drowning out the pleasant smell of the sage. Rachel tightened every muscle. Chemical energy surged throughout her body, readying her for an emergency.

She whirled at a sound. Saw nothing. Maybe it was a coyote looking for prey, or Mario trifling with her again.

"You rang?" Mario said.

Rachel turned. Although recognizable, he was translucent. He had that look of surly indifference, the look teenage boys everywhere learned to project.

"What are you doing here?" she demanded.

"Hey, you called me!"

"Not now. Not this moment. Why did you appear, instead of my father?"

"Now, Rachel, with all that boo-hooing, I slipped through when you weren't paying attention. Next question?"

"Why did you want to come back?" Rachel had no idea how to deal with the spirit.

"Got a score to settle."

"Were you responsible for that nice old man's death? And, what about the disappearing car keys on the ski basin road?"

"Rachel, really," Mario's voice was sarcastic. "The keys were just a little prank. But spirits can't drive cars. Don't confuse us with gods."

"I wouldn't make that mistake," she spit out the words. She felt contempt for this man, whatever he was. It was not lost on her that he knew about Abe Smith's death.

"Another woman with an attitude," he replied. "That's what's wrong with this world." He raised his arms in mock defeat, and then laughed. It wasn't a pleasant laugh, but one of sneering contempt.

At that moment, Rachel understood the feeling of one's blood running cold. It was an all-encompassing sensation: Cold to the bone, cold to the soul.

"What score do you have to settle?" she asked.

"If I told you that, you'd try to stop me."

"This is ridiculous. You're dead."

"Yeah, but I wasn't resting comfortably." Mario cackled.

"What do I have to do with it?" Rachel tried again.

"You provided the conveyance. It didn't hurt that you were close to the action."

"What action?"

"Now, now, don't trouble your pretty head with details." While she watched him, his sneer seemed to change into a kindly smile without a hint of malice. The transformation interested Rachel, but she remained leery. "Interesting talent, isn't it?" Mario said. "I can look many ways, depending on what a human wants to believe." The face returned to its former expression.

"You haven't answered my question." Rachel reminded herself that Mario was not of this world and she had no idea what he was capable of. She feared he had something to do with her father's death even though Mario died later the same day.

"Did I kill dear old dad?" He clicked his tongue in ridicule.

Rachel was repelled by his ability to hurt. How dare he turn the knife with so much pleasure? The natural reaction was to hit back with words, but that would only end in further pain and frustration. She remained quiet.

"A little unsolicited advice, Rachel." He lingered for effect. "Stay away from that stupid old Indian, if you know what's good for you." His words were charged with wickedness.

Rachel was stunned that he knew about Joseph and frightened at the innuendo. She felt certain that he meant the shaman no good.

"Well," he said, "it's been swell jawing with you but I've got things to do, places to go. I don't have to drive or even walk anymore. Ain't it cool?"

Mario heard the growl first. The whites of his eyes showed slightly as he scanned the woods. Rachel searched for the creature, seeing him as he strode from beneath the bows of a tree. It radiated the soft glow she had seen before. What she didn't expect was Mario's reaction. He had stopped speaking and his cockiness was gone, replaced by a sharp watchfulness. It occurred to Rachel that he was afraid. Every time the wolf took a step forward, Mario floated backward a few feet.

"What's with you?" she challenged Mario.

"Never liked dogs," he came back quickly, trying to cover his insecurity.

"Then it shouldn't be a problem," Rachel replied. "He's a wolf." She marveled that there was anything that Mario could be frightened of in his present state. Perhaps he had a vulnerability, but if so, how to use it?

"A fine distinction," Mario said, disgusted.

The wolf paced closer, snarling. His lips curled up viciously. Rachel took a step back. Maybe it wasn't her spirit guide. She held very still and took another look at Mario.

Mario's image suddenly fell in on itself and he disappeared with a snap. He took the awful stench with him.

The ash from the sage no longer glowed. She had no idea how much time had passed, only that her body was numb with cold.

The wolf vanished; swallowed by the night.

CHAPTER 26

The alarm shrilled. Rachel flung out her arm at near light speed to shut off the rude buzz. For a moment she wondered if she'd dreamed the whole episode, but the broken paho lay next to the clock. She'd really done it, talked with a dead person, one who talked back. "You're losing it," she mumbled, threw back Chloe's comforter, and placed her bare feet on the floor.

"Rachel, you up?" Chloe knocked softly.

"Yeah, come in."

"Morning friend. Tony's on the phone. Want to talk with him?"

"Sure. Can't think of anything more fun than talking with a former husband."

"If you want to pick up your things," Tony said, "I'll be here." Long silence. "I called because I'm leaving again tomorrow. Of course, you can come by anytime. I don't have to be here." The pain in his voice was apparent. Rachel felt her heart crack a little. It would be easier for her to get her things alone, but he so obviously wanted to see her.

"I can do it today, if I can find someone with a truck or 4-wheel drive."

"Rachel, use the Jeep."

"Tony, I don't ever want to drive it again. I'll ask a friend."

It was left at that. Before she could ponder whom to inconvenience, the phone rang again.

"Rachel? Logan. How are you?"

"Well," she lied. "How's everyone's favorite P.I.?"

"Looking for a lunch partner. Are you free?"

"I'd love to."

She asked boldly, "Would you be willing to put your vehicle to work by doing a little hauling?"

* * *

The Blackstone's north hills house already looked unfamiliar to Rachel. The street view was mostly of the three-car garage but there were walls enclosing the courtyard entry. Through the gate one could glimpse asters in full purple bloom, softening the sidewalk. Leaves from the Russian olive, scattered by the wind, lay on the walk. She knew an *horno*—meaning small oven, but in this case, a portable terra cotta fireplace—sat out of view. It had brought warmth and light to many pitch-black evenings. She'd have to buy one for herself someday.

Logan parked and looked to her for his cue.

"Are you sure it's okay that I'm with you? Your husband won't mind?"

"Ex-husband," Rachel whispered the word. "It's okay."

"I'll be here." He patted her hand to reassure her and was surprised to see her flinch.

Rachel pulled out her luggage, while Logan reached for the boxes stacked one inside the other. She carried the bags to the front door.

Tony opened the door before she could ring. He looked tired. His eyes were puffy and the sparkle was gone. "Who's in the SUV?" He offered no greeting. So this was how it would go. She should have come when he was out of town.

"A friend with transporting space." Rachel passed him in the foyer, being careful not to ding the walls. "I'll put my clothes in these. I've got some boxes outside for the rest of my stuff."

Tony walked into the courtyard to retrieve the boxes and came face to face with Logan while Rachel looked on with apprehension from the doorway. He shook Logan's outstretched hand automatically.

"How do you do?" Logan said. "Logan Masters."

"Tony Blackstone. I've enjoyed your work."

"Thank you. And I, yours."

"You've seen my work?" Tony asked, surprised.

"Yes. Your PBS series on the vanishing American wilderness was outstanding."

"Thanks. Sorry about the circumstances." Tony waved an arm as if it would magically change the discomfort they all felt.

"I am too," Logan said. "Very sorry."

Tony picked up the cartons. When Rachel saw he was returning to the house she quickly stepped back inside. Better to make this quick.

She tried not to remember much as she walked through their house. It was beautiful. Tony made good money and the four-bedroom house was evidence of that. It had striking tile and hardwood floors throughout. The walls were real plaster, instead of cheaper wallboard. The *vigas* and much of the wood furniture were handcrafted. Though neither of them cooked, the kitchen was a dream by anyone's standards.

In the master bedroom she took her clothes from the closet and folded them into one case, hangers included. The other suitcase would hold sweaters, shoes, and cosmetic items remaining in the bath. She closed the closet, which she'd never filled and turned to the carved armoire. There were stacks of sweaters in a variety of colors. She stuffed several at a time into the open bag. A quick tour of the room produced some lingerie and a few keepsakes: last year's Christmas photos, theatre stubs, and post cards from friends.

The bath, done in burgundy and beige tile, was flooded with warm rays from the skylight. Only makeup and lotions she no longer used were still there. She dumped them in the trash instead of letting them clutter her new, if not fully conceived, life.

She snapped the closures and carried the much heavier bags back to the entry. Her office was off the foyer, down a few stairs. Rachel loved the view of the courtyard from its window. There had been many pleasant and productive hours spent here with plenty of time to catch the antics of the yard birds. She would miss it. Tears filled her eyes and ambivalent feelings threatened her resolve.

Tony left the boxes on her desk and she hurriedly stuffed them with files containing research material for articles already written, clippings, correspondence, and just stuff. These filled two cartons. Her bulging Rolodex that she would one day move to her computer, knickknacks, desk accessories, phone, answering and FAX machines filled the other. She removed two framed posters, one a painting of downtown Santa Fe, the other an O'Keeffe flower reproduction, adding them to a carton.

Rachel carried her things to the drive. Logan quietly helped her load everything into the back.

"That leaves the desk," she said. "My father made it. Would you mind helping me with it? It's small."

"Of course not," he answered, his face full of concern. Rachel had seen that expression many times before on film. For a moment she wondered if he was acting. She searched his eyes for an answer. How could anyone ever be sure of an actor's feelings? It must tough on the actor too, with people doubting their sincerity. Rachel reminded herself she had no reason not to trust him.

They both went into the house to retrieve the desk. Rachel's thoughts went back to what had gone wrong. It happened all the time to relationships in Los Angeles. The entertainment industry was full of the tiffs and divorces of the rich and famous.

Rachel thought of calling to Tony for help, but didn't. She and Logan lifted the small, but solidly built, desk and made shuffling noises as they carried it to the car. They played musical boxes until there was enough space to squeeze it in.

"I'll be right back," Rachel told him.

"Take your time."

"Tony?" she called out, but there was no answer. She walked through the house looking into each room, remembering the good, the not so good, and the ugly. The Christmas tree had been beautiful next to the kiva fireplace in the living room. Each spare bedroom had provided comfort for Hollywood movers and shakers. The dining table had held steaming, fragrant meals, prepared by someone else, but delicious all the same. She avoided her office. That goodbye had already been done.

There was only one place Tony could be, on the back terrace. Rachel walked through the kitchen. The pottery they'd bought together lined the cabinet tops, intermixed with Pueblo baskets. They were not dusty. Sylvia had been picking up after them for years. She hadn't lost her touch.

Tony stood outside looking up at the ski basin, his back to the house. A tumbler of scotch rested on the patio table. It had become his constant companion over the past few years.

"Tony, I think I've got everything. I'm going to leave now."

"Okay." He didn't turn.

She hesitated, not knowing what to say. Marriages begin with celebration, but could end with a whimper. Surely, there was something appropriate for this kind of parting.

"I'm sorry," she said. "I wish . . ." But she didn't know what she wished. "I'll miss you."

He turned then, his face was flushed and he was unsteady on his feet. "I already miss you."

As she climbed in beside Logan her heart was crumbling. What was that song lyric? There's more room in a broken heart? At the moment it wasn't comforting.

CHAPTER 27

L unch had been a total bust. Rachel hadn't felt hungry and
stared into space without noticing anything around her.
She was grateful that Logan hadn't spent a fortune on their
meal. They'd gone to a sandwich joint near her office. Several diners recognized Logan and pestered him politely for his autograph,
which he obligingly wrote on a napkin, a menu, and an envelope
containing a water bill.

After lunch they left her stuff in the bedroom of Chloe's
house. The desk fit well under the window. The boxes she would
live with for a time. She didn't want Chloe to think she was moving in lock, stock and barrel. But she did place her laptop on the
desk. She would need it for work.

Julian had called a meeting at 1:30 at La Fonda's bar. The office was off limits, cordoned by yellow police tape. Plywood
covered the space where the front door had been. Workers would
soon haul off the rubble and construct a new entrance. The brightly painted walls had taken on a matte look. They were covered with
a thin film of stucco dust from the explosion. It was likely they
would remain that way.

It was difficult to call it what it really was, a bombing. Everyone, even John kept referring to it as the "incident."

La Fonda boasts 400 years of hospitality at this, the end of the
Santa Fe Trail. While it has changed hands and names over the

years, there has been an inn to host everyone from those with gold fever to those with plenty of gold. The current structure was built in 1922 and is of the adobe architecture that has made the city different from all others in the States.

Rachel crossed the street and entered the main door of the cavelike lobby. One can't accuse La Fonda of using too much electricity. The lighting is dim at best, or perhaps mood-setting, except for the brilliant light provided by skylights that bathe the restaurant located in the center of the street level. La Plazuela was surrounded in glass windows with whimsical painted motifs on the panes. It had originally been an open air courtyard with a fountain in the center. There was even a ghost story surrounding the fountain. It seemed a man, in a moment of anguish, jumped into the well and killed himself. There had been occasional reports of diners seeing the figure of a man diving into the center of the floor during the time the well was covered in tile. The fountain had been restored, but she had heard of no further sightings. A few people were eating a late lunch or perhaps dinner according to their home time zone.

She made a quick left at the check-in desk and crossed Saltillo tiles which had known the footsteps of the famous and infamous. Many of the tiles were deeply worn. She always felt as if she'd gone back in time when she visited La Fonda. And it was hard not to pick up on the excitement of visitors staying at the hotel. Chloe would say the energy was exhilarating. Rachel had spent many an evening in the hotel's Bell Tower watching sunsets and appreciating Mexican beer.

Shorty and Stella were relaxing at a rustic table with a couple of margaritas. Shorty was listening to Stella. A comic book lay on the table. They both laughed and Rachel marveled again that they could be so comfortable with one another. They could share a joke. Julian was talking on his cell in front of the fireplace. Rachel could see him listening as he looked across the lobby and absently pulled at his beard.

She dropped her bag on the floor and sat down next to Stella. "Where's the kid?" Julian asked, perturbed, as he joined them.

"Don't mean to defend him," Rachel said, "but I was nearly late."

"Nearly late doesn't count," Julian replied. Julian ordered a Modelo for himself and a Dos Equis for Rachel.

"Well, he doesn't report to me," Shorty mumbled, opening his comic book.

"He doesn't seem to report to anyone," Julian said. He had doubts about John's skills as a reporter, but it wouldn't be professional to share this with his staff. Most of the time he forgot these people worked for him and thought of them as family. At that moment, John walked in.

"Glad you could join us," Julian remarked.

"Thought you might like me to finish the interview." John's remark had a caustic edge. He made a show of setting down his briefcase just so. Then he sat and carefully checked the crease in his pants. Rachel had noticed he lined up his pencils. There always seemed to be exactly six yellow writing sticks in a neat row on his desk.

Of course, she must have something awry within the sub-basement of her mind that caused her to notice.

"You want something to drink?" Julian asked him.

"I don't drink alcohol," John said arrogantly. "My body's a temple."

Even Stella snorted at that one. Rachel nearly spewed beer across the table, but managed to grab a napkin in time to prevent another explosive incident.

Julian ignored the juvenile display and began the meeting. "I don't want to belabor this, but the police don't have any leads on the," he searched for a word, "attack. There's no apparent motive, except the general lack of respect for others that's rampant throughout our culture." Rachel watched Julian expressing his anger the only way he knew how, with quiet resignation. "Which means, it's likely no one will be arrested, and no restitution will be made. Of course, my insurance rates will go up." He deliberated for a moment. "That would mean I'm being punished for something I didn't do. That should console me in my golden years." Sarcasm. Rachel didn't mind, she used sarcasm too. It had helped her through many a bad occurrence.

"Anyway," he paused again and rubbed his forehead, the same way Rachel massaged her head at the onset of a migraine, "there will be a security system installed in the office."

John cleared his throat and adjusted his tie. Rachel gave him a brief look of annoyance and returned her attention to Julian. Great, Rachel thought, now I'll have to remember Chloe's code and one at the office. She despised this kind of technology or at least the reasons for it, but acknowledged it was probably a necessary evil at this point.

"Here's the rest of it," Julian called their attention back. "At least for a few weeks, I want you to let Stella know where you are going and when you expect to return." He turned to Stella with an apologetic expression. "I realize it's not like you don't have anything else to do."

"It's okay," Stella said, "I don't mind." She tapped his hand with two fingers. There it was again. Something had passed between them.

Julian made sure the reporters and photographer were progressing in a timely manner with their assignments. The magazine still had to publish by deadline. They adjourned. Rachel went back to Chloe's to do a little work. She wanted to finish the restaurant review. An hour later the polished story was complete. After e-mailing it to Julian, she left to meet Chloe.

CHAPTER 28

I t was a pleasant walk along Don Gaspar. She made a right on San Francisco, and quickly crossed the street. The Plaza is the heart and soul, and yes, major tourist trap of Santa Fe. The historic Palace of the Governors makes up the entire north side. Native artisans sell their wares every day under the long *portal*. Shops selling everything from pots to jewelry to wooden chickens make up the remaining three sides, intermingled with restaurants.

Because of the *touristas* and the prices, few locals ventured downtown, unless their jobs brought them. But Rachel and Chloe, despite being long-time Santa Feans, loved the excitement of the Plaza. If one could overlook the T-shirt shops, large silver belt buckles, and lavish displays of newly purchased turquoise jewelry, it was possible to enjoy the tall trees of the square and the old central city.

Rachel walked across the Plaza and made a right heading down Palace, past the Palace of the Governors. Most of the Native American vendors had packed up their treasures, but a few remained determined to sell one more ring or pot.

Mid-way down the next block, she took a sharp left and emerged into the courtyard of The Shed restaurant, called Prince Patio. There were scattered tables, sheltering umbrellas, and bright spots of flowers. Lights draped over the doors were already on and added a festive air. The Shed had been serving up a fusion of

Pueblo, Mexican and Spanish cuisine since 1953 when it was located in a real shed. But its long-time home in this former hacienda dated back to 1692. Rachel walked through the open purple door. In the anteroom a fire burned in the small kiva and a few people were waiting, having already checked in for dinner. The restaurant was popular with both visitors and residents. There was more color inside that accentuated architectural flourishes, as well as skylights, plants and a great bar.

Rachel chose the bar over a table, ordered a margarita and waited for Chloe. She glanced over the menu, but it was permanently catalogued in her brain menu file. She loved the green chile chicken enchiladas. The Shed's green chile was grown especially for them in Hatch, New Mexico and was a favorite of Rachel's.

Suddenly Chloe was climbing onto the chair beside her. She ordered the garlic shrimp and a pomegranate margarita which she proclaimed as healthier than the house drink. It just looked like a pink drink to Rachel. Pink!

Chloe wore an enormous turquoise squash blossom necklace, white shirt tucked inside a roper jacket over a shaped denim skirt that clung to her body. Her face was impeccably made-up. Rachel instinctively raised a hand to her cheek, momentarily wondering if she'd applied any blush at all.

The drinks arrived with salsa and chips. For a few minutes they crunched and sipped happily. In the courtyard, birds would be quietly pestering diners for tiny piece of tortilla chip. Inside? No feathered panhandlers today, although occasionally a bird would get inside the restaurant.

Chloe broached the subject Rachel wanted both to share and bury. "How'd it go today with Tony?"

"Awful. I hate shit like this."

"Rachel, you know that personal growth comes from proper closure of a relationship."

Rachel looked up at Chloe, whose face was perfectly serious. She wasn't joking, although Rachel was sorely tempted to laugh despite how much she hurt.

"Chloe," she began carefully—she knew this jargon was important to her, "I prefer to think in terms of moving on. And, I don't believe I have to learn some kind of lesson from every awful thing that happens in life."

"But what's wrong with learning from pain?"

"Nothing, I suppose, if you want to, but I prefer to get on with life."

"Don't you want a closure you can live with?" Chloe implored her.

This irritated Rachel. "What you're really talking about is a peace treaty—a conclusion with all the loose ends neatly tied and everyone involved goes on without ill will? Life doesn't happen that way in my experience. Both parties are rarely willing to create a sweet finale. I don't believe it's necessary to experience closure, the way you see it. Okay if we change the subject?"

"Sure." Chloe smiled sweetly.

Dinner was placed before them, plates steaming. Rachel took a big bite. "Hmm, delicious."

"Have to agreed," Chloe said and they clinked forks in appreciation.

"I did something last night you should know about," Rachel said. Chloe waited in anticipation. "I talked with Mario Peña."

"What!" Chloe said, excited. Her dark expressive brows at first rose and then knitted together as she concentrated all her attention on Rachel. "How?"

"Joseph told me to listen to my spirit guide. He thinks it is the wolf that has been appearing. I don't know if I received some kind of message. It wasn't apparent to me if I did. But I left a bathtub full of bubbles to call Mario out."

"My god, Rachel. What happened?"

"I threw a party for him, and he showed." Chloe started to comment, but let Rachel explain. "I made a *paho* and burned a sage stick up the hill behind your house. When I called him, he appeared; one ugly dude. It's as simple as that."

"Nothing's as simple as that. What happened?"

"He was still Mario: Nasty, defiant, scary. His features kind of drifted around, but I could hear him all right. He said he had a score to settle."

"What did he mean by that?"

"He didn't elaborate. Being dead seems to have made him cagier than usual."

"Why did *he* come back, instead of your dad?"

"That, I didn't quite understand, but something about me providing the opportunity and he slipped through. One thing is certain; he's up to no good. And, he says I'm close to the action, whatever that means."

"I don't like this, Rachel. Mario never had any visible means of support, yet he mingled with the rich and powerful."

"I know, like the brother."

"Rachel," Chloe touched her arm. "What about the bombing? Could he have been responsible for that?"

"I asked. He said spirits couldn't do stuff like that. Personally, I take that with a grain of salt. He was a liar, among his other dubious skills. Yet, I can't prove he had anything to do with it. If I went to the police, or anyone but you or Joseph, they'd laugh in my face." They were quiet for a moment. Rachel looked at her friend. "Thanks for not laughing."

"Hey. I'm a believer. I only wish we were dealing with a good soul. We must be very careful. This is a no rules situation. Anything can happen."

Rachel knew she was right.

"Oh, golly, I've got to go." Chloe dropped some greenbacks on the bar. "Walk me to my car?"

"Sure, where are you?"

"Up the street. Near good ol' city hall."

Evening had settled into an indigo sky, powered by the Milky Way. Chloe was fussing with her seat adjustment while Rachel waited impatiently on the sidewalk next to the car, chiding her compulsiveness.

"This damn thing's supposed to remember me," Chloe complained. "But here I am again, resetting it."

Movement across the street at the entrance to the city offices caught Rachel's eye. "Look. That's Alexander Robbins, Pueblo Blanco's PR rep."

"Gee," Chloe gushed, "he's quite a hunk. All I get to meet are cats with fat wallets. Maybe I should take up journalism." She instinctively pulled down the visor mirror to check her face. The car interior washed in a golden glow. It was enough light to catch the attention of the man across the street. Rachel wasn't sure if he recognized her, but his demeanor was troubling. This was an angry man. He pulled his coat about him, clenched his fists and walked rapidly down the street, as if he didn't want to be seen.

Well," Chloe said. "Looks like Mr. Gorgeous is in a pissy mood."

CHAPTER 29

Rachel gave up trying to sleep at one a.m. She'd been restless since seeing Robbins. It bothered her he'd been at city hall. She reasoned that it made perfect sense for him to be there, after all, he was involved in the housing development. Yet, there had been something strange about the afterhours visit.

Wrapped up in her robe, she made her way through boxes to her desk. Despite the size of Chloe's guestroom, all of Rachel's belongings made the room seem small. She opened her laptop and pushed the "power" button, and opened the story on Logan Masters.

Logan was only one of many celebrities who had invested in Pueblo Blanco. The enterprise had openly courted the beautiful people. That in itself wasn't surprising, nor was it illegal. Anytime you could combine name recognition with major bucks, any business or cause could clean up. And it happened repeatedly in Santa Fe.

With time on her hands, she printed out the original draft, and then began the revision. Quickly she marked with a pen the words and phrases to delete. Additional thoughts or questions she wrote in the margins. Julian might not buy this article because he hadn't assigned it. However, if he passed, one of the local papers or celebrity rags would print it. After completing the editing she made the corrections, saved it and powered off.

Thirty minutes later she dressed and slipped out of the house. The highway to Taos was deserted. Only the highway signs showed up along the unlit road. Rachel slowed to thirty-five and scanned the edge of the pavement for the turnoff she knew to be there.

She drove west on a rutted set of tracks fit only for a four-wheel vehicle, not a heavy, low riding luxury car. The road didn't have a name because it didn't go anywhere. Kids used it for dirt bikes and lascivious pursuits. Hikers used it to reach trailheads.

After two miles of kidney-crushing driving, she came to the end of civilization and backed beneath the shelter of some trees. By the light of the dome, she slipped two C batteries into a flashlight and stepped out of the car. From the trunk, she took a small pry bar normally used for removing wheel covers. She thought it might come in handy. The trunk lid closed with a whoosh of air.

The creek was dry, spring snowmelt but a memory. She allowed her eyes to adjust to the darkness. This expedition would be better done without the use of telltale light. Pueblo Blanco was to her north atop a low mesa. The *arroyo* ran along the back side of the development for perhaps a quarter mile before it petered out.

Rachel crossed the smooth stones of the creek bed being careful to keep her footing. On the far side, there was a path made by wild animals in their nocturnal prowling. She made better time. Occasionally, a prickly pear needle would grab and pull at her jeans, making her swear in pain.

Using the flash to look for the best place to ascend, Rachel spotted a gentle rise in the otherwise sheer ten-foot bank. She doused the light and made her way, using a small sagebrush, to pull herself up the wall of crumbling soil and sporadic stubborn flora. It would be difficult to find coming back. She found several rocks of different sizes and placed one on top of the other as a cairn to help her on the return trip.

With only chamisa and a cottontail for company she trudged toward Pueblo Blanco. When she reached the outer edge of the development she stopped and listened. No sound. There was a breeze, but it would offer little noise cover.

Since she'd been allowed in the main building and the model home, Rachel headed for a house still under construction. Skirting the white slabs already in place, she slid behind a few shrubs making her way to the back of a house. Once there, she looked around for signs of life. No people, no cars—unless parked in the garage, but there were no windows in that part of the house. She'd have to deal with the off chance someone might be in the vicinity.

The facade of the house was finished but nothing had been done to make it homey. There were no plantings, and the cover for the terrace wasn't in place. Adobe bricks were stacked, probably with the intent of forming the courtyard wall.

She crossed to the back door. Locked. There were two bedrooms on this side, both with locked windows. Paper covered the panes, but one piece was torn. Rachel pushed herself to tiptoes and peered inside. On a large table, instead of the expected building tools, it was stacked with pipe. She could see the outline of a lamp. Why would they need a small desk light for plumbing? No one would foolishly pay for night rates. Rachel risked using her flash. She placed it against the glass and flipped it on for a few seconds. A watch lay beneath the lamp, assorted small tools and gloves. On the floor were several boxes, all closed.

"What are they doing?" Rachel whispered to herself. She looked for another point of entry. The kitchen window was equipped with a pass-through for outdoor dining, but was locked as well. Rachel thought she might persuade it with the pry bar. It worked. The latch broke easily, along with one of the panes. The glass fell in a shower to the floor inside. It made a horrendous noise in the dead quiet. "Damn," she whispered and dropped to the ground, clinging to the wall, listening. Nothing.

Several minutes passed before she dared to stand. Her hand shook so much she was forced to discard the bar. Everything sane implored her legs to run back to her car, but the journalistic side of her brain kept screaming, "There's a story here!" All the suspicions she had about this place not being on the up and up came flooding back. She was going in.

There had been a time when she was wiser. Once while watching a rerun of the old movie, *Don't Look in the Basement*, she thought one pretty young thing quite an idiot because of her proclivity to go places sure to be dangerous, such as the basement of the asylum. That's a memory I could have done without," she muttered to herself.

Rachel picked up the bar again and ran it along the edge of the opening to make sure all the glass was gone. Waited a few minutes partly to make sure she was alone, partly to screw up her courage. With that done, she shinnied up the side of the house and pulled her body through the opening. It would have been an easier feat with more room to maneuver, but she managed. Fortunately, she was flexible; thanks to yoga that Chloe insisted she do. She actually enjoyed it, but wouldn't give Chloe the satisfaction.

As she pulled herself through the window she risked a quick look around with the flash. The cabinets were in place along the kitchen walls, but no counters, sink or appliances. Rachel carefully stepped on the edge of the unfinished cabinetry and lowered herself to the floor.

The house was a bizarre mix of completed walls and a maze of structural skeleton. Small pieces of wood, nails, and wallboard were scattered about the slab. The hall leading to the bedrooms was just outside the kitchen. Not yet enclosed, the hall could be made out thanks to the finished kitchen wall that formed one side. It ran about fifteen feet to the bedrooms which fanned out from the hall. The bedroom walls were completed.

As she continued to explore, she was painfully aware that she could be arrested for breaking and entering. That would look nice on a resume.

Rachel checked the two rooms on the front of the house first. Building materials were stored in both, along with a wheelbarrow, shovels, and several buckets of paint.

The aroma in the last bedroom caught her attention. It brought back recollections of her grandfather's reloading activities. Gunpowder has a unique odor. She experienced a powerful urge to get the hell out, suppressed it, having come this far. After she steadied her quaking legs, she dared to use the flash one more time. Immediately she wished she hadn't. Rachel didn't know much about making bombs, but could this be anything else? Lifting the lid of one box revealed several sticks of dynamite and fuses. Another box held nails and screws. The watch on the makeshift desk could be used as a crude timing device. She'd seen enough. Light off. Time to leave.

Rachel crept to the window and pulled back the torn paper. Clear, except for a coyote trotting along the brush. No, wolf! The sheer creature looked right at her as if it knew she was there. Rachel couldn't explain it, but immediately a picture appeared in her head. Two men were getting out of a car. The scene was followed by a feeling of danger that swept over her. She was too frightened to contemplate the details, but knew, it was imperative she get out of there. Unfortunately, it was too late.

She heard the scrape of a key turning a lock, but she hadn't heard the car. Maybe someone had been at the development all along. For certain, she was no longer alone.

There wasn't time to go out the way she'd come in. Footsteps were already echoing in the house. The only place to go: the closet. Or, in moments, she would be discovered. She opened the door and slipped inside. At first, relieved to be out of the room, she didn't notice the closet had not been enclosed. Rachel stood, exposed, in a labyrinth of studs, joists, and beams. Panic time.

CHAPTER 30

C hris Woods thought he was dreaming. No. He was awake
now, but had fallen asleep in the office. He must have
been deep under to feel this groggy after a nap. His fingers
felt the smooth leather of the sofa, then the fabric of his jacket.
Yes, he was awake.

He didn't miss Jennifer all that much, but he didn't like the
big, empty house. His office seemed a good place to sleep. Wives
were a ball and chain, something like an extension of a mother, put
in his life to control him. Then the boys came along and his life
became full of commotion. He preferred making the noise, if any
were to be made, especially at city council meetings where it
grabbed media attention.

Only one lamp was on in the mayor's office, the banker's
lamp on his desk that illuminated only a portion of the top. He
remembered sitting down to have a drink, but when did he nod
off? His neck hurt where he'd rested it on the wooden arm. Imitation Spanish furniture could be grossly uncomfortable. He rubbed
the painful muscle, but it continued to ache. Something felt wrong.
It didn't bother him to stay at city hall all night, but tonight he was
uneasy. Maybe the cleaning crew woke him. He reached for the
switch on the floor lamp that sat next to the couch. It didn't work.
That only accentuated his apprehension.

His hand found the spilled drink on the area rug. The fiber was wet where the whiskey splashed from the tumbler. He ran his tongue around the rim looking for a few drops but stopped short of tipping it back. A movement across the room caught his attention. Someone must have left a window open and the breeze moved the draperies. But he could plainly see they were both closed. That left his imagination, which had never been active. He wasn't one of those *creative* types like Rachel, given to flights of fancy and intuition, but firmly grounded in what could be touched or proven.

That left the possibility a drunk or homeless person wandered in looking for a warm place to stay the night. He tried the lamp again.

"Still doesn't work?" a voice reached him from the opposite side of the room. Now he was concerned. Who was in his office?

Chris, startled, demanded, "Who's there?!" Not waiting for an answer, "You have to leave. These offices are for city business only."

"Then why have you been asleep since midnight?"

This was a bit too creepy. How could this person just sit and watch him sleep? "Leave my office immediately, whoever you are." When he stood Chris felt a bit woozy.

"Hey, buddy, remember me? Your pal. The one you tried to shut out. Maybe you even tried to kill me."

Chris looked across the room to the chair placed in front of a window. The high back obscured the occupant. He wanted to flee but was curious enough to stay. It sounded very much like Mario Peña, his former ally. Friend was too strong a word for Mario. He could be trusted only within view. Despite that, he had been a nearly constant companion during Chris' ascent to the mayoral office.

"Thought you were dead." Chris pulled himself together. People like Mario Peña were experts when it came to disappearing.

"I thought you were married." Mario said. "Why aren't you dreaming at home?"

"You've obviously been back long enough to pick up the current chatter on my private life. The bitch left, and took the kids. Good riddance." Chris made the two steps to the liquor cart and poured himself another. "Want one?"

"No. Don't have much use for drink anymore," Mario replied.

"Yeah, right." Chris made him one anyway. Mario waved it aside. Chris set it on the table beside him and sat down at his desk.

"So, what's it going to be? Why are you here? I'd ask how you got into the building, but that would be futile. You were never one for sharing trade secrets."

"I'm here because you still owe me," Mario said.

"Like hell I do." Chris disagreed. Mario could sit for hours and not say a word. Chris' anxiety increased with every silent minute. He made a few notes on his papers that were incoherent even to him, busying his hands. That's when he noticed the odor.

"What's that smell?"

"Chris, what are you babbling about?" Mario asked.

"Man, what is that? That damn cleaning crew's going to catch hell for this."

"Oh," Mario replied, "I don't think it's the poor slobs cleaning up."

"What then?"

"Think of it as a calling card." Mario Peña faded away as Chris watched. Mario's laughter lingered. Chris found it difficult to draw a breath.

CHAPTER 31

In a second of rational thought Rachel realized this trouble might be more than she could handle. A man approached. He hadn't seen her yet, but there was every possibility he would in a few seconds. He passed the opening to the kitchen, dim light from the kitchen window reflected off his head. She noticed a fringe of grey.

Rachel's instinct told her to get low, but movement would be a dead giveaway. Her body shook. She sagged slowly to the floor. Regrettably, she had dressed in all dark clothing—her best cat burglar garb, but the stucco wall and door behind her was white. All she could do was look as much like a bucket of paint as possible and hope to escape discovery. She was far more frightened of this living person than Mario Peña's intangible form.

The figure stopped at the entrance to the hall. Rachel pulled back trying to fold into her body but she could get no smaller. He lit a cigarette. In the glow of the lighter she saw a face but not recognizable in the flickering. He turned in her direction and drew deeply. Rachel forced herself to avert her eyes, afraid he would sense her watching him.

She thought of her car, the huge, won't-fit-in-any-parking-space, scratched, wonderful car, out there waiting, if she could only reach it. Was he going to smoke that damn thing all night? Worse yet, they were in a structure containing gunpowder and dynamite!

As a child in a tight spot she'd made bargains with God, only to find she was unable to keep those promises later. She would make no further deals. Better to use her brain, if only it would jumpstart and come up with a brilliant evasion.

The cigarette finished, he stamped it out with his foot. Rachel held her breath. He walked toward her. His shoes made scraping sounds when he stepped on the litter that strewn about the floor. He stood abreast of her, his hand on the door knob. It wasn't possible to shrink into the gloom any further. The door opened and closed behind him.

Seconds later she heard the folding chair creak as he sat down. It was now, or forever be frozen in place. She slipped through the vertical supports, being careful not to crunch anything underfoot.

With each footfall she tested the concrete beneath her by carefully placing her foot to avoid stepping directly on clutter. She hoped to make a quiet getaway, but it was a slow process. Rachel crossed the dining room, avoiding the tubing that would heat the floor. The living room was easier because it was larger and most of the supplies had been stored in the rooms along the back. Upon reaching the foyer, she heard someone approaching from outside. She flattened herself against the wall.

This man was whistling. The door swung so wide the knob touched her. He needed to close the door without turning around. He didn't.

"Hey, what are you doing here?" he demanded.

"Testing you!" Rachel ducked and plowed into his unsuspecting body like a linebacker on Sunday afternoon. He gasped and sputtered as she hit him full in the chest. Pain shot through her shoulder and Rachel understood the need for football pads. The impact caused her to drop the flashlight and she bounded out of the house.

Someone shouted, "Get him!" He had mistaken her for a man. Good. Rachel was already running. If only she could get out of the open and into the brush she had a chance of reaching her car. There was an instant when she thought about guns, but remembered a moving target was hard to hit. Rachel did her best imitation of a jack rabbit and sprinted into the shrubbery.

Her chest heaved as she caught her breath behind a piñon. No one was coming after her. The two men stood looking in her direction, but they were not moving toward her. The taller silhouette pointed and instructed the other. The smaller man ran to the garage and tugged it open. Moments later he drove away from the house.

With frequent looks back, she jogged back to the *arroyo*. Without the light she'd never find her stone marker. She paced the edge. No luck. Rachel chose a spot, sat down, and slid to the bottom, slowing her descent by digging into the loose soil with her heels. The landing wasn't pretty, or painless, but nothing broke.

When she reached the Merc she hesitated. She hadn't thought to switch off the dome light. It took only a few seconds to get inside, lock the doors, and start the engine, but she felt like a duck target on the state fair midway until the light went out. She headed back to the highway across the washboard terrain, nothing to do, but hurry slowly.

Rachel reassured herself the worst was over. The police would apprehend the two men and confiscate the bomb paraphernalia. Seconds later she saw headlights in the rearview mirror.

CHAPTER 32

Weathered hands rubbed patiently at the chipped enamel dish. Satisfied, Joseph placed it in the dish drainer. There was no sewer system or indoor plumbing. Later the dish water would nourish his vegetable garden.

All day Joseph was alert, but going about his day. His early morning walk, revealed a new nest residing in a spindly tree and a rabbit taking its first independent hops. He enjoyed these things more than ever today.

In his eighty-three years he'd experienced many spiritual occurrences, but none worried him in this way. He was troubled about the woman reporter. She had stumbled into a wicked place. Years ago, as a young man, he dreamed about a day of reckoning. He believed this would be it.

As the hours passed and the late afternoon shadows stretched along the ground, he found himself experiencing the clues his dream had foretold: birds perched silent in the trees; the usually gregarious prairie dogs stayed inside their burrows; and most ominous reddish water appeared in the dry streambed behind his home—without benefit of rain.

Joseph wrapped himself in a colorful wool blanket. The shack was warmed only by a fireplace. He sat at the table facing the flames. The chair teetered a bit on the uneven earthen floor hardened by time. He lit the kerosene lantern and it cast lively patterns of light across his drawing papers. The soft lead pencil drew a stormy sky. He skillfully shaded the menacing clouds. Taking time to consider every stroke, he sketched strange triangular mountains. Cross-hatching gave depth and intensity to the eerie landscape. Carefully he added sagebrush, a single strong shrub standing alone.

For several minutes he closed his eyes to rest them and allowed his thoughts to evolve. To complete the drawing, he made jagged lines to form a bolt of lightning which struck, then bounced, from the sage. In the lower right corner he scribbled "Rachel Blackstone," instead of his own signature. By the time he had placed the drawing inside an envelope and stashed it behind the heavy breakfront, inherited from his mother, the lantern flame began to dance in an odorous wind. Smoke poured from beneath the door. He turned to face evil.

"I've been expecting you," he said calmly. The immoral ones always come in darkness, stealing light.

"Old man, you're interfering where you don't belong."

"You have escaped from where you belong." Joseph looked directly into its black eyes. The pupils were so large they could not be mistaken for human. The body was cloaked in fluid that resembled garments. If touched, a hand would pass through the putrid mist of the monster.

"You know I've come to kill you." A vile smile licked at the corners of its mouth, anticipating the event.

"You are not human. You cannot kill me." Joseph bluffed, anticipating what was to come.

"You're right, old man. I can't kill you with my bare hands or hold a weapon. But I'm quite good at creating weather phenomenon." The sinister mouth formed an "O." Joseph felt its breath and the lantern lost its glow. He was resigned to whatever was to come. It was obvious the spirit had already discovered its power.

"Spare the woman," Joseph said. "She inadvertently provided your portage to this world. There is no other part in this for her." He could only hope his death would not be in vain. Joseph was not afraid to die, but he did fear for Rachel.

"Oh, but she is involved. Thanks to her interference. She will have to pay a price. But I plan to have a little fun with her first. You won't be around to meddle. No more frantic calls to the good shaman." Its high, shrill laughter could curdle blood.

"You underestimate her," Joseph said. "She is stronger than you know."

"Yeah, right," it said. "Oh my, look at the time." Joseph glanced at the battery clock that sat on the table. But that wasn't what it meant. "The appointment you've waited so long for is now." The monstrous one began to laugh again, fading away. Its retreat shook the seams of the flimsy cabin.

Joseph sat on the floor, next to the table. He spent his last few minutes in deep concentration, ignoring the maelstrom created by the supernatural creature. Instead, he sent a warning to a woman a state away. He knew not if she would receive it, but he focused his last few breaths on her. Fighting would be in vain. Although he had prevailed in such battles before, he could not today.

The walls of the shack vibrated from hurricane force winds which loosened old nails and shook the rafters from their time-honored places. When they gave way and the roof fell through. The old man became young again.

CHAPTER 33

Rachel checked the rearview again. Her reason for being here was truly stupid. What had she found out? That a construction crew had dynamite, pipe, screws, and nails. Big surprise. Bigger surprise? They were pissed about someone snooping around.

She wanted to turn off the headlights in an effort to blend in with the night, but doing so would make the petrified ruts impossible to navigate. The earthen ridges grabbed at the tires, jerking the car back and forth. Worse, the car behind her was closing in. Even at school zone speed she expected a shock to break at any moment. The terrain didn't seem to be hindering the vehicle behind her. It was a no way out quandary. She had put herself here, alone.

It couldn't be more than two miles to the highway, but it might as well be twenty. The weighty car could not outrun the one following her. The car bucked across a washboard strip of road. Rachel yanked at the wheel in an effort to avoid sideswiping a large chamisa but the grooves won and the car tore through the shrub, emerging with yellow blossoms stuck beneath her windshield wipers.

The lights behind her were bright, illuminating the interior of the car. Why didn't he ram her? Surely, that was the intention.

Once she caught a glimpse of lights on the highway ahead. She feared it would be impossible to reach before the bozo made his move.

Rachel's arms ached from fighting to control the Merc's mad plunge through the back country. Her eyes strained to see every bit of the slender lane which led to safety, but as the car vaulted and jumped over a surface not fit for a lunar touchdown, she held on.

The vehicle causing all the trouble lagged a couple of car lengths behind her. Maybe he was only trying to scare her. If so, the ploy was a complete success. The temptation to pull over and take her licks came and was quickly brushed aside. It was an un-welcome combination of fatigue and fright.

Ahead, the trail narrowed even more. In the flash of her head-lights she could see a boulder, the size of a bus, on one side and a gigantic prickly pear on the other. She aimed the Merc slightly off center, toward the cacti. The highway was near now and her foot begged for more speed. In a few minutes she could break some more laws getting back to town. With this feeling of relief, she re-laxed one second too long.

Several yards before reaching the squeeze in the lane, her front tires hit something buried in the road. The Merc became air-borne. She stomped the brakes from habit and tried to hold the direction with the steering wheel. The Merc burst through the prickly pear. Cactus pads flew in every direction. It made a sound like bursting watermelon. In seconds she destroyed desert flora and landed in a small depression surrounded by piñon.

The harness system left her uninjured. There was no air bag in the 1985 model car so she didn't have to worry about decapitation, only the malicious intent of the person in the other car.

Briefly, she thought of leaving the car and going for the high-way, but the events of the wee hours had left her worn. At present she doubted she could outrun an aging tortoise let alone anyone bent on wiping out her existence.

That decision didn't exclude fighting in place. Rachel pulled the Little League baseball bat from beneath the armrests where she kept it. With as much dashing around as she did, meeting strangers, she thought some sort of weapon, short of a gun, had merit. The occasion to use it had not presented itself before, but tonight she was glad to have it.

A white pickup skidded to a stop. Dust engulfed them both in a suffocating cloud. Two men leapt from truck, headed in Rachel's direction. One was hollering something incomprehensible as he waved a flashlight.

The bat was small, but she held it like Albert Pujols at the playoffs.

By the time a face pushed up against the side window Rachel had released the seat belt. A minuscule surge of adrenalin flushed her body with readiness. The evening had spent most of her strength running and climbing. Was this how Custer felt?

The face at the window didn't seem to hold much malice. He spoke words, but all she could lip-read was, "Okay." Okay, what? To kill me? A quick look told her the other man was trying to open the passenger side door. Neither of them had a weapon. After a few seconds of pounding and yelling, they stopped. Rachel, confused by their lack of animosity, waited for their next move.

The young man on the driver's side must be about twenty-five. In her dazed condition, it finally registered that he wasn't one of the men back at the house, although they could have accomplices. He motioned to the other, who joined him. He too, was a young guy, wore glasses and looked like a computer geek. Curious that he would be in the outdoors at all, Rachel lowered the window about an inch.

The two calmly stood a few feet away from her car. The one with the spiky hair said, "I think we're scaring her." The other remained quiet. Rachel heard, "Ma'am, are you all right?"

She heard herself reply, "Yeah, sure, don't I look it?" It was then she knew how ridiculous she must appear, armed with a club, jumping about her car like some kind of wigged-out chimpanzee auditioning for a part in a Disney flick. She dropped the bat on the floor and passed out cold.

As Rachel faded to catatonic bliss, she heard Joseph's voice urging her to be careful, warning her. He seemed to be saying to call him, no, call on him. It wasn't clear, but it seemed he did not mean by telephone. This, she didn't understand. His words abruptly stopped as she came to.

The two guys still watched her with concern. The nerd said, "We called an ambulance." He pointed to the cell phone in his other hand.

Feeling like an utter fool, Rachel opened the door and let her would-be rescuers hold her up, protesting the need for medical attention while barely able to walk. She remonstrated all the way to the hospital, only to learn she had a minor concussion from hitting something inside of the car when she succumbed to self-inflicted hysteria.

Her guardian angels followed the ambulance to the hospital. The two insisted on calling someone for her. They contacted Chloe, who rushed to fetch her when a lack of insurance persuaded the financial office she didn't need overnight observation. Chloe kindly made arrangements to have her car towed from the outback. Rachel took to her bed.

CHAPTER 34

Morning arrived late for Rachel. At 11:30 Chloe touched base during lunch to find Rachel sitting on a kitchen bar stool in her night shirt, hunched over, examining her bruised legs. A cup of tea steeped on the counter.

"Counting bruises?" Chloe asked.

"Didn't take enough math for that," Rachel said. "Every muscle in my body is screaming."

"It's that fight or flight response. What you need is a psychic healer; someone who is well-trained in Reiki and toning. I could refer you."

Chloe was earnest. Rachel could see it in her face. She stifled the giggle scrambling for escape. "Thanks," she said, "but I think the hospital bill will be quite enough for me."

"Oh, I see," Chloe crossed her arms. "You don't believe in spiritual healing but calling back an evil spirit, well, that makes complete sense."

"I couldn't argue with you on that point," Rachel acquiesced. "Even if I had the energy.

"Who were those guys last night who ran me off the road?" She went for a subject change.

"Juan and Chad, two brothers with different *madres*," Chloe said. "Really different mothers. They claim you were driving erratically and too fast for the road, so they followed you to see if you were all right."

"What were they doing out there?" Rachel demanded, feeling the fool. She thought they'd been intent on murdering her.

"They asked the same thing about you, but as to your question: They were camping."

"Which one called you?"

"I believe it was Chad. You're lucky my guest had already gone home, or I might have left you at the hospital. Maybe they could've found a room for you with padded walls. What were you doing out there?" Rachel expected Chloe's toe to tap in motherlike impatience.

"I thought I could figure out what is going on at Pueblo Blanco if I did some looking around. That's all."

"So naturally," Chloe said, "you went out there in the middle of the night. You know that's trespassing?"

"Yeah, but it gets a little worse." Rachel recounted the whole humiliating adventure from the hike through the night to finding the dynamite to her encounter with the two men.

"A little worse? Oh dear god, you broke in. You can be arrested for that."

"It's okay. They didn't recognize me," Rachel said. "It's no big deal."

"No big deal. No big deal!" Chloe was beginning to get shrill.

"Sit down. Here, drink my tea," Rachel held the cup out to her.

"Thanks, but I'm going to need something stronger than tea." Chloe filled a glass with ice, opened a cabinet door and pulled out a bottle of Baileys, poured it over the ice and drank half.

"Isn't it a tad early?" Rachel asked.

"It's five o'clock somewhere."

Rachel grinned at her friend's consternation.

"I was certain they were chasing me on the road. It's mortifying to discover it was just a couple of guys enjoying a night out camping."

"That's the kind of thing that happens when you break laws and take ridiculous risks," Chloe admonished.

"What happened to my car?"

"Relax Rachel, it survived. Juan happens to be an auto mechanic, apparently quite a good one—owns his own shop. He felt so bad about scaring you; he asked that your car be towed to his garage. This morning he called me at the office and said it needed some realignment, and it will be good as new. Hard to believe, isn't it?"

"Very funny."

"You know, you don't have to drive that," Chloe considered what to call the Merc, "that hulk."

"I know, I know," Rachel held up both hands. "But I like the Merc. It has personality."

"So did the mammoths, I'm sure," Chloe said, "but they're extinct. Cars that big should be too."

Rachel ignored the remark. She was too tired to scrimmage. Chloe had already turned her interest elsewhere as she fumbled with the filters to the coffee machine.

"You're having coffee too?" Rachel inquired.

Chloe gave her an exasperated look. "It goes with the Baileys!"

When the coffeemaker was working, she spread out the newspaper on the counter. "My god," Chloe exclaimed.

"What is it?"

Chloe was still bent over the counter, reading intently. "I don't believe it!"

"What!" Impatient.

"There was a death at Pueblo Blanco last night."

"Huh?" Interest and dread twisted at Rachel's stomach.

"It says a man's body was found at the construction site this morning. There was no identification. Workers did not recognize the man as someone connected with the development. Foul play is suspected. Rachel, what have you gotten yourself into?"

"Hell if I know."

CHAPTER 35

The following day Logan called, inviting Rachel for a late lunch. She was happy to accept. Rachel asked him to meet her at the house for sale south of the Roundhouse.

She picked up the Merc that morning. Juan Hernandez had balanced the tires and realigned the front end, even pounded out a small dent resulting from the dive through the prickly pear. Rachel begged him to take money for his efforts but he steadfastly refused, apologizing repeatedly for frightening her. She tried to explain it wasn't his or Chad's fault, but he was firm. *De nada.*

Before she drove away, Juan had one final thing to do for her car. He called upon his ace mechanic, and American Indian healer, Lloyd Soretto, to bless the Merc. Soretto used a cigarette lighter to ignite white sage. He placed the smoldering herb, which represented fire, in a shell which he told her symbolized water. Then he used a feather to guide the smoke, the replica of air. He began near the ground and worked his way to the roof of her car.

"I banish the negative," Soretto said. "And ask that peace and love enfold this car."

When her car had been smudged, he paid homage to the seven cardinal directions: north, south, east, west, up, down and center.

Rachel found herself blinking back tears. Soretto was a beautiful mover and he seemed intent on banishing any evil from the

Merc. She thanked him. He ducked his head and backed away shyly.

Juan, who had been standing by, was taking no chances with her car. He cautioned her: "The brake pads are wearing. Bring her by soon. We will make sure she stops on a dime." Rachel privately pledged to patronize Juan's Auto Casa for all her days.

A few blocks away, she let go of the steering wheel. The car continued to go straight. She smiled.

* * *

She arrived first with *carne adovada* burritos stuffed into a greasy paper bag, a thermos of tea, and a morning paper.

As she stood at the curb of the small adobe house, it was apparent it needed someone to tend it. The need stirred a rare emotion in Rachel, that of the nesting instinct. The urge to weed flower beds and repair stucco was at juxtaposition to her desire for freedom. She admitted an interest in the house or there was every reason to be somewhere else. Rachel sat on the front stoop in the afternoon sun.

Logan parked his car across the street. She couldn't help but notice his incredible looks. He could stop traffic, especially if a woman was behind the wheel. What bothered her, on this flawless autumn day, was why they were seeing one another. He was married. This was no time to mess with her head by indulging in a stupid affair that could only end in pain for everyone involved.

"Morning, Rachel." Logan startled her out of her guilty thoughts. "You okay?" He saw the bruises on her forehead. She touched it gingerly, and told him about her nocturnal activities.

His face registered disbelief and awe. "Are you in your right mind?" He smiled, not knowing her well, but trying to joke with her.

"Wasn't the smartest thing I've ever done. Everything hurts," she wrapped up. And then, redirected. "How are you?"

"Great. With weather like this, it's hard to complain. So, tell me Rach," he had become more familiar and she was starting to like it, "why are we meeting here?"

"Chloe wants me to buy it. I can't show you the inside, except what you can see through the windows, but there's a nice patio in back. You up for a burrito?"

"Green chile?" he inquired.

"Red."

"How could I turn down an invitation like that?"

Their shoes made scraping noises as they walked down the old flagstone path scattered with debris. The wooden gate squealed as Rachel pushed it inward. She made a mental note to oil it, and then realized what everyone else had known all along, she was staying in Santa Fe. She was home. The recognition of how she felt let some of the weight of indecision slide from her shoulders. For a moment she stopped, her eyes filling with tears at the thought of having a place to call her own. Logan halted abruptly, expecting her to go on. "What's up?" he asked.

For a minute she remained quiet, composing herself. "Funny, how we make decisions. I just this minute decided to buy this place." She wondered if it surprised him. With his income he could afford anything he could dream.

"That's wonderful," he said. "May I be the first to congratulate you?" He gave her a quick hug, pulled the newspaper she held beneath her arm, and walked to the patio table. With his back to her, Rachel had a couple of seconds to deal with the feelings his embrace had left. First, there had been the flush of warmth from the pleasant surprise. She resisted the impulse to exclaim, "Wow!" This was followed by a wave of anxiety at what might happen if she didn't get a grip.

She joined him and placed the food on the table, giving Logan a napkin and then his burrito. There were two cups in the sack, which she filled with tea.

"This is a wonderful courtyard," Logan said. "I can see you here, under this tree, writing on your laptop." He took a large bite of burrito and sat back comfortably in the chair.

Rachel had to agree. The yard was a manageable size and would be gorgeous once cared for. She could imagine a sedum growing between the flagstones—she read about it once while cooling her heels in a dental office. The stucco wall gave not only privacy but a sense of being wrapped in the earth's arms. Here, nothing could go wrong. This would be her refuge. A squeak rustled her from daydreaming.

"Who's this?" Logan asked, already extending some of his burrito to the cat who gently rubbed his leg. "Never heard one make a noise like that; sounds as if she needs to be oiled." The tortoiseshell cat ate the offering hungrily, gulping it down and waiting for more. She didn't even flinch from the red chile; obviously, a native kitty.

"Chloe says the cat belonged to the former owner of the house, who was killed in some kind of accident. His parents live out of state and didn't know about the cat." She observed the creature with misgiving.

"You don't like cats?" he said protectively as though she had suddenly contracted leprosy. His hand never left the soft fur of the purring feline.

"Well, it's not that I don't like them. It's more, they don't like me." She was feeling defensive. She feared he would find great fault with her character if she didn't recover from this *faux pas*.

"She likes me," Logan grinned. By now the cat was upside down on his lap allowing him to scratch its stomach. "Why wouldn't she like you?"

Rachel had to admit the little multicolored animal seemed friendly. Hesitantly, she touched the silken fur. Some clung to Logan's black silk shirt and pants. He ignored it. The kitty righted herself and gazed at Rachel from green eyes. The kind of eyes that looked deep into the soul. She had a tan blaze down her nose. Her fur was mostly black, but accented by orange, tan and white hair. On her stomach was a large patch of orange tabby stripes.

"See," Logan said reassuringly to the cat, rubbing its ears, "she's okay. She just doesn't know about kitties. We'll make a cat mom of her yet."

Rachel thought she would be sick. A cat mom? Indeed! What happened to Logan's macho private eye ways? Actors act, she reminded herself. This was a side of his personality never shown on the screen.

"I'd buy the place just for the cat," he said. "She's obviously at home here, but needs someone to care for her. I think she's not getting enough to eat."

"I'll give it some thought," she said. "Maybe I can find a good home for her."

Logan smiled. Rachel thought it a knowing kind of smile— much like Stella's. It irritated her.

She reached for the paper, hoping to change the subject and got more than she bargained for. On the front page was a picture of a man. The headline read, "Body Identified." The man's name was Victor Chavez, the attorney she'd tried to talk with about Pueblo Blanco.

CHAPTER 36

"Package for you," Stella said a couple of days later. Rachel turned from the window. She'd been staring at the street where the tragedy had occurred.

"What? Oh." She took the thin cardboard envelope and placed it on her cluttered desk. "Thanks." Some items were of short-term importance such as press kits, releases, and photos. Phone messages, notes to herself, and rough drafts of her stories had a date with the shredder that seldom arrived. Her efforts to be efficient were always thwarted by her inability to part with something on the off chance it might prove useful someday. Files worked to a point, until they became filled to overflowing. The stacks comforted her. Rachel was certain Chloe could explain it with the perfect psychological term. And it would likely reflect poorly on Rachel.

She noticed the return address of the Hopi Nation in Arizona. No longer interested in her sloppy habits, she tore at the stubborn packing tape. Inside was an envelope with her name on it. It contained a drawing on a single piece of eight and a half by eleven white copy paper, the kind in conspicuous supply at any office store. Clipped to it was a small note.

Dear Ms. Blackstone:

Joseph died suddenly when his house collapsed in a storm. This drawing was found with him and has your signature. We thought you'd want it. He regarded you fondly. Sorry to send such sad news.

Sincerely,

It was signed by the director at the Hopi governmental office.

Joseph dead! She turned her back on the rest of the office to hide her emotions. His house collapsed? How could that happen? She rationalized, trying to understand. Arizona wasn't prone to tornadoes, but wind, yes, that could happen.

She felt surprised by her sense of loss at the death of the kind, old wise one. Rachel felt alone. Joseph would no longer be available to help her return Mario. That understanding chilled her. Unbidden, the Hopi word *maski*, came to mind. She understood it to mean the "corpse house." Joseph was now among the other departed spirits in the Underworld. She would miss him.

Rachel examined the pencil drawing with curiosity. Her name was written in the lower corner, but she had not drawn it. The stormy landscape depicted a single lightning bolt striking sagebrush, silhouetted in front of a mountain range. The mountains had odd sharp peaks. The picture had a savage intensity. There seemed to be figures sketched in odd places as if they weren't really there, yet somehow were. Each pencil stroke was strong and deliberate, but she hadn't a clue why her name appeared as the artist.

"Are you going to eat that?" It was Julian's brat nephew, the ne'er-do-well with her job. It was bad enough young John was not a good fit with the magazine. In addition, he always seemed to be hungry. You couldn't leave any morsel lying unguarded on your desk, without losing it the first time you had to make a trip to the loo.

"Yes, I'm going to eat it," she said evenly. "I eat anything on my desk, so back off." The retort was more vicious than she'd planned, but Joseph's death was too disturbing, and she didn't welcome the intrusion. Rachel pushed the drawing back into the safety of the envelope, tucked it under her arm and grabbed the half-eaten Twinkie. "See you later, Johnny." She knew he hated to be called that; all the more reason to say it."

She blew Stella a kiss. "I'm going to Chloe's office," Rachel said and left through the rear entrance. Carpenters were repairing the bomb damage on the front.

A moving van was parked in the Smith's driveway. Mrs. Smith was moving to her daughter's. Already Mr. Smith's flowers drooped, Rachel believed, from broken hearts.

Rachel marveled that the Merc was riding smoothly. It accelerated onto the street with renewed vigor. She hoped Chloe wouldn't be in the middle of the deal of the century. Rachel wanted Chloe's opinion of the drawing.

Chloe greeted her with, "Rachel, your aura is looking under the weather. You've got to get some rest."

Rachel raised one eyebrow and speculated as to what Chloe saw. "It's just the concussion and scattered bruising that you're seeing."

"Nonsense," Chloe answered, "I can tell the difference."

"Maybe you can shed some light on this." Rachel laid the envelope on Chloe's oversized desk and took a seat.

Chloe read the note and looked up at Rachel, "You okay?"

"Yes, but I could sure use some good news."

Chloe then turned to the drawing and scrutinized it. "I take it you didn't create this. What do you make of it?"

"I don't know; my ESP's on the blink."

"Very funny." Chloe frowned. It was all together charming when she did it. "Is it a message from Joseph? No one else at the reservation knew you, did they?"

Rachel shook her head slowly, and mumbled "No."

"Maybe this isn't clear now, because you don't need the information yet. You know, when the student needs help, the teacher appears. I think Joseph was probably an accomplished artist. The pencil strokes look confident, but this was done in a hurry."

Rachel had no other theories to offer so she replaced the drawing in the envelope. "I'll live with it for a while and see if I can make anything of it. I came for another reason too." She hesitated, not knowing whether to commit to something permanent. "I guess," her breath caught a little. "I want to . . . buy the house."

"There, that wasn't so hard," Chloe teased. "Course you were the only one who didn't know that. I stopped showing it to give you some time to think about what you wanted."

Chloe slipped one perfectly manicured hand inside the middle drawer of her desk and pulled out a contract. Rachel's name and information were neatly typed in the blanks. "Sign here."

CHAPTER 37

Chris Woods entered his home shortly after midnight. It had been a particularly stressful day. He was sick of budget meetings and that damned sissy city accountant. He'd spent the evening in the private dining room of his favorite club, unwinding with that appealing new clerk in the planning department. Her name? Betty? No, not right. Betsy? He thought that sounded close. No matter, she was young, fresh, and eager to please.

The quiet house that had been welcome right after his family left was becoming a tomb. He didn't miss the wife. The boys, he missed. Yeah, they could be noisy, but they were always glad to see him. His wife had filed for divorce. He'd heard from her attorney. Fine by him. Her parents in Minnesota could have her—and support her. She wasn't getting a dime, like he had any to spare.

Things were tough enough right now without having to dig deeper into his pockets. He couldn't afford the lush four-bedroom house in the hills even with two incomes. The bank let his mortgage go unpaid because of his position, and he planned to be mayor for a long time. That left what little money he made as city leader free for more pleasurable pursuits.

He poured a whiskey at the living room bar and sauntered into the kitchen for something to eat. The refrigerator light produced much ado about nothing. Trace amounts of milk were sour, the pastrami had green crap growing on it, and the bread was dried out. He dumped it all in the garbage disposal and let it rip. The cabinets produced a few stale crackers which he ate anyway, washing them down with his drink. He wasn't really hungry, but restless.

Slowly, between sips, Chris became aware of an odor, one not eliminated by throwing out the bad milk. The trash compactor was empty. Besides, it didn't smell like rotting food, but unpleasant nonetheless. Chris lobbed the remaining crackers into the sink in a fit of pique.

"You always were easily exasperated." He'd been sitting in the kitchen watching the whole time.

Chris pulled open the refrigerator door to get a better look. "Mario?"

"Yeah, it's me. Shut that damn thing." Chris let the door close.

"What the hell are you doing here? How'd you get past the alarm?"

"Got to activate it or it doesn't work."

"It was set." Chris said beginning to feel uneasy. "I turned it off just now. You still haven't answered my question."

"The one about what the hell I'm doing here? Interesting, you should use that term. Have you ever thought about hell, Chris, my pal?"

"Not since Sunday School." He reached into the pantry and pulled out another bottle of Glenlivet. The whiskey burned on the way down but left a smooth aftertaste. He suspected he was becoming an alcoholic, but it seemed a small price to leave behind his troubles.

"You ought to," Mario continued. "You never know when things might blow up in your face."

"There are all kinds of hell." Chris placed the glass on the tile counter, his hand steady. "What the fuck happened at that damn development?"

"What makes you think I know anything about it?"

"Let's face it, Mario, if it's bad, you know, even if you weren't directly involved."

"I suppose I do have a certain reputation."

"You think?" Acerbic. "Want one of these?" Chris shook the bottle and poured himself another. Sex made him thirsty, and Betsy had been accommodating.

"Nope, I gave up the stuff."

"So you said the other night."

"Right. Where have you been hiding out? Did you read the paper? You know you're supposed to be dead."

"Where I've been, we don't have much use for reading. But death is something I've had on my mind lately."

"You beat it, if you can believe the press," Chris said. "Now it's time to get back to business. This deal's been fallow too long."

"Let's talk about it," Mario said. "How about some light?" Chris reached for the switch that operated the lamp hanging over the table. What he saw made him take a step back. Mario was different. There was something strange about him. His eyes. Maybe he was high. Mario had always had a dangerous edge. There had been other times when Chris had watched him intimidate some poor schmuck. He thought Mario probably collected debts for local loan sharks, but hadn't wanted to know. Right now he felt as if he'd missed a payment.

* * *

The phone rang early. Rachel resisted wakefulness in favor of that protective place called sleep. It was not quite light. Slivers of gray sifted through the sheers. A mountain jay heralded the coming sunrise. Oh, maybe she could go back to sleep, just a few minutes, please. She couldn't resist Chloe's sharp knock on her door.

"Rachel, wake up. Something's happened."

Those words are as bad as "we need to talk" or "you better sit down" and are generally accompanied by "I'm afraid" or "I'm sorry." Any one of those goes before the news of a traumatic event requiring years of recovery. She waited for a few seconds before hearing what was sure to be bad news, as though it would change the outcome.

The persistent knocking roused her from the warm comforter. She was halfway to the door when Chloe crept in.

"I'm sorry," Chloe began, "to wake you so early."

"It's okay. What's up?"

"Now I don't know if this means something bad has happened to Chris, but . . ."

Rachel's stomach did a leap on empty. Chris could be a jerk, but he was the only family she had left. She fought back all the ugly thoughts coming to mind. "Just tell me." The words came out calmly, even though she didn't feel calm.

"His car was found abandoned along the Rio Grande."

"And Chris?"

"The police said there was no sign of him."

"You talked to the police?"

"No, they notified the city hall emergency number. His secretary called me. Tony told her we were friends."

"Were there signs of a struggle? Anything unusual?"

"Not from what she told me. Someone out for a morning run, noticed the 'MEMAYOR' car tag, didn't see anyone around, and called the police."

Rachel felt apprehension descend upon her. She looked to Chloe for some kind of affirming platitude, but she was sensing the same thing.

"He's in trouble, isn't he?" Rachel asked.

Chloe could only nod in agreement.

CHAPTER 38

The mayor was missing. The TV stations were constantly breaking into programming to report it again and again. Betsy Jones couldn't believe it. She'd spent the evening with Chris Woods, convinced he cared about her.

She was the classic American girl gone astray. All her life she had been pretty and it made up for her lack of intellectual ability. Extra effort on her part helped her squeeze through public school and college with a "C" grade point. The naiveté she couldn't seem to offset.

Repeatedly, she'd found men in authority difficult to resist. As long as they were nice to her, she saw nothing wrong with being nice in return. It started with one high school teacher, then several college professors, a couple of bosses during summer jobs and now the mayor. When he told her last week he'd been late to a meeting so he could be with her, she felt special. Not long after, he asked her out. Last night, they'd had a romantic dinner and wine— a lot of wine. He said he liked her, thought her pretty.

The clerk job at the planning department was a stroke of luck for Betsy. Her number hit the top of the list on the city roll on the same day the last clerk left. Apparently, there had been some trouble keeping the position filled. She didn't care why. She liked the job—and it came with benefits. Betsy enjoyed talking with people all day, though her supervisor was somewhat unpleasant. That didn't bother her because Chris Woods liked her.

Until this morning anyway, things were different now that he had disappeared. How could she find out about him? The police weren't going to tell her anything or the mayor's office. That's when she remembered the reporter in the planning department the other day.

Betsy dumped out her purse and located the card. The after-hours number was written on the back. She dialed her cell.

* * *

Two detectives sat on the edge of Chloe's chairs. Chloe sat next to her friend on the sofa in case she needed her. But she also knew that Rachel kept her emotions close to the cuff. Usually, the only emotion she expressed was anger cloaked in expletives and dripping in sarcasm. Chloe had learned to read what was really bothering her, but respected her need to handle it alone.

The older officer, Detective Flores, repeated what Chloe told her earlier concerning Chris' car.

"I want to reiterate," Flores continued, "that there was no evidence to indicate foul play. Normally, we wouldn't investigate a missing person this soon, but he is the mayor, and we don't want to take any chances in case criminal activity might be involved." His face betrayed his real convictions. He was having trouble looking at Rachel directly. "Because we're taking every precaution, I need to ask you a couple of questions."

"All right," Rachel murmured. These two could talk all day about how Chris could be okay. Rachel didn't believe them.

"Do you know of anyone who may have threatened him in any way?" Flores asked. He absently wiped his forehead with the back of his hand, betraying his nervousness.

"No," Rachel began hesitantly. "You must know, Chris is not the most beloved mayor the city has ever had, but I know of no one specifically." She passed on mentioning Mario. That he was up to no good, was a given, but as far as she knew, he and Chris were friends. Bringing up Mario would only make her look like a nutcase. With her recent history that would be all too easy to believe.

"Rachel has only just returned to Santa Fe," Chloe said. "She's been living in Tulsa for a few months."

"Nice city," said the rookie officer inanely. Until then, Rachel had forgotten he was there. "My sister and brother-in-law live there."

"Yes, it is," Rachel agreed and returned her attention to Detective Flores as he began speaking again.

"Anything odd happen lately that might be a factor here?" he asked.

The stitches in her finger itched. There's no such thing as a little itch, because the first one triggers the big, long-lasting one. They were supposed to come out in a couple of days, but that was one doctor's office visit she could forego. Rachel picked at them while she thought about what to say. She hated to bring her brother's personal life into it but decided it might be important. "My brother's wife recently left with their two kids. I think divorce is a possibility."

He made a scribble in his detective notebook and stood. Junior officer followed his lead. "We'll call you the moment we know anything," Detective Flores said. "Try not to worry."

She thanked them.

Rachel tugged at the stitches with her tweezers. All but one of the tiny black threads was out when the phone rang. Rachel swore as she pulled it through in a hurry—it hurt—and rushed to stop the ringing.

"It's for you," Chloe beat her to it.

With uneasiness she picked up the receiver. The small sweet voice on the other end came as a surprise. Rachel couldn't think of anyone she knew who sounded this untouched. The girl wasn't from the police. Instead, she was asking for Rachel Blackstone, the reporter.

"Speaking."

"Ms. Blackstone, I work in the planning department at the city."

Rachel's brain picked through the memory bank for the file on this one. Where oh where has my . . . uh, there it is! The young thing who helped her on the Pueblo Blanco development. At times it didn't pay to leave cards with people.

Although print reporters didn't get the attention of those in television, the nonmedia public seemed infatuated with anyone, however fringe, who wrote or spoke the news. Rachel was usually able to avoid this unwanted attention, but occasionally the minor celebritydom of her work caught up with her. She feared this was the case.

"What can I do for you?"

"I was wondering, since you're a reporter, if you know what happened to Chris . . . I mean the mayor."

Rachel swore she could hear a small sob after the question. Why would an employee on the lowest rung be upset enough about the mayor's disappearance to call a reporter, or did she know he was her brother?

"Why did you call me?"

"Because you're the only reporter I know." There was definitely a sniffle.

"Did you know the mayor?"

"Yes," the tiny voice said. "We knew each other socially."

Oops. Rachel knew what that had to mean. While the wife's away, the mayor will play.

"I've forgotten your name, would you refresh my memory?" Rachel wanted to get as much information as possible before revealing her familial relationship.

"Betsy. Betsy Jones."

"Thank you. Ms. Jones, I honestly can't add anything that's not already on the news. Please, would you tell me the last time you saw the mayor?"

"Sure. Last night."

Last night! "Have you told the police?"

"No," alarm raised the voice to a higher pitch. "Maybe I made a mistake?"

She was losing her. "Please, Ms. Jones . . . Betsy." Familiarity might produce the closeness she needed to keep her talking. "This is important. Did the mayor say anything that might help us know where he is, or where he planned to go?"

"I don't know. I mean I don't remember. We talked about a lot of things. He said something about a deal he was working on, but I don't know what it was. I better go. I didn't mean to bother you."

"Betsy, it's no bother. You see, I'm very glad to hear from you because the mayor is my brother, and I'm concerned about him."

"Chris is your . . . ?"

"Yes, that's right. Betsy, are you at home? Would you mind if I came by your house?" Rachel spoke those alarming words: "I think we need to talk

CHAPTER 39

Betsy Jones lived in the new Santa Fe, an area of town Rachel disliked. It was great for those who love suburbia but a sad environment for those who appreciated history and character. Except for an effort to make the houses and apartment buildings look adobe, they could be occupying any 'burb in the country. Here, the middle class could live relatively free of fear—of the different, the unusual, the spicy, while still living in a unique community the convention and visitors' center billed as a cultural crossroads. When family came to visit, you could always venture out, but the rest of the time you could live a nice boring life.

Southwest Santa Fe was what the real estate folks called *affordable*. There were kids all over the place. Rachel found a mixed neighborhood more fun. She found Native American and Hispanic people to be more family-oriented in a healthy way. Since she didn't have much of a family, she sometimes borrowed others. Food at gatherings was flavorful and consistently good, the music didn't make the Top 40 or the YouTube Charts, and the company was the best.

Rachel turned off Airport Road and headed south for the apartment complex where Betsy lived. Inexpensive, by City Different standards, and the land had been carefully scraped of any identifying flora. If chamisa or piñon were to grow here again, they would have to be planted, or wait many years for the vegetation to find its way back. A few intrepid asters clung to the sides of the road adding spots of purple. She found the apartment number and parked the Merc.

Betsy answered her knock cautiously, as if fearing Rachel might have transformed into a space alien during the last thirty minutes. The apartment's interior hadn't changed much since it was built. This one had four white walls and a short pile carpet of pale turquoise, the only southwest color in sight. The tiny galley kitchen to the right of the entry was furnished with cut-rate appliances. Vinyl parquet squares covered the foyer floor. Talk about oxymoron.

The young woman looked frightened. "May I come in?" Rachel asked.

"Oh sure, sorry," Betsy recovered her manners. "Can I get you something? I've got some, well, water."

"Thanks, a glass of water would be nice," Rachel said. The girl needed to do something normal or she was going to fall apart. Rachel picked one of two secondhand chairs that graced both the ends of a coffee table. A handful of red silk flowers rested in a salad dressing cruet in the table's exact center. Betsy placed two cork coasters on the table, followed by glasses of iced water.

"Are you really Chris' sister?" She sat on the edge of the other chair and observed Rachel suspiciously. Her fingers twisted her hair into unflattering tendrils. Rachel noticed the nails bitten to the quick. She was a young adult with little experience in handling problems. At the moment, Rachel felt grateful for her life experience.

"Yes, I'm Chris' sister." She tried to sound reassuring. "You may be one of the last people to have seen him before his disappearance." It was too much for Betsy. Her blue eyes searched the room for help. "What I mean is he may have told you something that might give us some idea of where he went."

Betsy was quiet so long Rachel thought she'd have to shake a response out of her. "He mostly told me how pretty he thinks I am." That's Chris, the silver-tongued devil.

"Is there anything else? What did you talk about? Movies, books, family?" Betsy only shook her head. "How about city business?" They did, after all, work at the same place.

"He did thank me for the errands I'd run."

"Errands?" Rachel nearly pounced on the poor thing.

"Well, yeah," Betsy's lower lip trembled, "before dinner he thanked me for taking several envelopes to the planning commission. Once I took a package to some guy I met at the farmers market. Chris said he couldn't trust a messenger service with something that important." Her lip stopped quivering, but her body language still betrayed her urge to bolt.

"What did the guy look like? The one at the farmers market." What a good place to meet someone clandestinely. It was a mix of locals and tourists looking for fresh produce or gifts. Everyone was exchanging sacks, envelopes and boxes. And in an obstacle course of haphazardly parked vehicles, one could disappear quickly.

Betsy thought about the question for a moment. "He was old. You know." Actually Rachel had no idea, but probably most people looked old to someone so young. "Kind of bald. The hair left was grey. He was pretty good looking, for his age." Betsy should hope she lived long enough for her hair to turn silver. Right now, she couldn't think past the pain of the moment.

"Did you know what was in the packages?"

"Oh no. I would never look. That wouldn't be right."

Integrity—hard to argue with—but Rachel could have easily forgiven Betsy for a quick look at the contents. It was possible the deliveries were on the up-and-up. It may have been Chris' way of getting to know her for his own lascivious purposes. Just because Chris was involved didn't indicate a conspiracy, at least nothing more than getting this fresh-faced kid into bed. That was unforgivable enough.

Rachel thanked Betsy for her time and headed back to the real Santa Fe. She stopped at a convenience store, something she rarely did, because that much convenience almost always meant expensive. But she needed a few things quickly.

Since she had to drive through the South Capitol area to return to Chloe's, she pulled over at the house that would soon be hers.

She glanced through a couple of windows, but the inside wasn't what interested her this time. Under the tall trees, she sat at the table on the terrace. There was something about Betsy's description of the man that rang a bell but not loudly enough for clarification. Rachel closed her eyes. It was quiet and she savored it. After about twenty minutes she realized she was no longer alone. There was a wee squeak from across the yard.

"There you are. What took you so long?" Her voice evoked a real meow from the cat as she marched bravely in her direction. The cat's bowls were near the back door. Thanks to Chloe, the water had been turned on. Rachel cleaned them as much as plain water would allow and filled the larger stainless steel container with water. She took the box of dry cat food she'd purchased and filled the other.

"You know it's not good etiquette to inhale your food." One black ear twitched in her direction. She chanced a quick pat on her satiny suit. That produced an undeniable noise from the creature, a soft rumble like a refrigerator motor, relaxing and reassuring. "This purring stuff's kind of nice," she noted. The feline paused long enough to look at Rachel. Jade eyes regarded her with part gratitude, part suspicion, but Rachel was tickled she acknowledged her at all. She thought that a peculiar reaction to the attention of a cat. It was a new start. Rachel poured a few more morsels in the dish and left.

Life was looking up, if only Chris's disappearance could be explained, so she could enjoy it.

CHAPTER 40

Chloe stood at the back door holding the phone, waiting for Rachel to come up the walk. "Tony, for you," she called. Rachel picked up her pace through the herb garden. She crushed fragrant lavender under her rubber soles, leaving the scent of a sachet.

"Did he say what he wants?" she whispered.

"No. I think he's concerned about Chris."

Rachel took the phone and walked a couple of steps, delaying the moment she must speak. The mountains received a dusting of snow overnight. If it didn't turn unseasonably warm, the skiing would be good by Thanksgiving. She didn't understand why talking with Tony was so difficult. There weren't many awful things between them. Chloe moved closer and touched her arm comfortingly. Rachel thanked her with her eyes.

"Hello, Tony."

"Rachel, I heard about Chris. Any news?" He was making it easy, straight to the point.

"If you've been watching the reports, that's pretty much everything I know. There was no indication of a confrontation in either his house or car. The police have searched the area but have come up empty-handed. I suppose it's possible he just walked. He's simmering most of the time."

"Would he stage his own disappearance for whatever reason?" Tony asked.

"Like, for attention?" She laughed and for a second forgot they were no longer a couple. "It's not like he doesn't get enough as it is."

"Yes, but with Chris," Tony said, "some of that is bad." Rachel readily agreed. Her brother had single-handedly alienated tourists since he took office. Chris couldn't be responsible for the entire downturn in the city's economy, but he'd been forthright about what he termed "ugly tourists."

"He could be antagonizing," she replied, not realizing she'd used the past tense.

"Call me if I can be of help. I'm sure he'll turn up, raising hell." Tony's words were reassuring but Rachel feared they didn't ring true.

"Thanks for calling."

"You okay?" Chloe asked, squeezing her hand.

"Yeah, life sure sucks sometimes." The tears were clogging up her sinuses but she refused to allow them out.

"I'd have to second that." Chloe averted her face to give Rachel time to recover. "Some good news; Logan called earlier. He wants to take you to dinner. Why don't you give him a call? An evening out would do you a world of good."

* * *

They met at an out of the way restaurant on the south side. It could be difficult to avoid a gossip-hungry entertainment media even in Santa Fe. Home to many celebrities, the local citizenry accepted them, but there was always time to fill on the insatiable cable entertainment shows.

Rachel ordered fajitas while Logan requested an uninspiring dinner of grilled chicken. "I've got to do a love scene tomorrow," he explained. "I don't want to run off the leading lady."

"Any news on Chris?" he asked.

"No. He seems to have vanished without a trace, as they say in the movies." She tried for a laugh. The stress of his disappearance was beginning to weigh on her. At first, she'd thought it was all a stupid joke. At this point she knew different.

"I believe he'll show up," Logan said, placing his hand over hers.

"I hope it's in one piece." Rachel nearly choked on her words. Maybe that was why she didn't see it coming. The flash caught them off guard, as intended.

"Angelique!" Rachel demanded. "Cut it out!" Angelique Dupré fancied herself a real Hollywood-style gossip columnist. She wasn't the least bit concerned about her image, stooping to ambush attacks, confrontations, and surveillance bordering on stalking. When her career as a big-time journalist failed due to her objectionable tactics, Angelique moved from New York to Los Angeles where she took up "entertainment news." Santa Fe had the misfortune of claiming her as, one would hope, a temporary resident.

"Married actor seen in the company of a recently divorced reporter? Makes a catchy headline, don't you think, Rachel?" Angelique wore enough makeup to give any supermodel a run for her eyelashes. The woman, a vile member of journalism, was just the kind of writer who gave all the rest a bad name. "Shouldn't you be at home brooding about your long lost brother? It doesn't seem fitting to be out on the town when some awful thing has happened to our poor mayor."

"Angelique," Rachel paused tiredly, "how nice to see you. Is haunting back in fashion?"

"Oh, Rachel, aren't you always the amusing one?" Angelique's teased and lacquered hair moved in tandem with her head. "Care to give me a quote?"

Logan was still smiling pleasantly, but Rachel detected a hint of anger in his eyes. She had to think of something fast or Angelique would fabricate to her heart's content.

"I'm interviewing Mr. Masters for *High Desert Country*." She pulled out her reporter's notebook and laid it on the table. Quick thinking under these circumstances was a gift from the gods.

"That doesn't explain the hand-holding," the boorish woman insisted.

"Of course not, Angelique," Rachel smiled, "but Mr. Masters heard about my brother's quandary. He was comforting me. Our dinners have arrived. Might we eat them in peace?"

Angelique smiled slyly, as one does when hearing bullshit. "Well, I guess that's better than nothing. Be good, you two." She was gone like the wicked old witch.

Logan winced. "That picture will be in the papers tomorrow?"

"'Fraid so," Rachel said. "You might want to prepare yourself for the possibility of it appearing in more westerly publications as well. Angelique is a bitch, and she always gets her man."

"Thanks for the warning," Logan said. "Do you still feel like eating?"

"Sure, she's gone."

"Good, because I have something to tell you."

"Sounds serious," Rachel responded. "Is it?"

"It's about the attorney found dead at Pueblo Blanco."

Yes?"

"The name sounded familiar," Logan elaborated. "Last night I did some checking. He was the front man when I invested in the development. Real fast-talker, but seemed to have his facts in order. Quite a few others from the entertainment industry also invested through him by way of their attorneys. My lawyer couldn't find anything untoward so I went ahead. Nevertheless, there's going to be a lot of people hurt, in the pocketbook, if this turns out to be murder. Not to be unkind, but stocks could fall overnight, a frenzied sale could result, and the whole thing could go down the tubes."

Rachel knew he was right.

CHAPTER 41

By morning, shit hit the fan. Angelique's column appeared on the front page of the arts section, above the fold. Rachel studied it over Chloe's shoulder at the kitchen counter. The photo showed Logan smiling tenderly at Rachel. The camera caught his hand over hers.

"Gosh, Rachel, the picture's not bad and she spelled your name right." Chloe teased. "Can't ask for more."

"How about the truth?"

"No one wants that. How 'bout I read you the story?"

"Can I stop you?"

Chloe smiled.

"'Logan Masters, star of the popular *Jake Weathers* television show, was seen at a Santa Fe hot spot last evening with writer Rachel Blackstone. Blackstone is a reporter for *High Desert Country*, and is estranged from her husband, well-known film producer Anthony Blackstone. Her brother, Santa Fe mayor Christian Woods, was reported missing when his car was found north of the city near a wilderness area. Although Blackstone's comments indicated she and Masters are strictly business associates, a picture tells a thousand words. Surely, Mrs. Logan Masters won't miss the hand-holding. Blackstone says the actor was comforting her on the disappearance of her brother. Time will tell.'"

Chloe finished and couldn't help but add, "She spelled all the words right."

"Yeah, Angelique is journalism at its finest."

"I know all you need is more bad news, but the story has already been broadcast on *E!*"

"The cable channel?" Rachel asked, disbelieving. "How could they have gotten it so soon? Never mind. I know the answer to that. Her blog. Not so much as an editor to keep her in check. That woman is such a pisser."

"She's got balls all right. I can't forgive her for doing this while Chris is . . . gone," Chloe said. "Her timing could have been kinder."

"Nuts to her," Rachel said. "I'm going to work. Julian's got several new stories for me. Maybe interviews will take my mind off everything."

When she reached the office, there were three reporters hanging out in the courtyard. Dave Marks approached her first, "Rachel, I'm sorry; you know I'm only doing my job. Will you give me a comment?" Dave was an okay guy. Rachel knew him to be an accurate, compassionate writer. She knew why he was here. He had to be.

"Regarding Ms. Dupré's column this morning," she began. "I am writing a story about Logan Masters and the series he's filming outside of Santa Fe."

"Thanks," Dave said. "What about the hand-holding allegation? The two of you have been seen at several locations around town. Is there anything to that?"

The other two reporters were scribbling in their notebooks; one, a woman from a local New Age publication. Rachel couldn't imagine why they would be interested. The other, a man she had never seen before.

"Mr. Masters heard about my brother—Mayor Woods—and was being kind."

"There's nothing more to it than that?" the unknown reporter asked?

"Who are you?" Rachel demanded. "Who are you with?"

"Sly Barrington, freelancer to the stars." When he smiled, his mouth twitched giving him a sinister look.

Ugh. Barrington was a bounty hunter, at least as she used the term—and he had changed his name to reflect the way he saw himself. Rachel knew of him, and his deplorable accomplishments. He freelanced for the muckraking tabloids. He'd helped ruin more than one Hollywood match. He seemed happy in his own skin even though it was likely to shed at any moment.

"Isn't it true, that you and Masters met at a private residence the other day?"

"I don't know you," Rachel said calmly. "I'm not answering your questions." She made herself walk slowly the few remaining steps to the front door. The urge to run was powerful, but she resisted.

"That must be some interview you're doing with Masters." Barrington wasn't about to let it go. "Must be in-depth reporting. Huh, Blackstone?"

He was still shouting rude questions as she closed the door, resisting the impulse to slam it. That would only add fuel to his story.

Rachel had no respect for people like him and couldn't understand why they thought it was acceptable to behave in such a manner. The average marriage had a 50/50 survival rate, but those born of Tinsel Town had virtually no chance of making it.

"Want me to run them off?" Julian said. He sat in the waiting area conversing with Stella. "Better yet, let Stella get rid of them. She's scarier than I am."

Stella glared at him in the familiar way she always did; part reproach, part adoration.

"No thanks," Rachel said. "Gives me something to do later."

"Interesting reading in the paper this morning," Julian said. "Did you happen to see the arts section, Stella?"

"I did."

"I would have sworn Rachel was in that picture."

"Dead ringer, all right." Stella was enjoying herself as much as Julian.

"Very amusing," Rachel replied. "First I have to deal with Angelique, the charming welcoming committee outside, then jokers at work. I'm truly blessed."

"Adultery is never funny!" John stated as he marched through the office and their conversation. Julian's smile faded. Rachel looked across the room at Shorty who was finding it difficult not to strangle on his morning bear claw.

"I hear there's a nice little place just waiting for you to move in," Stella changed the subject, completely ignoring the nephew's intrusion.

"You've been talking to Chloe again?" Rachel said.

"Good real estate information is hard to find," Stella said.

"Not to mention good gossip," Rachel said.

"That too." Stella smiled sweetly.

Rachel wished she could enjoy the good-natured ribbing more, but with Chris missing in action, it was difficult. Doubtless, she could add homewrecker to her resume, right next to breaking and entering—and raising the dead.

CHAPTER 42

The cat lounged in one of the patio chairs when Rachel arrived that evening, food in hand. Her ears pricked forward as Rachel came around the corner of the house. "I feed you once and already you're taking me for granted." At the sound of her voice, the tortie stretched and bounded from the chair. She reached the food bowl before the first hard nugget hit the bottom of the dish. "I see you enjoyed yesterday's serving," Rachel commented on the empty bowl.

She squatted and gently stroked the coat of many colors. "So what have you been up to?" The only answer was crunching. "I see, had a full day, did you? Got a stomping ground around the neighborhood?" The tail twitched happily. "Do me a favor, don't be a pest to the neighbors, 'cause I'm about to move in here." She gave the cat another pat and rose to leave. "See you *mañana*."

Before she could walk away, the cat stopped eating and laid her ears flat. Rachel took a step backward, afraid she had provoked it. As she watched the cat, the hair on its back and tail stood up. Her eyes widened and she hissed loudly. "What is it, sweetie? Did I do something wrong?" Then she recognized the odor. Rachel ran around to the gate, wanting to keep Mario away from the cat. He was there.

"What do you want?" she demanded, stopping as she rounded the corner of the house. Deep shade next to the house made her feel more frightened. There was only one way out of the walled backyard. Through the gate Mario blocked. There appeared to be no escape from the problem she'd created.

"Being human is such as drag." Had she heard the words or received them directly in her mind?

"Surely, there's a point to that statement." What a prick, dead or not.

"My dear Rachel, of course there's a point," his voice hostile.

Even ghosts get pissed off she thought. Good. "Notice how people, the living, need proof of everything?" He said. "That's why there are so many tests, to prove we know something. And court-rooms, to prove guilt or innocence. In the case of kidnapping, people want proof of that too."

"And?" She waited.

His body materialized in its hydrous form. It continually shifted as though static electricity energized its parts. Mario's eyes were so penetrating she feared he could read her thoughts.

"I arranged for a little gift to be delivered to your friend's house. Ms. Valdez is a very attractive woman. Nice house too. I think she was a little upset by the parcel."

"I swear, if you've hurt her . . ."

"You'll do what? Call the police? Send me back? It was only stupid luck you brought me here, fooling around with things you know nothing about. Do you really think you could say 'abracadab-ra' and I would—poof—vanish?" He snapped his fingers, but they didn't make a sound.

This was a conversation she didn't want to pursue. Unques-tionably, she felt she could not send him back. What had made her think this nightmare would ever be over?

"I'd like to leave now," she demanded.

"Oh, did the big, bad ghost scare the little human?" Mario's voice fairly gushed with mockery. Rachel's stomach felt queasy. The odor seemed to get worse every time she encountered him.

"Don't you want to know about my gift?" he asked.

"I'm sure you'll tell me when you get around to it."

"I hear your brother, the good mayor, is missing."

"What!" Suddenly, this skirmish was beginning to take on an even more ominous tone.

"It's a shame, things like this are commonplace." If he were alive, he'd be picking lint from his clothing, he was that nonchalant.

"What do you know about it?"

"That's why I sent the present, so you'd know what I know."

"And that is exactly what? Is he okay? He's not . . . ?" She couldn't bring herself to finish the question.

"Your brother's all tied up." Mario laughed. The sound made Rachel wince.

"What do you mean; tied up?"

"He's been detained, Rachel." It was the timbre used with a small child who refused to pay attention. "You might even say kidnapped, though of course, he's no kid."

"Who took him? Why didn't you tell me sooner?" Her voice was sounded shrill even to her. "Valuable time had been lost."

"Whoa, slow down, it's hard to process that many questions at once." Mario's face betrayed his words. He toyed with her.

"Mario," she said with uncharacteristic vehemence, "you were his friend. How can you withhold facts that could lead to his rescue?" She was unprepared for his laughter. His sick delight at her brother's quandary released the putrid odor of the dead. She recoiled several steps, covered her mouth with her hand trying to repress the nausea. His image shook in evil mirth. Rachel wanted to run, far away, but there was nowhere to go Mario couldn't follow.

He stopped laughing as if the joke hadn't been funny. "Your brother, my friend? The fine mayor of Santa Fe doesn't know the first thing about friendship or loyalty. He was willing to leave me high and dry before my untimely demise. Now he's learning about these things first hand."

"Are you saying you've kidnapped Chris?" She couldn't believe it.

"No, I'm incapable of doing anything so mundane. But I still have, hmm, friends would be too strong a word, but associates might fit the bill."

"Where is he?" Rachel insisted. The situation was all too clear. Mario had somehow abducted Chris, or had someone else do it. How could she have ever been so stupid? She'd made the assumption they were friends. They were together all the time. What did that make them—partners? In what?

"Oh my dear, don't strain your pretty head. I'll give you some clues. He's tied up and he's high and dry, at least for now. Soon he'll wish the monsoon would come again. Maybe some snow will fall and he can melt it on his tongue."

"Mario, what are you talking about?" she pleaded.

"Goodbye for now." Mario's likeness seemed to crumble, but instead of the pieces falling they evaporated along with the stench.

"Wait! Where is he? Damn!" Rachel was alone, except for the hissing cat.

The tortie, swollen twice her size, hissed again. Rachel, afraid to approach her, took slow steps and spoke soothing words. By the time she reached her, she began to calm. "Are you okay?" She hesitated to get within reach of those claws. The cat raced up the nearest tree where she sat on a large branch, her tail twitching frantically.

"I guess you're okay." She would have to be, because Rachel had to get to Chloe.

CHAPTER 43

An anxious Chloe waited for Rachel. Her hair was in disarray from nervously running her hands through it.

"Where have you been?" Chloe said with distress. "I've been trying to reach you." Chloe paced the foyer. "You've got to get a fucking cell phone!"

"I stopped by the house to feed the cat when unexpected company arrived, Mario. Then there was an accident on Peralta. I had to take Palace and come in the back way. Oh, never mind," she said breathlessly. "What is this about a delivery? Mario said it had something to do with Chris."

"A man came by an hour ago and left this. He insisted I open it. Look." Chloe held out the plain manila envelope.

Inside was a gold wristwatch with a black face. Rachel turned over the watch, but she knew what the inscription said because she chose the words herself: "For Chris, From Sis." Not all that clever, but it amused her at the time.

"He's got him."

"Who? Mario?"

"I think somehow Mario has kidnapped Chris."

"But he's not alive. How could he have done it?"

"I don't know, but he was at my . . . the house. He knew about Chris' disappearance. He admitted he couldn't do the abducting himself, but alluded to 'associates.'"

"What are we going to do? We can't call the police. They'd never believe us." Chloe dragged both hands through her hair, pulling it back from her face. It immediately fell softly down again. "What about a priest? Could a priest get rid of him?"

"I don't know," Rachel said. "Let's sit down. I need to think."

"You can't think standing?"

"I'm too worn out to pace." Rachel walked through the house to the deck. There she lowered herself slowly into one of the wicker chairs. Chloe sat across from her on a bench, elbows on her knees.

"I thought Mario and Chris were friends?"

"Me too. That's why I came flying back to Santa Fe. I figured Mario would go to someone or somewhere he knew. Of course, there are any number of definitions for the word 'friend.' I never knew why they hung out together. I thought Chris was keeping bad company. It occurred to me he might be cruising along the fringe of the law, but I didn't think he'd actually cross the line."

"You do now?"

"It's the way this thing is falling in place." She related the story Betsy told about making the deliveries for Chris at the farmers market. "He was definitely using the girl. I just can't figure out why. Why would he need this service performed by someone other than a messenger?"

"Something to hide?"

"You betchy. But what?"

"Look," Chloe said, "we both know Chris can't find his ass with both hands. Maybe he got caught up in something through ignorance rather than premeditation."

Rachel couldn't help but smile. That was Chloe, always there to give perspective or reassurance. "Thanks, but you know my brother's a scumbag."

"Yeah, maybe, but he's not in Mario's league," Chloe said. "Even if Mario managed to hide his true character in life, he's been abundantly clear in death. He's despicable. But is there anything we can do about it?"

"At the risk of repeating myself," Rachel said, "I don't know." She dropped her hands in her lap in defeat.

"How about going at this in another direction," Chloe said thoughtfully. "What do we know?"

"We know that Mario is here, whatever his status," Rachel replied. "Chris is gone and Mario claims to have had something to do with his disappearance."

"And we know that Chris enlisted a pretty city employee to make handoffs to a man who remains unidentified."

"Chloe, what did the man look like today, the one who left Chris' watch?"

"Hmm. Good looking, middle-aged guy wearing a baseball cap and shades."

"Anyone you know?" Rachel asked.

"Nope," Chloe considered. "Wait a minute. I thought at the time we'd met, but he said no, he would remember."

"How was he dressed?"

"Well," Chloe mulled, "he wore jeans and some kind of plaid shirt. He was in shape."

"Shit nothing. I'm beginning to think we don't know much."

"There's one more thing," Chloe said. "The man found dead at Pueblo Blanco was the attorney the developers used to negotiate with investors."

"Yeah, Logan mentioned it. When I called his office, he wouldn't talk to me and his secretary refused to acknowledge any involvement with the development."

"There's more to his death than made print," Chloe said. "An associate told me all his body hair was white."

"And that means?" Rachel asked.

"According to my friend who has connections at the coroner's office, there was nothing to indicate the man's death was murder: no wounds, bruises, poison, drugs, you name it. But when he left home the morning of his death, his hair was brown."

"Geez Chloe, are you saying he was scared to death?"

"My thoughts," Chloe said. "Who do we know who could pull that off?"

"Mario!"

"And that brings us back to the mayoral office," Chloe said. "Would Chris have anything to do with Pueblo Blanco?"

"He's always in front of a camera where the city and money are involved. Anything that feeds the city coffers, except tourism, gets Chris' enthusiastic support.

"As far as the development goes," Rachel continued, "that's up to the planning commission. The mayor doesn't do the approval of such projects. I'd bet on one thing, if that company's a dummy, any evidence to connect that attorney has been buried by now."

"That leaves us with questions." Chloe shivered. The sun had gone down during their conversation and the temp was dropping. A phone rang inside and Chloe left to answer it.

"Rach," she called. "Telephone for you; says her name is Betsy." Chloe stood at the kitchen bar, her hand covering the mouthpiece.

Rachel snatched the phone. "Betsy, what is it?"

"I can't believe it," she said excitedly.

"What's that?"

"I saw him."

"Who?"

"The guy. You know, who met me, the one I gave the envelopes to."

* * *

Chris had no idea how long he'd been here. It seemed like days. He felt wretched. His hands and feet were bound; his eyes, blindfolded. Efforts to dislodge the sticky duct tape from his eyes had not paid off. And, he'd lost hair in the process, his eyebrows too.

His hands had been securely tied in front. He'd been able to relieve himself but not from a standing position, necessitating a steady movement backward to avoid the flow. It wouldn't be a problem again if he didn't get something to drink. Dehydration was imminent. Even his eyes were dry beneath the tape.

The air felt cool. It was night or he lay in shade. At first he thought it all a dream but the constraints were real. So were the rocks scattered beneath him. He sensed an enclosure of some kind. Everything hurt from his attempts to thwart the damn bindings.

His head ached and he felt groggy. He remembered drinking with the young city clerk. This felt like more than just too much booze. Whoever had taken him had drugged him.

The last thing he remembered was a meeting with Mario, but that had to be a dream, because Mario died months ago. Yet, even through the haze, it seemed real. They'd been talking about hell—an odd subject.

No one had come around since he regained consciousness: Nothing but quiet, broken occasionally by the sound of birds, a breeze, or the rustling of his discontent.

CHAPTER 44

T hanks to Betsy, Rachel knew where the mystery man was. The woman had become an ally. When leaving work she noticed the man she'd met at the market. He was going into one of the downtown motels, not to be confused with some of the grandiose, excessively priced hotels that catered to visitors with more *dinero* than sense.

Rachel alerted Chloe of the need for a stakeout. "Give me fifteen minutes." Chloe rushed to her bedroom. In fewer than ten minutes she reappeared dressed entirely in black. The skintight leather pants looked great on her, and she'd topped them off with a silk blouse and wool jacket. Her feet were ensconced in boots with two-inch heels. She cut a dashing figure. Rachel doubted any self-respecting private eye would be caught dead, or any other way, dressed to the teeth for what might be hours of boring car sitting, but this was Chloe.

"That was very fast for you," Rachel said as she crammed some candy bars in one denim jacket pocket and a can of Coke in the other. At that moment a car pulled into the driveway.

"That's why I needed the extra five minutes." Chloe hurried outside. Rachel left through the back door and climbed into the Merc. Moments later, Chloe slid in beside her with a huge picnic basket. The brass tag on the wooden handle read, "Gourmet Grub Shoppe."

"Okay, ready," she said.

"Uh Chloe, stakeouts are supposed to be long and boring, interrupted by junk food or a suspect sighting."

"Well, that's just stupid," Chloe said. "It's never bad timing for good food."

It was hard to argue with Chloe. In fact, Rachel tried not to because her friend was a good debater. She could always sneak a candy bar later.

Downtown Rachel parallel parked across from the motel Betsy said she saw the man enter. She'd even thought to notice the room number, 204. Only a couple of these types of motels remained. Most had been converted to high-end joints. But these accommodations had their purpose too: Quick and dirty.

"Gee, Rachel, he must not have much class. Do you know what this place is? Yuck."

"Chloe, dear friend, your world is a bit on the sheltered side."

"I'm not sure we're even safe on this street. Are you certain you want to do this?"

"Don't worry, if anyone messes with us we can always hit them over the head with," she opened the lid of the basket, "champagne?" Rachel laughed until her eyes began to tear, remembering to keep watch on Room 204 in between wipes. Chloe sat across from her with a stern look, unable to believe Rachel's lack of decorum. That made Rachel laugh all the harder.

"Do we have that out of our system?" Chloe asked with reproach. It only set off another stream of hysterics. "Really, Rachel, you could be grateful I think of your health. You'd eat nothing but green chile cheese burritos if I didn't step in now and then to see to it you got a proper meal." She removed clear plastic dishes in various sizes filled with fruit, Camembert, salad niçoise, quiche a la Southwest and crème brûlée. A crusty baguette rounded out the feast. By the time everything was laid out across the dash, Rachel's books, maps, parking tickets, and gum wrappers had to go. She gathered these items and threw them on the floor in back. "I'll have your car detailed for your birthday," Chloe said.

The comment pissed off Rachel for a moment, but she decided to let it ricochet from her sleeve. Yes, her car was trashed, but that way no one wanted to steal it and she could find everything.

Instead, "My birthday was two months ago."

"How about Christmas?"

While Rachel was trying to think of a good retort, the door to Room 204 opened. "Look," she touched Chloe's arm. A well-dressed woman stepped out in high heels, her skirt swirling around her legs in the evening breeze. For warmth she wore a fur wrap. Over her arm, hung a large designer purse or good replicate.

"Lawdy," Chloe exclaimed, "is that a prostitute?"

"More likely a call girl."

"Isn't that splitting hairs, Rach?"

"See that bag and the chic clothing?"

"And, how would you know about such things?" Chloe asked.

"Not everything that happens in Vegas, stays in Vegas."

"I've been there several times," Chloe said. "How come I don't know about it?"

"Perhaps we observe different things," Rachel pointed out. Chloe likely hadn't noticed the pornography littering the streets either. Rachel did a lot of walking when she traveled. Chloe was more the cab or limo type.

"You know," Chloe said. "I hear they take credit cards. Bet she uses the Square card reader that hooks up to your phone."

"What's a Square?" Rachel asked.

"Uh, you'd probably have to have a cell phone to know."

"Oh what have we here?" Rachel said.

A man pulled the door closed joining the woman on the second floor walkway. He massaged the woman's chest for a brief moment. She backed away from him, said something, and left. "Guess he didn't pay for anything extra," Rachel observed.

It angered him and he made an unfriendly gesture the woman couldn't see.

"That damn-son-of-a-bitch-bastard-slut!" Chloe exclaimed.

"Slut?"

"I was running low on expletives," she explained. "Do you recognize him?"

"Not yet. Wish there was more light."

He stood on the landing until the lady of the night became a part of it. Taking the stairs two at a time, he reached the parking lot, pulled out a pack of cigarettes and lit up. After a long draw he walked through the cluster of parked cars, and stepped off the curb under a street light.

"Holy shit," Rachel said with satisfaction. "That's the connection we needed."

CHAPTER 45

S leep had been fitful for Chris. No match for the duct tape, he remained bound, gagged, and in horrible discomfort. It was night. His efforts to remove the tape from his head had at least allowed him to discern daylight or darkness, but time was out of reach. Even if he could contort enough to see it, he thought his watch missing, either that or his wrists had gone numb.

Footsteps dislodged rocks and shale. His sense of hearing had sharpened. He detected only one person. The odor of hamburgers preceded him. Chris' mouth watered with anticipation. He was hungry. Surely no one would feed him just prior to killing him, unless the murderer liked to eat afterwards.

Light flooded his prison. The lantern made scraping sounds as it was placed on the uneven floor. He remained still. Someone roughly grabbed his arm, and pulled him to a sitting position, pushing his back against cool stone.

"Mr. Mayor," the man said, "got a little something for you to sign."

Chris tried to question, but the gag stopped his words. A fingernail gouged his cheek and the tape ripped from his mouth. Chris feared his flesh had come off with it. He raised his bound hands to rub the raw skin around his mouth. "Who are you?" he said through dry lips. "Why am I here?"

"Who I am is of no importance to you. You're here because you got greedy. We're about to fix that." He shoved a pen in Chris' hand and placed a paper on his thigh. His hand was positioned on the document. "Sign," the man said gruffly.

"What the hell?" The cuff against the side of his head was so brutal the words were knocked from his mouth. For a moment Chris thought he would pass out.

"Smell good?" The hamburger shoved beneath his nose made him ravenous. Chris nodded, afraid to speak. "If you want to eat, you have to sign."

"Yes, I want to eat." The pen was replaced and his hand re-positioned. "What am I signing?"

"I see we have to take it from the top." The blow tore through his head. He struck the other side on the wall of his dungeon, causing another explosion in his skull. This time it was accompanied by nausea. Chris fought the wave that threatened to dehydrate him further. It was the only battle he would win.

"I'll sign it," he mumbled. He scribbled his signature.

"Here's a bottle of water." It slammed against his leg. Something landed lightly on the floor across the chamber. He hoped it was the hamburger. With that, his tormenter left.

CHAPTER 46

At 9 a.m., Rachel and Chloe swept through the door at *High Desert Country*. "Hi, Stella," Rachel said. "Is Julian in?"

"He sure is. Hi, Chloe, it's good to see you."

"The feeling's mutual. How's life treating you?"

"Can't complain. How's the real estate business?"

Not one to spend a lot of time with preliminaries, Rachel was about to jump from her skin. "You're both fantastic and in good health," she gushed. "Can Julian see us?"

Stella gave her a sigh indicting Rachel should stop and smell the roses. "Shall I buzz him or would you prefer to walk the fifteen feet to his door and ask him yourself?" Stella and Chloe exchanged smiles.

"I'll stick my head in the door," Rachel said.

"Don't leave it in there. Can't find anything in that office as it is," Stella replied in a stern tone.

"Hilarious," Rachel quipped over her shoulder.

Julian tried hard to stifle a smile, having overheard the exchange in the outer office. "Losing your head again, Rachel?"

"Is everyone in this office a wannabe stand up?"

"Everyone but John-Boy." She guessed Julian didn't care for his kin.

"Chloe," Julian exclaimed. "What a nice surprise. It's been ages. I'd ask how you are, but Rachel obviously has something on her mind. Would you like to sit down?"

Chloe breezed past her and took the only chair not occupied by stuff. Rachel moved the pile of papers from the other chair. There was some dust on the seat, but she didn't bother to brush it off. Her jeans were well-worn.

"So," Julian began, "what's up?"

"Remember I told you there was something fishy going on at the Pueblo Blanco development?" Rachel began.

"I do recall your mention of said development."

"I was right." She ignored his legalese response. "We did some digging at the city offices this morning. Chloe, that part's your gig. Go ahead."

"You might remember, Julian," Chloe began, "another developer tried to build something on that same plat. I didn't know why the plans fell through. There can be many reasons: easements, soil problems, even endangered species issues."

"Tell me there's a blue mountain pipsqueak that held up the project," he said. "I'll thank it personally for stopping the overdevelopment of Santa Fe."

Rachel snickered. It was funnier when at someone else's expense. Chloe continued her explanation.

"In this case it appears there was a soil problem. According to the records, the development is in danger of being washed all the way to the Rio Grande when the next flash flood occurs."

"Geez, you're saying the houses wouldn't stop until they found themselves bobbing in Cochiti Lake?" he asked.

"Pretty much."

"Then the development may be a scam?" Julian asked.

"Possibly," Rachel said. "There are a lot of upscale folks: celebrities, CEOs, socialites, who have invested money in the project, many of whom don't plan to live there."

"She's right," Chloe said. "There must be several hundred investors. The promoters billed it as even more exclusive than Wilderness Gate. The press reports indicated they were looking to counteract the economic downturn by luring big money back to town."

"It might be as significant as the Homestake oil swindle that occurred in Oklahoma during the early 1970s," Rachel added. "There were hundreds of people taken in by that deal. The promoter was a smooth-talking, pinstripe suit who appeared to be legit, but was actually perpetrating a classic Ponzi scheme. The losses were in the tens of millions."

"That brings us to the big question," Julian rubbed his beard. "How has that development been allowed to continue? Someone had to falsify documents, pull strings or call in favors to get this by the planning commission."

"That's where I think my brother comes in."

"The mayor?"

"'Fraid so." Rachel said. In solving this puzzle, she feared it might put her brother behind bars.

"What do you think he's done?" Julian prompted.

"He had an affair with a young clerk in the planning office. When he disappeared," she choked a bit, "this girl called me. It seems she made special deliveries for Chris. Now," she added quickly, "we don't know this was anything illegal. The clerk didn't look inside the packages, but since she was instructed to meet a man at a busy place, the farmers' market, it likely wasn't aboveboard."

"Particularly after last night," Chloe interjected. The stakeout had proved a memorable evening for her friend.

"The woman called me last night," Rachel resumed the dialogue. "She told me the man she'd met was at one of the downtown motels—you know the ones." Julian nodded. "Well, we parked outside." She paused. Would Julian buy it?

"And?" he cued.

"It was Alexander Robbins, the guy I interviewed at Pueblo Blanco."

"I see."

"It gets worse," Chloe said. "A friend in the know said the cause of death on the man found at the development was officially listed as a heart attack. But get this; his hair was completely drained of color. It's possible he was literally scared to death."

"You're saying this incident is tied to the possible swindle?"

"Julian, he was the attorney for the development. Chloe ran across his name while talking with a client. I tried to contact him for a comment, but got the brush-off. Chloe suspects the company is a shell. If that's true, the instigators may remain undisclosed."

"You think the organizers killed the man?" Julian asked.

"Could be, but why?" Rachel said. "Every time we answer one question, another raises its ugly head."

"The note you received, and the bombing here at the magazine, was intended to scare you," Julian said with resignation.

"I suspect the speeding car that killed poor Abe was too," Rachel said, feeling solemn. "Maybe the plan was to run me down, but the bad guys weren't counting on little Davy being in the way. We were all trying to save him." Tears filled her eyes. Chloe slipped her a tissue. They were quiet for a few minutes.

"Rachel," Julian asked gently, "how do you think your brother is involved?"

"I can't be sure he is. He's always lived in grey areas. I think he's been marginally over the line of the law before."

"What can I do to help?" Julian asked.

"I want your opinion as a former investigative reporter and as a friend," Rachel said.

"The reporter in me is screaming S-T-O-R-Y," Julian said. "You know *High Desert* isn't the right type of publication for breaking news. The managing editor at the *New Mexican* is a friend of mine. He might be interested. Or the *Journal* in A-B-Q, since your father wrote for them.

"As your friend, I'm concerned you may end up in trouble if you don't back off, but then I've never known you to do that," Julian leaned back, hands behind his head as he often did when considering options. "I think you should tell the story."

Rachel had been listening intently to Julian, so she wasn't certain when she first noticed Mario close by.

She rose abruptly, before Julian became aware. "Thank you, Julian. I appreciate you listening."

"My pleasure. It was good to see you again, Chloe."

Once outside Chloe touched her friend's arm. "Did you smell it?"

"Yes," Rachel replied. "Why would Mario care about our conversation?"

Chloe sighed. "So many questions, so little time."

CHAPTER 47

Rachel spent the rest of the day keeping company with her laptop, writing the story of Pueblo Blanco as she wanted to tell it, leaving out all ghostly references. She was tired. It was the good kind of tired, brought on by a productive day. She would drop the CD containing the manuscript by the *New Mexican* in the morning. Julian's friend had agreed to read it.

She walked along Chloe's deck, watching the mountains go to sleep, listening to her lug soles making soft thumps on the planks.

Rachel gently pulled back a branch and stepped into the clearing where she had confronted Mario. The ashes of the sage remained, waiting for the right amount of wind or rain to brush them to the earth. She sat on a large rock, leaning into the arms of a 100-year-old piñon, and let the dusk surround her. With her eyes closed, she could almost forget the upheaval of her life.

How she wanted to feel normal again, whatever that would be. A new start as her own person, as opposed to being someone's daughter or wife, would be exciting and daunting. She looked forward to moving into her house, if only everything wrong would right itself.

Suddenly aware her solitude was being invaded, she rose to her feet. Every muscle and fiber in her body was taut with anticipation. Rachel turned slowly, scanning the hillside for a glimpse of Mario.

"Behind you, bitch."

His inflection had changed. Where he had always been unpleasant and sardonic, he seemed full of anger tonight. Gooseflesh
pebbled Rachel's skin. She tried to hide her fear and turned to face
him.

"What do you want this time?" Her own voice amazed her as
she unconsciously meted out an equally angry response.

"You are a very stubborn woman." His face wavered in the
half-mortal, half-supernatural way she had come to expect. "You
have been warned several times and yet you continue to meddle."

"In what?" she demanded to know."What is it that you think
I'm meddling in?"

"Your failure to heed warnings has resulted in others dying."
Mario's eyes were black as soot. There was no mistaking his words.
"Don't publish the article. If you do, next time death may come to
someone close to you."

"What article? I don't know what you're talking about. I must
have a dozen stories in the works."

"It's a shame you worked so diligently today. It must not be
published. It could spoil my plans."

"The Pueblo Blanco story? Why do you care about what happens with that development?"

"That is my concern," Mario fairly roared.

"You're threatening people I love, yet you aren't going to tell
me why? Whatever's going on at Pueblo Blanco may involve Chris,
but I'm willing to write it anyway. What difference could it possibly
make to you?"

"Just like your father." It was aimed to hurt. The mention of
her dad by Mario left Rachel reeling. Trying to recover, she
searched her mind's vast data base in an effort to understand what
Mario's statement meant. She groped through for an explanation,
and found none.

She looked for a way out, but no person could outrun or hide
from a ghoul. Grief spread throughout her as she wondered if
Mario had murdered her father.

"Did you kill my father?" There, she finally said it. She needed
confirmation.

When Mario spoke it was no longer with his voice, but that of
another. Rachel took two involuntary steps backward. She knew

this person. How could it be? There are those who believe more than one spirit can inhabit a metaphysical being. One could be virtuous and the other wicked. She longed to look into his face, but was afraid to do so.

"Did you hear me?" it spoke, and kindness flowed with the words.

"Yes Dad." Rachel fought back tears.

"It's all right to look at me," her father said. She was still afraid. It could be another horrible trick by Mario. He would be pleased at her pain.

"Have you noticed?" he said. "The stench of Mario is gone. What has taken its place?"

Rachel inhaled tentatively. The odor she had come to fear was gone. In its place was one more familiar, a happy memory. She closed her eyes and sighed. Her senses were flooded with childhood hugs from her dad, wrapped in Old Spice. When he was off working on a story, Rachel would think of him at sea experiencing high adventures. He was an old-fashioned kind of man when it came to the basics. His drink was bourbon—straight up. Yet, he always remembered candy for his kids on Valentine's Day. As a man and journalist, he was principled.

She lifted her face to see him, braced for a sick joke. But it was not a trick. He looked very much as she remembered, except there were no lacerations from the accident that took his life. Rachel still had nightmares from identifying his body. Her brother hadn't been "available." Although his reflection had the same swimming effect she'd witnessed with Mario, his was full of light and love.

"How . . . ?" Rachel was overcome with happiness but caution would not let her be euphoric. This wasn't real. But he understood her question without her stating it.

"When you called me back," he said, "I didn't want to come. I know that sounds heartless, because you are still earthbound. But once you've left, it is indescribably, by human standards, beautiful and serene. One simply has no desire to return.

"But Mario is a vengeful spirit and has found no joy in death. Because you opened the way and because he and I were connected in life, he was able to push through."

Rachel could not believe what she was hearing. "So why are you here," she said, hurt, "if you didn't want to come back?"

"Mario is dangerous. I came to help you, but I am not as strong as he is, therefore I cannot offer you absolute protection. I have tried many times to move him aside and speak to you, but not until you asked him if he killed me did his power diminish enough for me to show myself. I haven't much time. His potency is strengthening as we speak. That is why you must listen to me. Mario cannot return to his death unless you make him. You must not allow him to remain here. It is not his place. He will continue to cause harm." Her father's last few words sounded tired.

"Please, Dad, don't go."

"I have no choice. And I may not be able to talk with you again. You must send him back."

"But how?" Rachel cried, wiping tears from her face. She was five years old again. Instead of her father fixing this he was telling her she had to do it herself.

"Call upon all your strengths. You must want him to return as much as you wanted to see me."

"I don't understand. What strengths?"

"You have friends, some are no longer here, but they have great power and wisdom. What you cannot do yourself, they can help you with." She leaned forward to hear. His voice was fading. He spoke once more. "I love you. Love yourself. You can do anything." A sound like the opening of a vacuum seal followed his words. He was gone. Rachel found herself on her knees in the dark, alone, consumed with anguish and confusion.

How could she put the genie back in the bottle?

CHAPTER 48

Rachel burst through the kitchen door, gasping for air.

"What in hell?" Chloe exclaimed, dropping her box of takeout.

"Mario," she panted, "he threatened to hurt someone close to me."

"Why? What's his problem?"

Rachel staggered to the *banco,* which ran the perimeter of the kitchen table, and flopped down on the padded bench. "He doesn't want me to publish the article."

"The Pueblo Blanco story? The one you worked on all day? What does—did—he have to do with that?"

"I've no idea. He wouldn't elaborate." Her pulse still raced. "I think my father knew."

"What?"

"He was on his way to meet me when he was killed in the car wreck. Mario said I was just like him. I believe Mario killed him and then was murdered himself. Somehow he's tied to that development."

"But Rachel, what are you going to do about the story?"

"Publish it," she said with conviction. "Can you leave town for a few days, until this thing is over?"

"No way. I'm staying put."

"Chloe, Chris is already in trouble. I couldn't bear it if something happened to you too."

"And you think I could escape a spirit by leaving the state?" Chloe said. "Have you considered Mario might be responsible for Joseph's death?"

"Damn. You're right." Awareness streamed into Rachel's consciousness."That must have been the reason for the drawing."

"I think we should take another look at it," Chloe headed for Rachel's room.

While the two searched the hastily filled boxes, Rachel thought aloud about the drawing. "It was simple. A storm. Lightning. That's all. I can't imagine what it could mean. Maybe nothing."

"Nevertheless, we need to examine it again," Chloe said. "*Voilà!* Here it is. You're right," she said with disappointment. "Just a storm, but he signed your name. That has to mean something."

They sat on the floor among the boxes that held Rachel's belongings and were thoughtful for a few minutes.

"This is hopeless. How are we going to make any sense out of it?"

"Look," Chloe pointed, "the lightning is striking the sagebrush. See how it seems to hit, then bounce off? Could that have any significance?"

"Sage is burned in many Native American ceremonies but I don't see anything suggestive about its representation here."

"Didn't hurt to look." Chloe finished repacking the cartons. "I'm tired. Think I'll turn in early." She paused momentarily. "You sure about the story?"

"Yes," Rachel nodded. "I feel I owe it to Dad, to finish what he started."

"Okay. 'Night."

Hours later, Rachel gave up trying to sleep, pulled out the drawing again and continued to study it from all angles. All she could do was hope it would become clear.

* * *

By 10:30 the following morning Rachel delivered the story to the *New Mexican*. When she reached the reception area on her way out, someone called her name. A young woman, held a small envelope in her hand.

"Are you Rachel Blackstone?"

"Yes."

"This is for you."

Rachel took it, looking for a return address. There was only her name, typed across the front. "This was left for me? Do you know by whom?"

"No. It was in our drop box this morning when I arrived."

"Thank you."

Marcy Street was in full bustle. A UPS truck blocked the lane of traffic going west. An angry horn blared.

Rachel crossed the street to her car which waited next to an expired parking meter. Once inside, she opened the envelope with her thumb, leaving a jagged wound from which she pulled a white sheet of mundane copy paper.

In the holy water you will find

If you get there in time

The clue to the mayor's powder

Hurry, before it loses its power.

"What the hell?" Rachel sat upright with a start, looking around her as if someone would come forward and admit to this nonsense. She wadded the note, crushing the paper into a ball and tossed it on the floor along with the discarded stuff from the stakeout. Some prankster obviously needed to get a life. She was about to start the Merc when it occurred to her, this might be the real thing. If there was even a chance it could lead to Chris, what harm could it do to follow the directions?

She smoothed the page open with her hands and reread the instructions. As she gave serious thought to the game, her body shuddered with a quick chill. What if this was not someone's idea of an amusing diversion? What if it was a high-stakes hand?

Because of the reference to holy water in the first line Rachel assumed the writer must be alluding to one of the many Catholic churches in town. There were several in the downtown area to choose from. Our Lady of Guadalupe was the farthest from her. San Miguel Chapel, the oldest church in the country, was likely overflowing with tourists. Like the San Miguel, Loretto Chapel was a haven for visitors looking to marvel at the miraculous staircase. That left St. Francis Cathedral in the heart of downtown just a block from the Plaza. It did have small receptacles of holy water attached to the walls of the sanctuary.

Rachel pushed as fast as the traffic congestion would allow all of twenty miles an hour, until she could turn onto Washington. A herd of walkers at the Palace Avenue stop sign slowed her progress. She made a left and hoped for a parking spot. She cruised past the cathedral. A couple of blocks down, she snagged a space with time on the meter. It wouldn't have mattered, she had no change.

She jogged back up the street. Cathedral Park, a treed lot next to the church, was fenced, preventing Rachel from taking a shortcut through the lawn. The building's planned ornate twin towers were never completed, although the north one is taller by one row of bricks. Perhaps money had run short, or maybe patience. She thought the church was beautiful, sans steeples. The Romanesque Revival architecture with its rose window held the view of all who looked upon it.

Inside, Rachel passed the tiers of candles near the front door. Through the second pair of doors the grand altar appeared between rows of wooden pews. The church was incredible with soaring arches and Corinthian columns. Another time, Rachel would have taken her time in the peaceful haven of worship. Today she hastily looked for the meaning of the rhyme.

The floor of the cramped aisle along one side of the pews offered nothing. She checked the benches. Having exhausted one side, she was about to cross to the other when paper sticking out of one of the holy vessels caught her eye. That didn't belong. A folded piece of paper protruded from one of the small basins. She carefully pulled the note from the water, which had already softened the paper to the point of tearing. Unfolded, the ink had run, but the message could still be read.

They gave them a home
For the prairie dog to roam.
But to get closer to his honor
You must see them holler.

"Say what?" Rachel sank into the nearest pew. The only prairie dogs she could think of, besides those which built their homes helter-skelter throughout the city, were at one of her favorite spots. Jackalope was a junkyard gone big-time. The retail place specialized in terra cotta planters and pots, folk art, southwest furniture, food, plants and even kept a petting zoo. Centrally located among the several large buildings was the prairie dog farm. But, what did the reference to "holler" mean? "Of course!" she said way too loudly for her surroundings. Lunch. Her watch showed 11:38 a.m. If traffic wasn't a nightmare, she could just make it.

CHAPTER 49

T raffic was at bottleneck proportions so close to lunch. It was a mere four-mile drive to Jackalope from downtown, but in the hustle of lunch time traffic, combined with last chance road repairs before winter, Rachel thought it unlikely she would make the midday prairie dog feeding.

She bristled as the Merc's turn signal patiently declared its intent to move to the right, stood landlocked in the middle lane of traffic in the never-never land of St. Francis Drive. There was no way she'd make the turnoff to Cerrillos if someone didn't exercise their good family values and let her the hell over. "Shit, I should have taken the Old Trail." Rachel smacked the steering wheel, hurting her healing finger in the process. While massaging her knuckle she heard a soft honk. Looking up, she saw a driver motioning her over. Frantically waving her thanks, she made the turn with moments to spare.

Not only was Cerrillos motel heaven, it was home to several schools, many restaurants, large and small shopping centers and hundreds of miscellaneous businesses. And, it connected to I-25 and the rest of the world.

The Merc crawled along as horns sounded and middle fingers were exercised. Rachel thanked her lucky stars the car still had a New Mexico tag. Those with out-of-state license plates were sometimes treated with more enthusiastic rudeness than were locals. Visitors were likely to see a bumper sticker reading: "If it's tourist season, why can't we shoot them?" Nice.

By the time she reached the College of Santa Fe, it had been nearly twenty minutes. Jackalope was still several blocks away and difficult to get into coming from the north. Around Second Street, she had a chance at the inside lane. Now, Rachel flipped the car's turn signal while waiting for a few dozen vehicles to go by. When finally there was a break, she left some rubber behind. It was 12:07 p.m.

The prairie dog enclosure at Jackalope was close to the entrance. Rachel made straight for furry ground-burrowing creatures, passing pottery and beautiful handmade furniture that any other day she'd stop and admire, maybe even buy. Jackalope had acres of shops and thousands of items to choose from. It was the one place where she actually enjoyed shopping.

The open air pen was surrounded by a wall perhaps three feet high with flat rocks cemented to the top making a shelf of sorts. It was easy to lean across the stones and watch the tiny *dogs* munch on alfalfa or carrots. Two prairie dogs stood guard while the others ate. Upon sighting Rachel, the lookouts cried to alert the others. A couple stopped chewing momentarily, sensing no danger, continued with their meal.

Rachel walked around the enclosure, seeing nothing on the ground surrounding it, nor anything remotely resembling a piece of paper that might hold the contents of another message. She stepped back to make a larger visual sweep when she noticed a folded piece of paper lying under some alfalfa inside the enclosure. A prairie dog was dining precariously close. One back foot was firmly placed upon the white note. What to do? Jump in and risk getting permanently evicted from one of her choice haunts or was the greater risk in not plucking it from the heap of dirt that was home to a couple of dozen of Mother Nature's cutest. That's when she noticed the kids.

She walked around and approached the two children, one shy girl with her thumb in her mouth and an older boy, likely her brother. Childless by choice, Rachel was not good at guessing a child's age, but he couldn't be more than nine or ten.

"Hey, kid. Want to make five dollars?"

"Sure," he eyed her suspiciously. "How?"

"See that piece of paper lying inside?" Rachel pointed.

"Yeah."

"Well, it shouldn't be there. Paper's not good for prairie dogs. If I lift you in, would you get it for me?"

"Will they bite me?"

"No, they'll just run down their holes," Rachel said, hoping it wasn't a lie. Shit would definitely happen if one of the little beasts bit the kid. But, it was the least intrusive way to get to the note. The boy wouldn't be noticeable to anyone while she lifted him in because her own body would hide him.

"Okay, where's the five bucks?" Smart kid or blooming shyster? She produced the bill.

He jumped up onto the ledge and Rachel quickly lowered him in. The prairie dogs scattered, a few ran to the far side of their home, while most fled downward through the bolt holes that dotted the mound of earth. The nimble child grabbed the note. Rachel hauled him out. That was right before all hell broke.

The tiny girl had somehow extricated her thumb from her facial orifice and was screaming clichéd bloody murder. Mommy and Daddy dearest were running from a stack of terra-cotta pots toward their precious toddler whose face was turning redder with each decibel level. Daddy stepped right in a fragile clay planter, shattering it to bits on the gravel. By the time they reached the pen, big brother was standing on the wall as if he'd been there all the time.

"What's going on here?" Mommy charged. All little sister could do was wail and point at Rachel.

She smiled weakly, pretty sure she was doomed.

* * *

Stella placed an envelope on Julian's desk. "This came for you by messenger."

"Thanks, Stella."

Julian slashed the envelope with a letter opener. The phone rang before he could slide its contents from the wrapper. He dropped it on the messy desktop and reached for the phone. When he looked for a notepad, the envelope disappeared under a page proof.

CHAPTER 50

"What are you doing with my son?" Daddy grew a bit calmer, but his face was a near match for his daughter's. From the corner of her eye, she saw the boy push the note into his pants pocket.

"She was just helping me see better," he said, much to Rachel's amazement.

"Did she touch you inappropriately?" Mommy asked.

Rachel looked at the young mother, completely dumbfounded. Of course she would like to get her hand in the little guy's pocket, but only to get the note, not because she was a budding pedophile.

"No, Mom," the kid groaned. He must have been thoroughly schooled in inappropriate touching. His foot scuffed the ground in embarrassment.

Mommy picked up the squealing sister. Bouncing by the right person terminated the high-pitched shrieking and caused the thumb to pacify her once again.

"Darling, we should probably report her to the police," Mommy said. Rachel started to mention how unnecessary that would be, but the two began a heated discussion of the pros and cons of getting involved with the police in a strange city. Apparently, they had been vacationing for nearly two weeks. Tension was nearing Middle Eastern intensity.

Rachel thought she could slip away without their noticing, but she didn't have the verse for the next clue. It was nearly 12:30. The minutes were ticking by and she still had no idea where to find her brother. The boy was paying attention.

While his parents were arguing about Rachel's history as a possible subversive, he pulled the paper out and dropped it nonchalantly on the ground. He winked at Rachel before joining the fray.

"I'm hungry," he whined. His parents didn't hear. He tugged at his dad's pants leg, but was quickly brushed aside. Rachel seized her opportunity, picked up the dusty paper and shoved it in her jacket pocket.

Before she could make a clean getaway, a store employee rushed over to them. "Hey, buddy," he said. "Who's going to pay for the busted pot? That's an $8 item."

"Here," Rachel said. She shoved eight dollars in his hand. "Put your kid through college." She shouldered passed him. Once in her car, she guided it onto a side street. Several blocks away, she stopped to read the note.

Ringling Brothers has the big top
But SF has one of a lesser scope.
Don't you wish you knew?
Where to go to rescue?

"No shit," she mumbled. "Big top? He's talking about a frigging circus. The big top?" She mulled the various animals used and abused by the circus, the performers from trapeze artists to clowns, but nothing made sense. At one time, there had been a carousel at the Villa Linda Mall, but that had been removed.

It was 12:43 and counting. "Damn." That little altercation cost precious time—back to the circus. They frequently traveled by train. Santa Fe had a train to Lamy and one to Albuquerque. Was her brother in either of those?

Was time running out for Chris? She had a crushing sense of urgency. He probably deserved the mess he was in. She loved him despite his ability to create trouble from air. "Where are you, Chris?"

* * *

"Julian," Stella's voice came over the intercom. "Just got the strangest call."

"What's that?" He was preoccupied, proofing the next issue.

"Someone just called and asked if you'd read the letter that was messengered here a while ago? It sounded like a kid."

"That it?"

"No, he said you'd miss the biggest story of your life if you didn't read the letter."

"Well dammit," Julian was exasperated. "I don't see it, and right now checking these proofs ranks high with me. Did you tell him *High Desert* isn't a daily? He should send his hot tips to the *New Mexican*."

"I explained, but he insisted the message was of the greatest importance."

"Shit. I'm going to have to find it first."

* * *

Rachel couldn't think what to do so she found a pay phone and called Chloe. The receptionist told her politely that Chloe was out of the office. "Can she be reached? It's important."

"What's your number?" Rachel gave her the pay phone number. "I'll ask her to call you," she said.

"Thanks." To herself: "Maybe I should get a cell," she said to the stupid, silent pay phone, "You know you hate most of the latest technology." The items on her unnecessary-to-live list included: Smart phones, iPods, and FedEx. Whoever needed something absolutely, positively overnight, unless it was an organ transplant? Even computers made her list, although she liked hers and needed it for work.

The black telephone shrilled, jarring her from the mental tirade on technology. "Hello!" she shouted.

"That's the thanks I get, after interrupting my showing," Chloe bristled.

"Sorry," Rachel mumbled, and commenced telling her about the strange day she was having. "What do you make of the last verse?"

"Geez, there are performers, wagons, rip-off games, and animals."

"Yeah, and tons of shit, but that doesn't help me find Chris." Rachel was surprised by her own voice. There was noticeable panic.

"He's going to be okay, Rach. We've just got to figure out what it means. Have you called the police?"

"With what? Gee, Mr. Police Officer, I've been finding these poems all over town. Care to evaluate them?"

"Honestly, Rach, it wouldn't hurt. Read them to me again and I'll write them down. We're going to have to split up in order to cover the most bases. I'll contact the police and relay the messages."

"What should I do?" Rachel asked. "Drive out to Lamy?"

"You know," Chloe said, "there's one more thing that's part of a circus."

"And?"

"The big top, from the first line of the note. Maybe it's the tent we need to be looking for. Santa Fe has its own version."

"You're the best."

"Just go. As soon as I'm finished with the police, I'll meet you there."

"Hurry," Rachel said, but Chloe was already gone.

CHAPTER 51

Rachel made a dangerous left turn into traffic. The Merc choked in protest. "Don't you start," she railed. "Cooperation is of the utmost importance." Her foot gave it a blast of gas.

It bucketed down the busy thoroughfare toward the promise of Interstate Twenty-five. When finally she found herself on the four-lane ribbon to Albuquerque, she pushed the car up to seventy and hoped memory would tell her which road to take. The La Cienega exit flew by. She'd only visited this place once and the directions were in her fuzzy recall file. She did not know if it was Santo Domingo, Cochiti or San Felipe Pueblo road that she needed. They were all clustered nearby.

The Cochiti exit sign shrank in her rearview mirror, the nowhere land of already traveled terrain. "They're the ones with the dam!" she slapped the dash in frustration. She'd have to wait for the next exit and turn around. It would be faster to cut across the median. "What the heck," she said aloud and moved into the inside lane. A good spot to cross appeared. She made her move.

The car bellied out over a small stand of infant sagebrush but otherwise Rachel thought the turnabout went rather well. Only one person honked at her and she was on her way to the exit she needed. That was before the flashing lights of a Highway Patrol car caught her eye.

* * *

Julian stacked the proofs to one side. Every month it seemed more of an ordeal to get the magazine to press. He needed another full-time person on board to help with the design and publishing, a delegation he was looking forward to. He was waiting to make a decision. It was likely Rachel would stay in Santa Fe. When she left a few months ago he thought her return a given. But he understood her need to take some time to think.

With her back on a permanent basis, he could move on to the next thing. Rachel was his best writer. He thought with her around, John might look to greener pastures more along his political persuasion. Julian didn't relish letting him go and having to face the family outcry. Unfortunately, John wasn't a people person and he'd received several calls complaining of his lack of courtesy. Rachel could be politely persistent when she needed to be, and the experience to remain cool under fire.

He gathered the proofs in preparation to leave and noticed the mystery letter delivered earlier by messenger. "Damn," he sighed wearily. "That's just what I need, the story of a lifetime." In as much as he had covered government corruption in D.C., breaking news and the thawing of the Cold War, he doubted seriously that anything in Santa Fe could compare.

Inside the envelope was a single piece of paper. Unfolding it, he read:

What happens to snoopy reporters
Who don't heed good advice?
Follow the directions
Or she ends up iced.

Julian raised an eyebrow as he puzzled over the message while noting the hokey poetry. Too much had been going on to ignore it. He quickly read the finding directions typed below the freakish verse and left his office. "Stella, please take these proofs to the printer. There's somewhere I have to go."

"You okay?" she asked.

"Yeah. I've got to take care of this." He walked out the office door, forgetting his own instructions to let Stella know his whereabouts.

Stella watched him go. She had a bad feeling about that special delivery.

* * *

Chloe walked into the police station and was confronted with chaos. The lobby was filled with demonstrators. Adults with signs protesting ill treatment by a local employer sat on the floor, having overflowed the limited seating. The strike had gotten out of hand, resulting in the arrest or detainment of dozens of people. Chloe felt momentarily nostalgic for her college days.

She wound her way through the humanity; the place already reeked like a locker room. The officer manning the front desk looked weary. He was keeping a careful eye on the masses, some of whom were softly singing *We Shall Overcome*. There would be no shenanigans on his watch.

"Excuse me," Chloe said. "May I speak with Detective Flores?" His was the only name she could remember from the brief visit they'd paid to Rachel.

The no-nonsense uniformed officer quickly scanned a single piece of paper tucked into a low-tech clipboard. Chloe thought he'd be cute if he let his hair grow out of the closely clipped cut hugging his nearly bare head. Course, he'd have to get a sense of humor to complete the package. She doubted he had the inclination to have fun.

"It's his day off," he finally replied, dismissing her and going back to monitoring the crowd.

"Officer," Chloe said, "this is important. Is there someone else I may speak with?"

"Lady." Chloe cringed at the word. It not only made her feel older than her years, but it was said with some contempt. "We've got a lot on our hands at the moment. Is this something that can be handled tomorrow? Flores will be back then."

"No," Chloe allowed a hard edge to enter her voice. "It can't wait until tomorrow. Is the mayor's disappearance important enough to warrant seeing one of your superiors? That would be virtually anyone here other than you. Right?" Chloe gave him her best contemptuous look. It was effective, but made him mad as hell if his flushed face and bulging veins were any indication.

Pride wouldn't let him go immediately for another officer. "You have information about the mayor?" he asked doubtfully.

"Yes," she replied evenly. "Please get someone to talk with me."

He picked up the phone and turned away from her, talking in hushed tones. His shoulders shrugged a couple of times and finally he turned to face her. "Someone will be out in a minute. Have a . . ." The absence of seating and lack of order was causing him immense discomfort. She hadn't met many laid back police because the regimented employment didn't attract them. But then, she hadn't met all that many police, except for brief encounters where she collected yet another speeding ticket.

"I'll stand," she quipped, retreated three steps back and leaned against the wall next to the desk. She glanced at her watch: 2:47 p.m. She'd hurried through the showing, but the trip across town, in the absence of freeways, had taken a precious half-hour. She needed to talk with someone soon.

Chloe wondered if Rachel had found Chris. And if so, was she in danger too?

CHAPTER 52

He was taking his sweet time. Rachel watched him in her side mirror. The officer completed his call checking to see if the Merc was stolen—like someone would actually steal it. A Corvette or Mustang, even a Camry, but not this. No, the only way anyone would steal this particular vehicle was if their getaway car stalled after the holdup.

The officer walked slowly toward her. She slipped out her driver's license and dug the registration from the glove compartment. She thought about asking for help, but the explanation would take too long.

"Good afternoon, ma'am," he said politely.

"Hello, Officer." She tried to keep the gravity of her situation from showing.

"Are you aware that a U-turn across the median is a violation?" He watched her carefully, lest she pulled a sawed-off shotgun from beneath the junk that littered her car.

"Yes I am," she said. "I'm sorry, but I have to use the bathroom and it was closer to go back." She'd written a story once about a woman stopped for speeding that had used this excuse and gotten off with a warning. Those things never worked for her. This was no exception.

"Afraid I've heard that one a few times," he said, still polite. "I'm going to have to write you a ticket."

"Is there a law against peeing in full view of other motorists?" she asked, immediately sensing it was the wrong thing to say.

The officer's face hardened a bit. Rachel figured she'd just upped the price of the ticket several decimal places. He tore off the page and handed it through the window. "Next time, get off at the exit. There's usually a service station where you can use the facilities. Have a good day." He nodded, his duty done.

"Thanks," she said. What else could she say without getting into more trouble? The clock in the dash read 3:22. Sunset was getting closer by the minute. She flipped on the turn signal before carefully merging into traffic. She wondered if there was any way she could find Chris before dark.

* * *

After waiting restlessly for forty minutes at the police station, Chloe finally talked with someone. One harried Sergeant Friendly, who was not friendly, half-listened to her story and completely tuned her out when she began the poetry reading. All this took place in the waiting area where detainees from some kind of protest wailed in song, sweat and confusion.

"Look," Sergeant Friendly told her, "we have every available man looking for the mayor. These notes, uh poems, sound like gobbledygook. Someone's just trying to get attention. It happens all the time in these cases."

Before he could leave her standing in amazement Chloe said, "You do understand these notes were received by the mayor's sister?"

"Look," he started again, "no offense intended here, but the mayor's sister has been known to go a little overboard on occasion. She's riled people before with her reporting. As you can see, we have more than we can handle right here." He turned tiredly and began walking away.

He would have disappeared in a second had Chloe not stopped him in her own subtle way. She launched forth a series of loud profanity—all in French. The room finally fell silent.

* * *

The way to Tent Rocks wasn't exactly a secret but it might as well have been for Rachel. She was sure she'd gotten the exit right. Back on I-25, she found the turnoff to the Cochiti Dam. It was eerie driving along the base of the dam, keenly aware of the many million tons of water applying pressure against the other side. The tricky part came after making the curve on the highway. A Forest Service road provided access to Tent Rocks. She thought it was a couple of miles and slowed to look for it, took a wrong turn and lost precious time. Eventually, a small sign showed her the way. The road was every bit as bad as the one she'd taken during her Pueblo Blanco night moves. Juan would have to align her car again. Rachel made a note of the mileage. She would have to get out of here in the dark and she wanted to be sure of the distance. Four and a half miles later, bumping and grinding all the way, she crept into an open spot used for parking. It was thick with soft dirt.

She spotted a familiar car. On closer inspection she realized it was Julian's. What was Julian doing here? She would have ridden a tiger for that man. He had always been fair with her and she cared for him. He just couldn't be a part of this.

The Merc moved forward at her urging. She passed through the small opening and hid the car in the desert shrubs.

CHAPTER 53

T he high light grey spires of Kasha-Katuwe Tent Rocks National Monument rose starkly against the gathering dusk. Born of the volcanic eruptions six to seven million years ago—the same disturbances that created the Jémez Mountains— the ash had been carried east to fall in this area. It was reported to be a quarter-mile thick. There was enough hot ash to have cooked a moderate-sized city. Some of the cone-shaped formations were 90 feet tall. Wind and rain over the centuries abraded the ash into pinnacles of layered heaps. Many of the hoodoos balanced rocks on their peaks, much as a seal perches a ball on its nose.

The area was strange and bewitching during the day, but when the sky darkened to indigo, it might as well be another planet. Rachel took one of the paths through the ponderosa pines and sagebrush on her first visit. A canyon 200 feet deep was so narrow at times that it was impossible to pass through. She wanted to avoid this route.

The larger obelisks resembled tepees and contained chambers hollowed by time or humans. Many had provided overnight lodging to guests of a more modern generation, if the contemporary petroglyphs were any proof. Happy faces and other recognizable motifs decorated the interiors in a few of the formations. Whether the chambers had evolved naturally or were made by human hands, they were a handy place to roll out the old sleeping bag. The ceilings were stained black with the remnants of campfires.

Rachel stopped, conflicted. She didn't want to go into the rocks alone and without a flashlight. But if Chris was here and in trouble she couldn't wait for backup. Then there was Julian's car. What were the chances the two of them would find themselves in this place at same time? Unless he was involved somehow? When she thought of their relationship and all they had experienced, it was hard for her to believe he would ever mean harm to anyone. His presence, however, made her cautious.

Desperately she wanted to wait for Chloe and the police. What if the police didn't believe Chloe? In that case, no help would be forthcoming. She couldn't wait. Her feet began moving, skirting Julian's car.

"It's probably all a hoax anyway," she muttered, remembering that Chris's car was found north of the city and Tent Rocks was southwest. Being alone in this otherworldly place caused her wildly fluctuating thoughts or what Chloe called free-floating anxieties.

She opted not to pay the parking fee and located the trail near the kiosk the Bureau of Land Management had erected. She dreaded what might be at the end of the trail. What if all she found was Chris' body? What if there was nothing at all? "Oh shit, stop thinking," she whispered.

Rachel walked, stumbled, a quarter mile into the canyon before stopping for rest and reorientation. A boulder made a convenient place to sit. The fact that it had tumbled made her slightly nervous, but Rachel was more concerned with why she had been lured out here, than with what nature might have in store.

Despite the cool autumn evening, her face was covered in tiny beads of perspiration. Feeling her way into the chasm had left her hands dirty and scratched.

A twig snapped. Her warning system engaged. Rachel scanned the immediate locale. The white cliffs reflected the light of the moon, deepening the shadows. She heard footsteps. What to do? Confront whoever it was or find a place to hide? She opted to hide—it was better to know the enemy. With more stealth than she thought possible, she backed alongside the boulder to a handy crevice. She held her breath.

A man came into view. Walking rapidly, without caution, he made no attempt to hide his presence. Rachel remained motionless, watching him.

He stopped. Rachel clinched her fists in apprehension. Both hands on his hips, he swiveled, scrutinizing the canyon. Rachel unconsciously withdrew farther into the cover of the fissure. Her shoe slipped on a small rock. The scraping sound seemed to reverberate throughout the gorge. She felt every bit on the abyss, sure to be discovered and dispatched in some ghastly way.

He moved toward. Rachel closed her eyes. When she timidly opened them, he was listening intently. "Is someone there?" he asked gruffly. She gasped softly, covering her mouth with her hand as she recognized Julian's voice.

Rachel wanted to run to him, throw her arms around him, but she didn't dare. Not until she knew why he was here.

Julian strode off through the gloom of towering rocks. Her body sagged in relief. She stepped back onto the path to follow him, stopping occasionally to listen for his progress, not wanting to betray her own.

* * *

Julian grew angrier as each wasted minute passed. First the mysterious note with its not-so-veiled threat, then the twenty-mile drive to the middle of nowhere. The author of the note was obviously a fiction writer.

As he walked deeper into the canyon, he felt another presence. It was one thing to meet someone with a story, and quite another to walk headlong into a trap. He was suspicious, this must be the latter. Some instincts may go dormant from lack of use, but his reporter's intuition was still strong.

The wind picked up. It funneled through the confining space between the rocks. There was a nearly imperceptible sound from ground he had already traveled. Julian faced the breeze, all senses on alert. He was giving this ridiculous rendezvous ten more minutes. Resolutely, he resumed the trudge.

A flickering light caught his attention near a break in the wall of the pass. He retraced several steps. To get a better look, he balanced on a fallen log, hoping it hadn't decayed too much to hold his weight.

On the other side of the ash barrier, the high rocks curved around a small natural enclosure with a ceiling of stars. The light of a fire penetrated the darkness. It was only luck that he'd noticed it.

With effort, he scrambled up the rough hardened ash. Frustrated, he could not get through the opening. He cursed years of eating chile rellenos. He'd have to find another way in.

CHAPTER 54

As Julian's silhouette disappeared into the night, Rachel crept forward to the spot he'd just vacated. She clutched the pillars with both hands, pulling her body up so she could see. The rubber soles of her shoes clung insecurely to the rough surface. There was flickering in the clearing. She squeezed through the opening, and climbed the ash column to get a better vantage point. The effort resulted in new scrapes on her hands, but she hardly noticed. When able to straddle the seam where the rocks met, she sucked one thumb absently. It tasted salty.

She landed with an audible thud. With one hand bracing her body, she took a few moments to restock her oxygen. She considered going back. Her concern for Chris was precariously balanced with her concern for her own safety. Rachel crept forward.

Her progress went unnoticed as she negotiated the bumps and blobs of ancient ash. Every time she lost her footing, she stopped and listened; fearful she had given away her position.

It felt as if she'd been trapped in the maze of ash cones for hours. Darkness had brought with it poor depth perception in the murky contours. She was now close enough to hear the crackle of the fire. Its light cast long irregular shadows everywhere. Rachel stopped to observe and listen.

When she was convinced no one had seen or heard her. She walked softly into the clearing, where a bonfire roared. It was reminiscent of those set around Santa Fe at Christmas, only much larger. The flames licked heavenward toward the gathering clouds. Smoke from the blaze rose and then flattened out when a breeze caught it, carrying it away.

She stood mesmerized, not just by the fire, but with what was going on around it. Pale figures engaged in chores from another era. One scraped the hide of an animal. Another stirred something in a pot. Horses were being tended by others. Rachel tried to discern reality from everything she was seeing. The area is considered sacred by Native Americans. She was stupefied when a gauzy substance floated by her. She felt it, more than heard it, "There is danger. You should leave."

But she couldn't leave, because there was something even more terrifying beyond the glow of the fire. Choking, Rachel inhaled smoke as she pushed herself forward. Her face felt the heat.

Looking past the fire, it appeared there was a giant insect struggling in an equally large web. The thought brought back every horror movie Rachel had ever seen. She wished she'd worn boots. Good lord, a spider that big—could it be real? She allowed that horrible thought to permeate every crevice in her mind. At the moment she couldn't remember the name of a single nonpoisonous spider. Her skin hurt from the vicious scratching she was giving her thigh, but thoughts of behemoth crawling creatures had immediately caused her skin to crawl.

"Get hold of yourself," she whispered nastily.

The only way to see what tussled beyond was to get closer. Fists tightly clenched to stop the shaking; she took a few speculative steps along the edge of the crackling fire. Newly formed ash from the blaze drifted in the air. Rachel touched one of the fragile pieces, watched it disintegrate.

Maybe she could have discerned what was going on from several paces back. Maybe she hadn't wanted to. Whatever, she could see now. A human floundered in front of her. It pulled at the webbing, hopelessly entangled.

Rachel stepped aside to allow the light of the fire to illuminate the macabre entrapment. The man, she thought it was a man, was lashed to a huge dream catcher. Native Americans made the delicate creations to catch nightmares while allowing the good dreams to come through. They were round frames, covered in leather, with the open center stitched like a web. Feathers of religious significance were attached. In recent years, non-Natives made dream catchers to sell as souvenirs.

Still trying to comprehend the situation, she remembered covering a festival a couple of years earlier when the giant dream catcher was built. It had been a great hit with the crowd at the time. But this one held a nightmare, instead of preventing one.

The man's hands and feet were tied spread-eagle across the contraption, preventing all but the smallest movement. He hung upright between two stout poles, gagged, or surely he would cry out. He had to know she was there because by now, her body would be silhouetted by the fire. She had slowly worked her way around the boulders, dead wood and loose ash.

Rachel gasped as she recognized her brother. The horror of his dilemma was put off some by her joy at finding him. The happiness she felt seeing Chris alive made her careless. She rushed to him.

Chris vehemently shook his head. Even through the gag she could hear the word "no" said over and over. "Hold still so I can untie you." He continued to battle her efforts to release him. She peeled back a corner of the silver tape. With one calculated movement she ripped it from his mouth. Chris moaned in pain.

"Get away," he implored her through chapped lips. Dried blood caked at a corner of his mouth.

"No. I'm not leaving without you."

"Too weak," he gasped. "Go."

Her hands shook as she tried to untie the rough bonds. His battle against the shackles had made them so tight it would take a knife to release him.

"I'm sorry, Chris. They're going to have to be cut. I've got my key chain with the X-ACTO blade. It isn't much, but I'll try it." The key holder had been a promotional gift to *High Desert Country* from a printing company looking for new business. It had come in handy many times, but this would be the most important chore it had ever performed.

The twine frayed as she cut through it. "You'll have a free hand in a moment," she tried to sound encouraging, but it was tough going with the small blade.

"No," Chris said. "Go. You don't know . . ." His voice trailed off as his eyes fixed on something behind her.

CHAPTER 55

Rachel whirled to confront Julian. He stood inside the light of the fire. "What are you doing here?" she barked. "Do you have anything to do with this?" Reason was not forthcoming, only anger.

"Of course not," he rushed forward. "We've got to get him down."

"Stop where you are," Rachel pointed the blade at him, knowing full well it was nearly useless as a weapon. "Why are you here?"

Julian stopped, raising and spreading his hands in a gesture of peace. "I received a note at the office. It said to come here. That's all I know."

"I don't get it," Rachel said. "Why would anyone want you here?"

"Let's figure it out later," he said. "Right now, let's get Chris out of . . . Julian didn't finish his sentence because he crumpled before Rachel's eyes.

She blinked. Rachel thought the firelight must be playing tricks on her, but no, Julian lay in a heap on the ground.

Rachel rushed to help Julian, but was stopped by Chris.

"Get out," Chris said behind her, his words forced.

"Too late for that." It was Alexander Robbins. He stood near Julian, holding a gun in his hand.

"You killed Julian?" Rachel yelled above the roar of the fire.

"Not dead, just out, but things could always change." Rachel thought him the cruelest looking man she'd ever seen. Gone were the smiling eyes. Robbins radiated evil. He had the swagger of a person in total control. She had been right about one thing, he wasn't the marketing type.

"I see you've found your long lost brother. Too bad, he's all tied up," he sneered. "Oh, I seem to have interrupted your inept attempt to save him. How thoughtless of me." He noticed the tape was off. "I'm afraid hizzoner is a bit shopworn. Food's been a tad sparse out here."

Rachel could take no more of this madman's mockery. "Why have you kidnapped Chris?" she asked coolly.

"Oh dear," Robbins said. "So you really don't know. He said you didn't."

"Know what?"

"Your brother made a deal with me, and another associate. We had a sweet thing going, but the mayor got greedy."

"What are you talking about?" Rachel interrupted. "What could Chris possibly have to do with you?"

"Rachel. Do you mind if I call you Rachel?" He didn't wait for a reply. "Chris was kind enough to push through some paperwork at city hall to clear the way for our little enterprise."

"You mean Pueblo Blanco?" Rachel asked.

"Of course. It was all going so well. The stupid rich people were lining up to invest in our venture, then Santa Fe's economy went in the dumpster and our partner got in a hurry for a payback."

Suddenly, things started falling into place. "Mario?" Rachel said. Even as she mentioned his name, she could hear the thunder rumble as the storm neared. It sent a chill down her rigid body.

"Yes," Robbins said. "How did you know?"

"Wild guess." He had no idea how wild. Rachel inhaled smoke from the fire, which made her cough. She still held the small blade in her hand, but knew it would be useless against a gun. It seemed important to keep him talking. "Did you kill Mario?"

"Rachel, for once, don't ask questions," Chris said. "Better not to know." He groaned as he tried to move against the restraints.

"Why not?" Rachel said without caution. "He's going to kill us anyway. Isn't that what this is all about?"

"That depends on how cooperative you are," Robbins said. "You see, your brother refused to give me the number to a very important account in the Caymans."

"What's he talking about Chris?" Rachel asked.

"It was dear brother's job to take care of the money brought in by the investors," Robbins answered for him. "But he did the job a little too well." Julian stirred on the ground. Robbins, with a bored look, landed a kick to his kidney. Julian stopped moving.

"Stop!" Rachel screamed.

She had to do something. Could she run for help? Certainly Robbins would probably shoot her in the back. Maybe she could keep him talking long enough for Chloe to arrive with the police. She held her ground helplessly.

"You didn't answer my question," Rachel said. "Did you kill Mario?"

"Hell, yes," Robbins spat out the words. "Bastard had it coming. The guy was a loose cannon. He threatened to queer the whole deal if we didn't pay him off. Even went to the press."

The horror of Robbins' words hit Rachel full force. The "press" had to be her father. Her thoughts immediately went back to the winding ski basin road, the appointment her father had and the horrible incident that ended his life. The rage within her was overwhelming. She raced at Robbins, heedless of the gun.

"Stop right now," he shouted. She skidded in the ash, facing the business end of an automatic. "Move over there." He waved the gun toward her brother. Terror was etched into every line of Chris' face. His eyes willed her to comply.

"Why is Julian here?" she asked. He was still unconscious, but she squatted next to him and found his pulse. It was there. "What does he have to do with this?" Rachel stood.

"I owed him a favor," Robbins said. "He fingered me. It was a lifetime ago when I was kid named Alec Robertson. I spent years in prison because of him. It was one of the reasons I chose Santa Fe for this deal. Kill two birds with one stone, so to speak."

"What do you want from me?" she asked. "I don't have any idea where this alleged account is."

"Never thought you did," he said. "Chris hasn't been very co-operative, but I believe with a little persuasion he'll experience full recovery of his memory."

"I don't get it." But she did. She was there to make Chris give Robbins the account number. If he wouldn't do so, Robbins would probably threaten or torture her until Chris talked. Once Chris divulged the number, they would all be killed.

"I see the wheels are turning," Robbins said with the calmness of a practiced killer. "Having you show up as the reporter was icing on the cake. Now, I'll finally be through with interference from your family. Shall we get on with it?"

Rachel unconsciously took a step back, but Robbins quickly closed the gap.

CHAPTER 56

With one arm twisted painfully behind her back, Rachel had little choice but to go where Robbins steered her. He holstered the gun, pulled out a knife. It was an ugly thing with a serrated blade more than six inches long. Light from the bonfire shimmered as it was reflected along the blade.

"Okay," Robbins said to Chris, "it's do-or-die time." He slid his arm beneath hers, holding her wrist with a crushing grip. She struggled to extricate it, but his grasp was absolute. The edge of the knife rested across the palm of her hand, the one she'd removed the stitches from a few days earlier. "We'll start simply," he said, "and work our way up." He gave a sick smile.

Robbins stared at her brother, waiting for a reply. "Surely, you don't want me to cut her?" The blade pressed hard. Rachel felt it settle onto her skin. It hurt. A thin line of blood appeared. She suppressed the urge to whimper, not wanting to give him any satisfaction. Robbins' eyes were still fixed on Chris so she made her move.

The energy that had been tightly on hold, erupted into one deft moment. She turned into Robbins grasp instead of pulling away, which caught him off guard. Her other hand blasted upward. She followed through with the weight of her body and was satisfied to feel her open hand strike Robbins' nose. Blood spurted from his nostrils. His face contorted in pain, but he still held her arm in a viselike clench. Rachel felt a searing sting as the knife creased the skin of her hand. She stopped struggling, frozen in fear and pain. Blood dripped from her fingers and mingled with his on the ground.

"For god's sake, stop it," Chris croaked. "I'll tell you."

It was Rachel's turn to plead. "Don't do it, Chris. Once he gets what he wants, we're dead."

"I can't let him hurt you. It's only money."

"Then why get involved in the first place?" she shouted angrily.

"Mayor's job pays . . . nothing." He swallowed, fighting the dry throat. "I've got a wife and kids."

"And girls on the side," Rachel said hatefully, resentment boiling within her that Chris would risk their lives for cash.

"Yeah." He made no effort to deny it.

"I hate to break up this endearing family chat," Robbins wiped blood from his face. He moved behind Rachel, twisting her cut hand up against her back. He positioned the knife across her throat.

Chris twisted sharply, pulling at the ropes. "I've already told you, I'll tell you what you want."

"I'm waiting." Robbins didn't move; nor did Rachel.

She was aware of everything: the cold blade against her neck, the clotting blood on her hand, the heat from the fire warming her calves. Even in the surreal surroundings, with death possible, she found herself in love with life. Breathing was a gift to cherish. Pain was a sign she continued to exist. She made herself focus on preserving that life.

Chris spoke, after what seemed liked hours. "Do you have paper?"

"Just tell me the number," Robbins said, angry at what he thought was another delay.

"It's long." Chris looked quickly at Rachel and back at Robbins. In the second their eyes met, Rachel saw his were swimming in tears. She wanted to run to her brother, but Robbins' had not relaxed his hold on her. Worse, every time she swallowed, she could feel the pinch of the blade.

Rain drops splattered lightly, causing the fire to sizzle in protest. The rumble of thunder grew closer and lightning scattered across the desert, a downpour was imminent.

Chris began reciting numbers. Robbins listened intently behind her. She could feel his breath in her hair. As they all waited for Chris to finish the number, he stumbled over the figures.

"Just a minute," Chris stopped. "That's wrong." The blade tightened in anger against her. Rachel tried to shrink back, but Robbins body wasn't budging. "The first three digits were correct." He began again, buying time.

The storm grew closer. Rachel became aware of something familiar. With everything going on, the significance was fuzzy, but the atmosphere had taken on another element—Mario! If Robbins or Chris noticed it, they did not let on. As Chris spoke the fourth number, the sky opened. A bolt of lightning hit the top of a nearby rock. The deafening crack of thunder caused them all to duck defensively. Rain poured in a torrent.

Rachel took a quick step backward, put her knee to the back of his and pushed. It had always worked in the schoolyard. He lost his balance and landed hard on the ground where runoff was already forming. Without deliberation Rachel brought her foot down on Robbins' hand. He yelled in pain. His fingers released the weapon. She grabbed the knife. Her first impulse was to free Chris, but Robbins still had a gun.

Words appeared in her mind, *can I kill him?* Rachel thought she could, but maybe she wouldn't have to. "Take off your belt!" she shouted. He hesitated. "Take if off or I'll cut you." If he had any doubts, the set of her face told him she meant it. And in his present position, she had the upper hand and had to be reckoned with. He slowly pulled the belt from its loops. Rachel shouted. "And forget about the gun!" He obeyed. She was about to cinch the belt around his wrists, Mario's signature became stronger. She looked up to see him standing before her.

"I'll take it from here," he said.

It was odd. He'd always appeared to be held in some kind of fluid, but even in the cloudburst, but his features seemed dry while Rachel's hair was plastered to her head.

Robbins began shivering uncontrollably from cold and shock at seeing him. Rachel glanced at Chris, who now looked more terrified than before. They could see Mario too!

"What are you going to do?" Rachel asked Mario.

"Let him go," Mario commanded. Rachel backed off, letting Robbins' belt drop on the muddy ash. Robbins stood shakily, then quickly drew his gun and fired at Mario, whose figure convulsed with each shot but reconverged to its original form. It didn't stop Robbins, who continued to fire until the magazine was emptied. Robbins began to run. Mario jumped in front of him. Robbins surged through his image, screaming in disbelief and horror. Mario followed him.

Rachel ran to Chris, cutting the ties that held him. The sharp knife sliced cleanly through each one. Chris crawled off the web and stood unsteadily. "I can't walk," he said simply, holding onto Rachel. He was only a couple of inches taller than her. She braced him up as best as she could. Both were transfixed by the showdown going on in the clearing.

Mario stood on a boulder, with both hands raised as if conducting an orchestra. Every time Robbins took a step, lightning would strike so close his hair stood on end. He was so terrified, Rachel felt sorry for him. Like a caged animal knowing its slaughter was near, he raced back and forth, never exceeding the bounds of his electric prison.

When Mario tired of amusing himself with lightning, the wind picked up. At first it was gusty, and then it was fierce. It was impossible for Robbins to stand upright without swaying. Rachel helped Chris take cover behind a large boulder, then watched, mesmerized by Mario's supernatural power.

Hurricane strength aerial currents swept under a powerless Robbins carrying him above the smoldering fire and slamming him against one of the rock spires. He fell to the rocky canyon floor. He made an attempt to get to his feet. Mario materialized before him. Robbins cowered, no longer strong enough to defend himself, but not weak enough to acquiesce.

The wind and rain abruptly stopped. Rachel could hear Robbins, the tables turned, ask, "What do you want?" He rubbed his red, swelling face.

"Revenge," Mario said. "Did you really think you could get rid of me with a few sticks of dynamite?"

"Mario, it wasn't me," Robbins lied.

"We both know it was you," Mario said. "Hey, I'm dead. You can't hurt me anymore, but," and he lingered momentarily savoring his power, "I can do a lot of damage to you and never touch you."

"Mario, please," Robbins pleaded.

Mario's answer was another powerful funnel of wind that encircled the horror-struck man. Rachel recoiled and huddled next to Chris, instinctively wrapping a protective arm about his shoulders. She could feel him quiver. Blood pounded through her own body.

Robbins jerked skyward. They watched as he was thrown back and forth in the vicious circle of wind. Firewood and stones were caught up in the vortex. His body was struck over and over. His clothing disintegrated, exposing his fragile skin. Then he was pelted with jagged pieces of hail all created by the monster. Rachel covered her mouth in repulsion as the ice mauled his body. Small chunks of bloodied flesh fell to the ground. Mario watched with no expression at all. When satisfied his retaliation was complete, a dead man fell to earth.

Rachel crouched in the shadow that enclosed her and Chris. Unreasonably, she hoped Mario could not see them. She knew better. She allowed herself one paralyzing question. What would Mario do to them?

CHAPTER 57

Cringing in fear seemed to be the only thing to do. Chris could barely walk and Mario was infinitely mobile. Staying was easy, but fighting? There was nothing physical she could do to stop Mario from carrying out whatever he wished. She shivered at the thought of what that sleazy, other world leftover might do should she launch an attack on him. Outsmarting him was the only option left. Was it possible to outwit an evil spirit?

Joseph had told her not to think logically and to go with her Great Spirit. She then remembered the drawing. Joseph depicted a storm in the desert. What were the details? The wet and cold was taking its toll and making it difficult to think. Chris was slipping into hypothermia. Whatever she did, right or wrong, she had to make her move.

She thought back to the drawing: the strange pointy mountains, the sagebrush, the lightning. "Hell, this isn't helping."

"What?" Chris asked weakly. "Is it over?"

Rachel took one of his hands. It was icy cold "No. It's not over. I'll think of something."

"Better make it quick," Mario said. "Little brother has to pay."

She couldn't see him clearly, but the constant flashing sky allowed her to keep track of where he was. He seemed to exist, his form bending and changing, at once a part of their world and yet part of the tempest. The storm had played out the heavier rain, leaving stubborn droplets, but it was churning into quite an electrical disturbance. Mario was capricious.

"Come up with anything?" Mario asked cruelly. "This shouldn't take too long. Robbins nearly wasted him anyway." His focus was on Chris, who sat on his heels trying to hold in his body heat. He stared straight ahead at nothing.

"Mario," she implored, "haven't enough people died over this? He'll pay for his part."

"How touching, the sister begs for her brother's life when he doesn't deserve to live."

"No one deserves this." She wanted to be sick as she added, "Even you."

"It's a little late for that. Robbins saw to my demise."

Joseph said she was a believer and therefore could find a way, but what way? Another bolt blasted the air near them. She instinctively ducked, it was so close. The concussion from the thunder must have knocked some sense into her because she realized, in an instant of clarity, Joseph had sent aid. The drawing wasn't meaningless after all. She knew how to get Chris out of danger.

"Come on." She tried to lift him to his feet but he was too heavy. "Get up," she shouted. "I can't do this alone."

"What do you want?" Chris was elsewhere, in a daze of cold incomprehension. The lack of food had dulled his senses and his will to live. She half-carried him away from the grotesque scene. Rachel wanted to take Julian with them, but she couldn't help two injured men at once. Julian had moved a little since Robbins' last attack. He was alive, but she had no idea how bad his injuries were. The least she could do was lure Mario away from him.

Mario pranced, keeping pace, watching her every move. "Really, Rachel," Mario eyed her skeptically; "do you think I'll just let you walk out of here? I've come a long way—thanks to you," he winked, "I'm not going to let him get away."

"So you kill Chris, then what? Me?" Her brother moaned the cry of an injured child. Her heart quietly broke. She had to stall until she could get Chris to safety. They both had a better chance if she could stand unencumbered against Mario.

"Why would I kill you, dear Rachel? You haven't betrayed me. Have you?"

241

"I wouldn't know how to answer that. How can one betray a ghost?" Her hand throbbed. Chris was moving only one foot, the other dragged through the muck. Rachel feared she couldn't support him much longer.

It was then Mario figured out where she was going. Whether he read her thoughts or instinctively knew, she couldn't guess. He stopped short and raised his arms. "Rachel, I must commend you. You are obviously a more formidable opponent than I judged." As his hands slammed together, a headwind hit them full force. Rachel floundered. Tears streamed from her eyes. Chris sagged at her side. She tried to urge him on, but he couldn't hear her. The roaring wind wrenched away each word in turn.

If they were to survive, she had to get Chris to the one desolate sagebrush a few feet away. It was clear to her, from her memory of Joseph's drawing, that sage was a sacred plant and would provide them refuge. Even the lightning had glanced off its protective shield in his sketch.

"I'm sorry," she yelled at Chris, "I have to drag you." She let him slump to the ground and grabbed both his ankles. With her back to the wind she schlepped her brother. Pulling dead weight through the quagmire was backbreaking. Her feet slipped. It was all Rachel could do to stay upright against Mario's blow. Chris tried to help, but though his effort was great it was of little help. The knife wound on Rachel's hand tore as she strained. She suppressed the urge to cry out. Fresh blood oozed, then ran from the cut. It was a bad gash, but it was the least of her concerns. There was no choice, but to soldier on. Their energy must go against the dark apparition who held all the cards. She did so gasping for breath.

Mario jigged at her side, laughing hideously, enjoying their plight. There would be plenty of time for dying. The two siblings, one too weak to help himself, and the other too stubborn to quit, moved inch by inch. One of Chris' shoes slipped off and was whipped away. Rachel grasped his ankle and continued to haul his body. Mario taunted them. The windstorm pelted her body with desert debris: thorny cholla, chamisa blossoms and small stones. The projectiles smarted as if hail assaulted her. If she gave in to the horror of the event, surely, fear-induced paralysis would result. Rachel could not think of the ruthless death Robbins endured only minutes ago, or the attorney who died of fright on a lonely mesa.

Nor could she think of poor Joseph crushed beneath the rubble of his cabin or Julian's fate. Fear is infectious, give in, and risk one's sanity.

Just as she thought her arms would be pulled from their sockets, the wind stopped. They had reached sanctuary. Rachel felt hope; transitory as it was. It renewed her strength. But she feared it was only the eye of the hurricane that provided a false sort of hope. Rachel helped Chris sit up and leaned him against the sage. "Stay here," she commanded.

"Not going anywhere," he mumbled.

Rachel stood, hands on her hips, and faced the devil's advocate. "Okay, Mario, it's just you and me. Your serve."

"I could have killed you both," he said. "I didn't."

"Yeah, I figured that. So what stopped you?" Rachel was aghast to find her teeth chattering. Her clothing was soaked with rain and sweat. The temperature must have dropped to forty.

"You." He looked her over like a creep appraising a whore. "You've been so much fun to play with. Besides, I don't have to do anything," he continued. "I can wait for exposure to get you both. I'm not cold, and I have infinite time."

Rachel was certain Mario would let them die. He was getting a kick out of their suffering. Whatever had happened to Chloe? Something must have gone wrong. But expecting help would arrive wasn't going to save them now. She had to send Mario back. Mario was proof the ceremony worked. Somehow she must reverse the process. There was no time to make a mask and she had no photos or cherished mementoes of him.

"Don't even think it," Mario grinned. Evil seeped from the orifice in the form of abhorrent goo. It collected on his chin and dropped in gelatinous globs to the ground where it seemed to burn small holes in the earth. Rachel resisted the impulse to look away. Everything about him made her want to retch.

At that moment, Julian hobbled out of the rocks into the clearing where Rachel stood defiant in the face of wickedness.

"Hey," he called, rubbing his head. "Are you okay?" He either could not see Mario or was too dazed to comprehend what appeared before him.

"Damn," Mario cursed. "I'll take care of this interruption."

"Mario," Rachel appealed. "He isn't a part of this. Leave him be."

Mario vaporized, only to reappear seconds later near Julian. "Julian, run!" Rachel shouted.

In desperation Rachel gazed upward and recalled Joseph. His benevolent weathered face materialized, illuminated in a warm glow. *Help me, Joseph. Please help me. Or we will surely die.* She sent the message in thought form. Joseph smiled ever so kindly. Was she actually seeing him? His eyes were dark, but they were the eyes of a celestial being, different from the dark malevolent eyes of Mario.

My dear, I have helped you. Is your brother not safely in contact with the holy sage?

Mario may not be able to hurt us here, but he can wait for the cold to finish us off. I must send Mario back, but I don't know how.

In the distance she saw Julian fall backward as Mario literally blew him off his feet. Julian scrambled away. Rachel ached to help him, but she could not stop Mario's rampage. She returned to Joseph.

He's going to kill Julian if you can't help me.

Joseph bowed his head and transmitted. You must first insure your protection by encircling the sage with stones.

Rachel scrambled around, but as she did so, Mario darkened the sky to black. Not even the few stars that had been showing through the clouds were left. It was no use. She couldn't see.

She thought of giving up. Realistically, how much more could any of them take? There are situations one just can't prepare for— nor can one study for them.

"What the hell?" she said. There was a light here in this dark place. A figure of white materialized. It was the wolf! It glowed. The creature looked over its back at her and then dipped his head to the ground as if directing her. Its blue eyes showed the way.

No longer afraid of the wolf, Rachel followed it as he led her to stone after stone. She grabbed each and tossed them into a crude circle around the shrub. There was no sign of Mario, who she thought to be frightened by the wolf, but he unquestionably was at hand.

Before the perimeter of stones was finished Mario appeared again and moved toward Chris, brandishing his arms in intimidation. His arms seemed to form wings, but they were not made of feathers, but green and black undulating fluids. Rachel quickly placed the last of the markers, completing the rough medicine wheel and enclosing herself and Chris inside the safe area. Mario rushed them repeatedly, but could not penetrate the circle.

"No!" Mario screamed, enraged.

Rachel tried to block his image from her sight as he hovered like an angry helicopter. He dove and charged at them. Heinous sounds assaulted their ears as he shrieked and seethed in rage. Unearthly vomit spewed from his contorted mouth. He yanked his arm from his torso and putrid green blood surged from his pseudo body. The stench made her recoil against the shrub.

Repulsed and horrified, she focused on Joseph. *Now, Joseph. It has to be now.*

His message appeared in her mind. You must barricade these shenanigans from your mind. Visualize his journey. Think of nothing else. Allow the power to flow through you. Don't try to capture it. You wish only to borrow it.

Carefully, her body shaking, she pulled off pungent sage leaves until her hands overflowed with the herb. She turned to face Mario. His expression told her she was ridiculous. "Stupid girl, you can't do this. I'll kill your Julian if you try."

Rachel understood that he could, would. She raised both hands toward the heavens, offering the sage. She blocked Mario's frenzy from her mind and she felt Joseph's warmth nearby. He knew she was a believer. She felt her strength grow in intensity. Not knowing how to begin, she visualized a tunnel, a concourse to wherever Mario came from. In a flash, she was back in Tulsa, on the rug in front of the fireplace, the swirling fog engulfing the room, the strange sounds consuming the quiet.

Rachel heard Mario shouting, "I'll kill you!" but she squeezed him out. She would no longer engage him in human communication. It was crucial to remain in an altered state.

Although her eyes remained open, she could see only geometric shapes. Circles, triangles, and zigzag lines converged in front of her obscuring the rocks, the storm, and even Mario. It was Joseph's drawing in its most primitive form. The clouds of the storm became circles, the Tent Rocks triangles, and the lightning bolt represented the zigzags that rippled before her. As the trance continued, the true shapes of this sphere slowly integrated with mathematical configurations. Rachel's consciousness spanned both worlds. Whatever was to come, she would abide.

The ground beneath her feet began to shake. She feared her body would be thrown flat, but her soles held fast. The earth responded to her anger. Her arms trembled violently; the sage tumbled from her hands and was cast about. Energy rushed into her body, her soul. It was potent. It was foreign—unlike anything she had ever experienced. *Don't try to capture it.* She let it go through her. It returned, again and again, bolstering her strength and courage. She stood tall, straight, feet braced apart, hands held high and wide. It seemed she was looking down upon the planet aware of what was going on, but removed. Chris huddled against the bush. She was standing next to him. Mario blustered, but from her new perspective, he appeared so small, insignificant.

When it was time, she somehow knew. Full of a force she had never before known Rachel slammed her hands together, once, but did not feel the sting of her injury. Again, lightning ruptured the sky in pandemonium. This time, she was its master.

She observed Mario dispassionately, as if he was a character in a movie. Every crack of thunder depleted his potency. He was no longer in control. This storm was all hers. She heard him beg her to stop but his words were a nuisance. Electricity charged the night and Mario fought for his existence. He savagely lunged at her over and over, but never entered the circle. His powers weakened.

The storm stopped, the clouds blew away in a whisper. The silence was absolute. Moonlight illuminated the canyon. A thick fog enveloped her body. It was not yet time to return to reality. The swirling cloud crawled from beneath the desert veneer and lifted, slowly engulfing Mario's image. As his evil power drained away, he howled, "I'll be back." It was the cry of a beaten bully, part bluster, and part defeat. He became the night. His body dissolved slowly, taking away the ugliness. He was gone. Rachel collapsed.

* * *

There it was again; Chloe's voice. Calling, calling and calling. God, that woman could be irritating. Couldn't Chloe see she was trying to sleep? Rachel opened her eyes, but her body was too weak to move. In the distance, lights bobbed as men and women carried flashlights. Their steps were loud and the sound carried through the ground.

"Rachel! Rachel!" It was Chloe again. Dear, sweet Chloe. She seemed so near.

"I'm here," Rachel rallied, but it was only a murmur. Languor compelled her to withdraw. She was vaguely aware of Chris. He seemed so peaceful. Where was Julian? She looked for him, but could not find him in the bobbing rays of light.

"There they are!" Chloe shouted and it seemed a million feet thundered in her direction. Chloe swept Rachel into her arms. "Are you all right?" she cried, looking at her face, rubbing her cold hands. "Dammit, Rachel, you always start without me."

CHAPTER 58

T he glow from the new lava lamp cast a pink blush throughout the kitchen. It stood on Rachel's desk, in the breakfast nook, its faux magma rising and falling quietly.

The move into the new house was easy. Rachel was nearly devoid of personal possessions. The alcove made a fine office with a window to the world of her backyard. She'd opted to keep some of the former occupant's things, but had purchased a new bedroom suite and upholstered furniture for the living room. None of it had been delivered yet. She'd been slumbering on the floor in a sleeping bag over Chloe's objections.

Chloe's profane outburst in French at the police station nearly landed her in jail. The obstinate police officer threatened to charge her with disturbing the peace. She countered by calling the New Mexican on her cell and offering them the story if they'd help her find Rachel and Chris. In minutes, people began arriving in the parking lot armed with lights, cameras, and notepads. By that time two police cars had been dispatched to Tent Rocks, along with sheriff's office personnel and an ambulance team.

Dear Julian recovered at home from a concussion and two broken ribs. He returned to work after a few days. They hadn't talked about what happened yet. Maybe they wouldn't.

Rachel won a national journalism award for her story on the scam and her brother's involvement. She left out anything not of the quick. It not only paid some bills, but she had completed her father's work. For a moment at the awards ceremony, she noticed a hint of Old Spice in the air. Sure, someone on the dais might have been wearing it, but she didn't believe that. Her father being there in spirit meant more than the award.

Several job offers had rolled in. Ah, to be in demand. She was considering each, but right now, she just wanted to be here.

The kettle on the stove cast off steam. She poured hot water over a tea bag and set it aside to steep. Her hand hurt from the gash Robbins inflicted. Thirty stitches had been required to put it right. She was referring to it as her Frankenstein hand because of all the sewing done to it.

Logan had called. It wasn't the first time, and she had to admit, she hoped it would not be the last, but his marriage wouldn't permit more than friendship. His series had been renewed and he would be back in a few months to begin filming.

Despite the divorce, Tony was a true friend. He was there when Rachel, Chris and Julian were deposited at the hospital. His support wavered a bit when he observed the doctor suturing Rachel's hand, but he had remained conscious.

Jenny, Chris' wife, arrived to hold vigil while Chris recuperated from exposure and dehydration. Reconciliation had been rumored, but Rachel expected bad feelings would recur now that her brother's illegal activities were exposed. Their father's suspicions that Chris was entangled in the whole mess had been correct.

After a short hospital stay, Chris was cooling his heels, compliments of the city. He didn't have the money for bail so the former mayor was sitting in his own jail. Someone else was minding city hall. It was a good bet Chris would do some time in the state pen.

His signed confession had been found among Robbins' possessions. In this coerced statement he admitted sole guilt in the real estate scam. Of course, the other perpetrators were dead, and that left him holding the bag. Chris' legal problems were long from over. It remained to be seen if the money would eventually be returned to investors.

The scheme had been Mario's idea. Chris had been easy to convince because of his great thirst for a high-rolling lifestyle. Mario met Robbins while in prison for other bad deeds and learned of his Santa Fe connection to Julian. Robbins wanted revenge on Julian for his incarceration and bombed the magazine office in retaliation. Robbins planned to kill Julian at Tent Rocks, but didn't live long enough. Mario didn't care about Robbins' retribution as long as he got what he wanted in the process.

Chris provided the connection to city government that was needed to get the approval for the development. He made provisions with the attorney for the dummy company and the secret account in the Caymans. The lawyer who died at Pueblo Blanco acted in good faith and had not been a part of the illegal endeavor, but his honesty did not save his life. No one would ever know what had happened to him. The official cause of death was cardiac arrest. Rachel would always believe he was frightened to death by Mario.

Robbins' demise was more difficult to explain. Chris claimed he was too out of it at the time, to observe what had occurred. Rachel wasn't willing to describe all the phenomena either. Law enforcement had to be content with death by freak weather conditions. But Rachel would carry the memory of Robbins horrific passing for the rest of her life.

She tried not to think about what had happened. It was too unbelievable. There had been no other conversations with Joseph. No sightings of the wolf, and no encounters with spirits. Rachel figured it was a one-time thing. She didn't care for a rematch.

A plaintive cry from outside penetrated Rachel's thoughts. For a moment her body tensed. She reminded herself that Mario was gone, never to return—at least not by her doing. She'd sworn off Native American rituals, well, unless, of course, it was absolutely necessary. The meow was louder this time. Insistent.

Rachel scrambled to the door for a look. There in the cold Santa Fe rain the little tortie stared at her. A more dismal, sad thing she had never seen. Water dripped off the bedraggled fur and her ears drooped in defeat. She invited the miserable creature inside, but it hesitated, not quite trusting this new benefactor.

"Come on in," Rachel implored, bracing against the cold wind. "I don't want to get wet." Still, the cat wavered. "Okay," she said with resignation. Into the muck she went, water slopping out of a puddle into her slippers while the rain soaked her clothing. She swooped up the cat with her uninjured hand and hurried back inside where it was warm and dry, her tea ready, and God in her heaven. She placed the tortie on the floor. She shook violently. Water sprayed the kitchen cabinets and Rachel's ankles. The cat alternately viewed her with distrust and tended to her fur.

"You know," Rachel said as she opened some cat food, "your fur reminds me of the chiles in the fall when they begin to turn from green to red. There are a few days when they are dappled in several colors at once. What you say I call you Chile Pod?"

The cat kept her gaze on the food process, not wanting to miss the moment when it was ready.

"I'll take that as a yes," Rachel said and set the bowl of food in front of her. Her nose twitched with interest, but she wouldn't move away from the spot between Rachel and the door.

"You know, little one, I'm not a cat person and you don't trust people, but somewhere along the line we've got to come to an understanding." She thought for a moment, sat down on the floor, raised her right hand and said, "I, Rachel Blackstone, promise never to hurt you, Chile Pod, to keep you fed, and scratch your ears all you want." She waited. "Now you."

A second passed, and another, then she came to Rachel, brushing her head against her leg, claiming her.

"Well," Rachel said with satisfaction and a bit of emotion, "Chloe would be so proud—a mutual growth moment."

Did you enjoy Reluctant Medium?

If so, please consider writing a short review on Amazon or Goodreads. Thank you for reading.

G G Collins

Check out the blogs:

https://reluctantmediumatlarge.wordpress.com/
https://paralleluniverseatlarge.wordpress.com/

ABOUT THE AUTHOR

A seasoned reporter, G G Collins has racked up a lot of column inches, a few awards and a fellowship at Duke University. She never met a story she didn't like, although some interviews were challenging, a few obnoxious. But reporting is always exciting, exploring the rooftops of skyscrapers, meeting in clandestine locations, getting an exclusive, and occasionally being a tad alarmed at someone's behavior. (Know where the exits are!) It's all in a day's work. Of course, one never knows how to dress: jacket for the interview with the visiting entertainer, or jeans for the aviation hangar story? Forget wardrobe, make sure there are plenty of notebooks and extra batteries.

But there was another side lurking, just waiting to write its way out. This side of her personality is fond of the strange, the frightening, the paranormal. An avid reader since childhood, she started her mystery reading career with Shirley Jackson's We Have Always Lived in the Castle. From there, the works of Stephen King were but a small leap.

The day she discovered the Hopi ceremony to call back the dead, she just had to ask the question: What would happen if the wrong spirit came back? Read it for yourself.